Sign up for our newsletter to hear
about new and upcoming releases.

www.ylva-publishing.com

OTHER BOOKS BY JAE

OTHER BOOKS BY ALISON GREY

Hot Line
Contract for Love

The Vampire Diet Series:
Good Enough to Eat

Alison Grey & Jae

good
enough
to **EAT**

ACKNOWLEDGMENTS

We'd like to thank our invaluable beta readers—RJ Nolan, Erin, Michele, Marion, and Carol—as well as our stellar editor, Nikki Busch.

CHAPTER 1

A VAMPIRE WALKED INTO AN AA meeting. It sounded like the beginning of a bad joke, and maybe it was. Other Girah would certainly think so if they knew where she was.

Yeah, but you're not exactly walking into an AA meeting, are you? Coward! Robin sat in her car in the church parking lot. She had driven all the way to Brooklyn from her Central Park condo to avoid running into anyone she knew. Her fellow Girah wouldn't be amused if they saw her hanging out with a bunch of human alcoholics. For at least half an hour, she had been staring across the street at the Romanesque building with the tall spire but couldn't make herself go in. It wasn't the crucifix above the main portal that stopped her from entering. Her kind had been around much longer than Christianity, so, despite what humans might think, crosses didn't harm or repel her. The color of the side door seemed to mock her, though: a rich, bright crimson exactly the color of fresh blood.

Three humans stood outside the door, smoking and joking around with each other. She doubted they were there for the AA meeting. They looked too healthy. Too happy. Too normal.

Robin was neither happy nor normal, and after not drinking blood for four days, she didn't feel very healthy either.

This isn't right. She didn't belong here, to this group of humans. But where else was she supposed to go? She grinned wryly. It wasn't as if she could walk into a Bloodsuckers Anonymous meeting. She had tried Overeaters Anonymous, but the sight of all those well-nourished humans made her feel as if she'd walked into a restaurant with an all-you-can-eat buffet.

Just thinking about it made her gums ache, and she started to sweat. She pulled down the visor to check if she could still pass as human. That was another myth about her kind that humans seemed to believe in. The vampires that Robin's fellow authors of paranormal fiction portrayed in their novels didn't have reflections, but she did. Her reflection looked flushed and shaky, but the people in the AA meeting would probably attribute it to alcohol withdrawal. Thankfully, her fangs hadn't protruded, so her teeth looked entirely human.

One of the men smoking in front of the church looked over.

Quickly, Robin pretended to check her teeth for any leftovers from dinner. When he directed his gaze elsewhere, she snapped back the visor and went back to staring at the church. Her legs were shaking, but she couldn't tell whether it was nerves or withdrawal. If she didn't get some blood soon, at least the synthetic type, she would become dizzy and pass out, possibly even die. Synth-O was expensive, though, so she usually waited until later in the evening to drink a bottle of the stuff. But before she could drive home and guzzle a bottle of Synth-O, she had to get through this AA meeting first.

The number eighty-two popped into her mind, and she realized she had been counting the bricks in the church's pale façade. She thought she'd shaken that old habit, but apparently, it was back.

Growling, she opened the car door and got out.

Her breath condensed in the cold January air. The smell of laundry detergent, oil, and chili powder assaulted her nose, making her realize for the first time that Saint Mary's was located between a Laundromat and a fast-food restaurant that served fried chicken and waffles. She wrinkled her nose at the weird combination of dishes. But then again, human eating habits were weird. She had eaten human food on occasion, trying to fit in, but it didn't have the nutrients she needed or the taste she preferred.

On legs that still felt slightly shaky, she walked across the parking lot and past the three smoking men, ignoring their curious gazes. No lightning struck her as she entered the church. *No spontaneous combustion either.* She grinned and shrugged. *Guess I'll take it as a good sign.*

The website listing AA meetings had said that the self-help group gathered in the basement, so she made her way down the spiral stone staircase.

Laughter trickled up the stairs.

For Robin, her addiction wasn't a laughing matter. It was a matter of life or death—hers or that of a human. She didn't want a repeat of New Year's Eve. One human hanging lifeless in her grasp had been enough.

She reached the bottom of the stairs and proceeded down a hallway.

More laughter came from behind a door.

Was she really in the right place? Well, only one way to find out. She opened the door at the end of the hall.

Twenty-one people sat on folding chairs, some chatting, some staring off into space, all of them drinking coffee from paper cups. A glance and a quick sniff showed Robin that they were from all walks of life—ranging from a man in a suit who smelled as if he'd been counting money all day to a guy in paint-spattered work pants. Unlike the people in Overeaters Anonymous, most of them were men.

One more reason to switch to AA. Robin had a taste for the fairer sex and not just in the bedroom. She would be less tempted to bite one of the men.

She let her gaze trail through the rest of the room, which looked as if it doubled as a daycare center. Children's drawings hung next to posters with AA's twelve steps. A giant coffee pot, a pile of stale donuts, and a stack of paper cups sat on a table in the corner.

The door opened, and the smell of smoke preceded the three men she had seen outside into the room. The seats were filling up quickly, so Robin rushed toward the only unoccupied chair along the back wall. A thick, blue book lay on it. "Excuse me." Her throat was dry and burned with thirst, so she had to pause and clear it. "Is this seat taken?"

The gray-haired man to the left of the chair with the book shook his head and gave her a friendly smile. "No. Please, sit." He took the book off the chair, put it on his lap, and trailed his fingers over the letters carved into the hardback cover. "You're new, aren't you?"

Robin nodded and hunched down in her folding chair.

"Feel free to get yourself a cup of coffee," the man said, pointing at the snack table.

Robin shook her head. She had never understood why humans were so obsessed with that bitter brew.

"Then how about a donut?"

Again, she shook her head, wishing he would just shut up.

Of course, he didn't. "Have you been to a m—?"

She jerked around and looked into his eyes. *Shut up!* She used just enough thrall to make it an order he couldn't help following.

His eyes glazed over, and he closed his mouth so quickly that his teeth clacked together.

Finally, some peace and quiet. As much as being a blood-drinking Girah could be a pain in the ass, at times like this, she really appreciated the mind control her kind could exert over humans. She blew out a breath and looked away from Mr. Blabbermouth, releasing him from her hypnotic thrall. She hoped his survival instincts would kick in now and stop him from trying to have a chat with her again.

The teenager on her other side was chewing a hangnail. He was dressed in black, his baggy pants hanging loose on his scrawny frame. The smell of something worse than alcohol clung to him. Heroin? Amphetamines? Robin wasn't sure, but whatever it was made him pretty sick. His skin was so pale that he looked much more like a vampire than she did—or at least more like the image humans had of vampires. His knee bounced up and down, and Robin caught herself counting the bounces.

She jerked her gaze away. The whole situation was surreal. *What am I doing here?*

Just when she was about to bolt, a bearded man stood. "For those of you who don't know me, my name is Brian, and I'm an alcoholic. Welcome to our AA meeting."

The others murmured greetings, but Robin remained silent.

"Okay," Brian said. "Now please all join me in the Serenity Prayer."

Oh, great. More prayer. The Overeaters Anonymous meeting had been the same. It had left Robin staring at the wall, not knowing how to pray to the human God.

All around her, people started to mumble the words with Brian. "God, grant me the serenity to accept the things I cannot change, the courage to change the things I can, and the wisdom to know the difference."

Robin shuddered as she flashed back to New Year's Eve, to Meghan turning toward her, blood dripping from her fangs as she said, "Why are you fighting it? You can't change who you are."

Instead of discouraging her, the memory of that night made Robin determined to try even harder. She gripped the edges of her folding chair. *Maybe I can't change who I am, but I can change what I do.*

That thought made her stay where she was, despite the urge to flee while Brian read the AA preamble and other members took turns reading from the blue book.

Most of what they read seemed more spiritual than practical. How were those corny mantras, the psychobabble, and the spiritual hooey supposed to help her?

Robin counted the number of times they mentioned God or a higher power, just to keep herself entertained.

Right when she started to consider putting them all in thrall and making a quick escape, the man who had been reading closed the book and Brian asked, "Are there any newcomers tonight?"

The teenager next to Robin stopped chewing his hangnail and looked up from where he slumped in his chair. He stopped bouncing his knee and lifted his hand. "Hi, I'm Kevin, and I...I guess I'm an alcoholic."

"Hi, Kevin," the group said in unison. Their greetings echoed off the walls of the basement.

How amusing. Here she was, a paranormal creature, yet Robin felt as if she was the only normal one trapped in this weird cult.

"Anyone else here for the first time?" Brian asked and looked directly at her.

Reluctantly, Robin raised her hand too. She didn't want to give her name or lie, so she said, "I'm just here to listen."

"That's fine. Everything in this meeting is confidential, including whether you want to introduce yourself or not." Brian smiled, half hidden by his beard. "Tonight's speaker will share her story now. Everyone, please welcome Alana."

Beautiful name. Robin itched to pull out her ever-present notebook from her back pocket to write down the name so she could use it for one of her characters. But when she caught sight of the woman now striding toward the small podium at the front of the room, she forgot about the notebook.

Alana was as beautiful as her name. With her trim body, pretty face, and hair that shone with a copper glow, she didn't look like an alcoholic at all. Then again, Robin knew only too well that looks could be deceiving. No one at the meeting would think she looked like someone who longed to sink her teeth into Alana's carotid.

Alana's steps were steady and her gaze never wavered as she took her position behind the lectern, but Robin could smell her nervous sweat and hear the blood rushing through her arteries and veins, calling to her. The pulse thudding in Alana's neck taunted her. *Bite me! Bite me,* it seemed to shout.

As if that weren't bad enough, Alana's smell revealed that she was O negative. That blood type was Robin's comfort food—like a pint of Haagen-Dazs, a large pizza with double cheese, and a piece of chocolate cake all rolled into one.

Yum. Dessert has just been delivered, a voice in Robin's head said, sounding strangely like Meghan.

Thirst flared. She could almost taste that smooth, salty tang on her tongue. *Stop it!* She was here to fight that urge, not to indulge in it. Wrenching her gaze away from Alana, she started counting—the number of chairs in the room, the leftover donuts on the table, the syllables in the twelve traditions displayed on a wall poster, the buttons on Alana's blouse.

Like a human under thrall, her gaze kept wandering back to Alana. Finally, she gave up trying to ignore her and listened to what the woman had to say.

———————— • • • ————————

Alana held on to the lectern with both hands. Feeling something solid beneath her fingers usually had a soothing effect on her, but today it wasn't working. Her gaze darted over her audience and lingered on the group's two newbies. While the fidgeting teenager stared down at his bouncing knees, the new woman's gaze was so intense it made Alana want to squirm. Her shortish, dark brown hair and fair skin weren't really unusual. Quite the opposite. Except for her deep blue eyes, she didn't look remarkable at all, but even at a distance, Alana sensed that there was something off about the newcomer. *How would you know? It's not like you still have any powers left.*

Someone cleared his throat.

Get a grip! She's just someone looking for help. Like you. Alana took a deep breath. "Hi. My name is Alana, and I'm an alcoholic."

Brian, Pete, and the others gave her encouraging smiles. "Hi, Alana."

The new woman still stared at her. Her face showed a strange mix of emotions, some unreadable. But Alana could have sworn she saw surprise and something like lust.

Shaking her head at herself, Alana focused on Brian. Even though he already knew her story, it helped to imagine she would speak just to him. "My beverage of choice was gin." She chuckled. No one but her could recognize the irony in that. "Gin Fizz, Fallen Angel, gin straight out of the bottle, whatever I could get my hands on."

Someone coughed, and Alana waited until the room quietened again.

"I started drinking after I found my girlfriend in bed with her catcher." When the new boy frowned, Alana said, "She was into softball. When she told me she needed to bond with her teammates, I had no idea she meant that kind of bonding." Alana shrugged, hoping to appear indifferent, but she doubted that anybody fell for it. No matter how many times she told this story, it still hurt. "Call me stupid, but I really thought she loved me and softball—in that order. Turns out she played softball just to hit on women and never loved me at all." She clasped the sides of the lectern until her knuckles turned white.

"On that evening, I drank alcohol for the first time in my life. I went to a bar and told the bartender to give me a drink—any drink. He suggested a Suffering Bastard, and I accepted. It sounded fitting." For a moment, she closed her eyes, remembering the fresh, slightly bitter taste and the numbness that soon followed. When she opened her eyes, she met the gaze of the female newbie.

But the stranger broke eye contact and looked down as if in shame.

I guess she has a similar story. Alana focused on Brian again. He winked.

"For those of you who don't know this cocktail, it's a mix of brandy, ginger ale, lime juice, a dash of bitters, and—you might have guessed it…" Alana smiled when everybody spoke together with her, "Gin." She sobered. "I drained the glass in seconds and ordered a second one. My whole body started to tingle, and the more I drank, the better I felt. When I woke up the next morning, I was back in our apartment, lying in the bed I shared with my girlfriend. Well, ex-girlfriend, I guess. Somehow I had not just made it home but also managed to make a complete fool out of myself, begging my ex to take me back, as if I was the one who had messed up."

Several group members shook their heads in sympathy.

"Looking back, I'm not sure what was more humiliating. Finding out my girlfriend was cheating on me or waking up naked beside her while she sported a grin as big as the cat that ate the canary."

Alana rubbed the wood under her sweaty fingers. "I moved out the same day. First into a hotel, then into an apartment of my own. I was alone. And by alone I mean I had nobody. A suitcase with some clothes was all I had." She closed her eyes for a moment, remembering the hopelessness she had felt. "I had given up everything for her. My life, my family, my friends. And there was no going back. My old existence had been lost forever, and the person I had sacrificed everything for was a fraud. I was such a fool. How could I ever think that it would be a good idea to go against everything I was?" Her words were more whispered than spoken. "Anyway, I couldn't get back to being the person I was before, but I had no idea who I was now, without her. So for more than two years, not a single day went by without gin. Alcohol made me lose my self-control. The more I drank, the more I wanted."

When Alana looked up, she met the penetrating gaze of the female newbie. A profound understanding shone in those blue eyes, as if this woman knew exactly what she was talking about.

Mentally shaking her head, she continued. "Without gin, I had no energy. I couldn't function. I drank to feel normal."

This was the part of her speech she hated the most. Bile rose in her throat, and it was as if no time at all had passed. She was behind the wheel again. Lights of oncoming cars blinded her, and the screams rang in her ears. "I had lost a case that day, so I went out and drank even more than I usually did. Not that I needed any excuse to drink by that point." Staring down at the lectern so she wouldn't have to meet anyone's eyes, she hesitated and then said, "On my way home from the bar, I lost control of my car. I swerved onto the sidewalk, barely missing a woman with her little baby boy." She swallowed and forced herself to look up and face her friends.

The faces of some people in the audience reflected relief. Most could probably empathize with the experience of driving drunk and narrowly avoiding disaster.

She cleared her throat and forced herself to continue. "I plowed into their dog—a yellow Labrador. He was instantly dead." She wiped away her tears when she felt them trickling down her cheeks. "When I saw what I had done, I was horrified and threw up in my car. I love all creatures in this world. The guilt I feel over killing an innocent animal, all because I couldn't face my life sober, will follow me to my grave." Her voice was shaking when she added, "Just a few inches to the side and I would have killed the mother and her baby. They could have been dead too." The last words were barely more than a whisper, and she had to swallow against the lump in her throat. "The judge sentenced me to attend AA and community service." She looked down at her friends. "When I came here, everybody was a stranger. I felt lost, like I didn't belong here. I couldn't imagine even one day without gin. How could I do my job or go to sleep without it?" She exhaled. "It wasn't easy, and AA sure wasn't the instant cure I was hoping for. I still wake up every morning wanting a drink, but these wonderful people here took me under their wings and taught me that it's not about not craving anymore; it's about being strong enough to fight it." New tears came when Alana remembered what a special day it was. "Today I'm eighteen months sober."

The group applauded.

Alana wiped away her tears and stepped back from the lectern, smiling. Whatever happened, no one could take this accomplishment from her.

Still clapping his hands, Brian stood and stepped onto the podium. He gave her one of his famous bear hugs before pulling a key from his pocket and opening the case at the bottom of the lectern. He smiled as he took out a gleaming sobriety chip with the number eighteen on it and handed it over.

The chip felt good in her palm. She had earned it, and she was proud of it, especially since, other than becoming a lawyer, it was the first thing of importance she had accomplished without the skills she'd once possessed. Grinning like an idiot, she held up the chip for everybody to see.

The group cheered.

Robin stared in envy at the bronze chip arcing through the air as Alana flicked it up and then caught it smoothly on her way down from the podium. The sobriety chip had the number eighteen on it.

Eighteen months of sobriety.

Robin's respect for the woman grew. She knew she wouldn't even make it to eighteen days without drinking blood. She would die if she tried. But maybe what Alana had said was true. The words still rang in her ears: *It's not about not craving anymore; it's about being strong enough to fight it.* She would fight the urge to get blood fresh from its preferably human source and make do with synthetic blood, even though it was expensive and tasted like licking a dirty nickel. If she had to write a few extra short stories so she could afford a few pints of the brew, then so be it.

Maybe being here, among these humans who couldn't understand the nature of her problem, wasn't so useless after all. She had wanted to tune out Alana's story but couldn't help listening. As different from hers as the story was, it still struck a chord. The stories were different, but the emotions behind them were the same.

The more I drank, the more I wanted.

Those could be her own words, even though Alana had said them.

She started, wrenched from her thoughts, when the humans stood and formed a circle.

"Let's finish up with a prayer," Brian said.

Robin mentally rolled her eyes. *Great. Another prayer.*

Everyone joined hands.

When Robin hesitated, Brian waved her into the circle, directing her to take a place between him and Alana.

Bloody hell, no! She didn't want to hold hands with any human, least of all the alluring Alana. Just the thought of feeling the blood rushing through her arteries made her dizzy.

But Brian grinned at her. "Don't worry; we don't bite."

Yeah, but I might. Her stomach churned as she took a step forward, then another. Before she could change her mind, Brian grabbed her hand. His palm was rough, full of calluses, but then another hand, warm and soft, slid into hers on the other side.

Energy tingled up Robin's arm and ran through the rest of her body like a current. She wanted to wrench her hand away but knew she would only call attention to herself. Startled, Robin turned her head.

Alana looked up from where her gaze rested on their joined hands and smiled at Robin. Her green eyes were as deep and mysterious as a hidden lake in the forest. As if sensing Robin's urge to flee, Alana squeezed her hand.

Not knowing what else to do, Robin stood still like a statue as the group recited the Lord's Prayer. She didn't know the words, but she moved her lips, faking it.

Alana stood silent too.

Through their linked hands, Robin felt the pulse of her blood with every heartbeat, drowning out the words of the prayer.

Her teeth started to ache, and she forced herself to stare straight ahead instead of turning her head and ogling the smooth skin of Alana's neck.

When Brian finally said, "Amen," she pulled both of her hands back and stuffed them into her pants pockets.

Instead of dispersing, most group members hung around, drinking more coffee and talking to each other.

Robin eyed the door, but before she could make her escape, Brian cleared his throat to get her attention.

Alana still stood next to him, and Robin was only too aware of her presence.

"Let me welcome you in person," he said. "I'm Brian, and this is Alana."

Robin thought about giving a fake name, but with one glance at Alana, the truth rolled out of her mouth. "Robin Cald—"

Brian held up one hand. "Just first names in here."

Duh. Robin smirked at herself. *Did you think they're called Alcoholics Anonymous for nothing?*

"So, what did you think of your first AA meeting?" Brian asked.

Robin shrugged. "It was okay, I guess." She risked a quick glance at Alana. "I liked your speech."

A bright smile seemed to light Alana's face from within, transforming her features from pretty to breathtaking. "Thank you."

"So you'll come back next week?" Brian asked.

Everything in Robin screamed *yes*, but she wasn't sure if it was her bloodlust talking or the part of her that was looking for help. "I don't know yet."

"We always advise newcomers to go to ninety meetings in their first ninety days of sobriety," Brian said.

That might work for humans. At least at the meetings, there was no alcohol around. But for her, attending an AA meeting meant facing a room full of temptations. If she got hungry enough, even the men would start to look like tasty morsels. "I don't know," she said again. "I'm not sure this is the right place for me."

Brian reached out as if to pat her arm, but then his brow furrowed and he pulled back before he could touch her.

Seems alcohol hasn't completely killed his survival instincts. Robin suppressed a smirk.

"Well," Brian said, "you've got time to figure it out. Maybe having someone to talk to one-on-one would help. You'll need to find yourself a sponsor. Someone you can call for support. Normally, we prefer a same-sex sponsor." He glanced to his left. "I'm sure Alana would be glad to take you on."

Robin wasn't sure who looked more shocked—Alana or she. They stared at Brian and then at each other.

There was no way to politely refuse the offer, but she couldn't accept. Not when the blood running through Alana's arteries and veins was her version of gin. *Shit. What do I do now?*

———— • •• ————

Alana stared at Brian in disbelief. He had a wicked sense of humor, but this went too far. She was in no condition to be a sponsor to anyone, let alone such an attractive woman. Where had this thought come from? Sure, Robin was a good-looking woman, but Alana hadn't been attracted to anyone since Kelly. She cleared her throat. "Brian, I don't think—"

"I don't need a sponsor," Robin said.

Brian frowned. "But it's one of the things that make AA such a success. Having a sponsor can be a great thing whenever the craving for alcohol becomes—"

"I don't have an alcohol problem," Robin said, her face a stony mask.

Yeah, sure. It was always the same. When people came to a meeting for the first time, they all thought they didn't belong. Not that Alana had been any different. She had been just as deeply in denial as most others, maybe even more. She had told herself that there was nothing this bunch of humans could offer her. How were they supposed to help her when they didn't even understand who she was—or rather who she had been? But time had proven her wrong, and it would probably be the same for this newbie. She couldn't be the one to help her, though. She wasn't in the position to be a sponsor and a shining example for anyone, least of all for a woman she found herself strangely attracted to. Every instinct screamed at her to stay away and not risk her sobriety. "Brian, maybe you should ask Pete or Caren to take her on."

"That won't be necessary." Robin glanced at the exit. "If you would excuse me. I need to go."

Alana watched her leave.

"What was that?" Brian asked.

"Huh?" Alana snatched her gaze away from Robin's retreating form and looked at Brian.

He gestured to Robin's back. "Don't you think she could use some help?"

"Of course she could. She's a typical case." But at the same time, Alana felt there was more to this woman than met the eye. Something about Robin was different, but for the life of her, Alana couldn't put a finger on it.

"Then why don't you want to be her sponsor? I didn't hesitate to take you on when you first came here. Don't you think it's time to pay it forward?"

Alana lowered her gaze. Her shoulders drooped, and she nodded. Brian was right. Robin probably felt just as lost as she had during her first meeting. Maybe she had no one to support her. Without further hesitation, she grabbed her jacket and purse and hurried after her.

When Alana left the church, Robin was already halfway across the parking lot.

"Robin!"

The woman stopped and turned around as if in slow motion. "Yeah?"

Alana came to a halt in front of her. "I always denied it too."

For a second, Robin seemed to look at a point below Alana's face, but then she lowered her gaze and stared at the ground. "Don't take this the wrong way, but you can't help me." She turned away from Alana and strode toward a light aqua Toyota Prius. "But thank you anyway," she said over her shoulder without looking at Alana again.

Alana nibbled on her bottom lip. She couldn't force Robin. Getting sober had to be her choice. All Alana could do was to offer her help. Right? Right. But a nagging feeling told her to try one last time. "Wait." She ran after her.

Robin opened the driver's side door but still didn't look at her. "What is it?" Her voice sounded strained.

Alana foraged through her purse, but instead of a piece of paper to write on, she found only one of her business cards. She hesitated. One of AA's basic principles was anonymity. Should she really...? *Just do it!* She grabbed a pen as well and wrote her private numbers on the back of the card before holding it out to Robin. "If you need anything, call me."

Long moments ticked by as Robin stared at the offered card but made no move to take it. Finally, she gingerly tugged the card from Alana's fingers and put it into her pants pocket. "Thanks." She climbed behind the wheel, closed the door, and drove off without looking back.

"That went well," Alana mumbled and strolled to her own car. She wasn't in the mood to go back inside and tell Brian she had probably scared off the newbie for good. It was time to drive home and face her empty apartment. A lot of work was waiting for her anyway.

CHAPTER 2

With trembling fingers, Robin closed and locked the door to her condo behind her. Her breathing was coming much too fast. Cold sweat formed on her forehead, and her legs felt like two slender trees tilting from side to side in a storm. She leaned against the door, pressing her hands against the solid wood, and counted the boards in her hardwood floor.

By the time she reached one hundred twenty-four, a nice, even number, she felt calm enough to step away from the door. She crossed the living room and stood by the floor-to-ceiling window. Normally, the sight of Central Park below had a calming effect on her. From her condo on the eighteenth floor, people, trees, and park benches looked smaller, and any problem that might plague her seemed more unimportant.

Not today. Today, the park pulsed with life, and she imagined the hammering heartbeat of a jogger, sweat dribbling down the human's neck, blood rushing through her arteries. The jogger's green eyes, the same color as Alana's, darkened as Robin lowered her mouth toward her neck and—

Abruptly, she turned away from the window. Maybe a pint of Synth-O would help. She was starving, so no wonder she couldn't focus on anything but blood. She opened the fridge and took out one of the bottles.

The Synth-O came in brown bottles with labels that read corn syrup. If Robin's neighbors saw her coming back with her groceries, they might wonder how she stayed so slender while going through half a dozen quarts of syrup each week, but otherwise, the bottles wouldn't draw any attention.

A drop of condensation slid down the bottle, and she traced it with one fingertip before twisting off the cap and putting the bottle to her lips. For a moment, she expected the heavenly taste of fresh blood, sweet and salty at the same time, but instead, the artificial taste of Synth-O hit her taste buds. *Ugh.* She shook herself, pinched her nose between two fingers, and choked the rest of the brew down as fast as possible. The unpleasantly cool temperature of the drink didn't help either. Usually, she preferred her blood at body temperature, but the synthetic blood would spoil if she didn't keep it in the fridge. Even though her mind and her taste buds protested, the rest of her body didn't care where the blood was coming from. Her senses came alive, and the trembling in her muscles instantly stopped.

More, her body shouted. While the bottle provided the sustenance she needed, the rush of the hunt was missing, that sweet moment when—

She roughly shook her head, interrupting the dangerous thoughts.

After closing the fridge with a loud bang, she went into her office and powered up her computer. It was time to replace one obsession with another.

She was determined not to supplement her diet with fresh human blood that wouldn't cost her a thing, so she had to sell a couple of short stories until her next royalties came in.

Good thing paranormal romances were in high demand since *Twilight* had made it on the *New York Times* best-seller list.

Robin growled, and her fangs protruded, as they always did whenever she thought of that ridiculous series. *Sparkling vampires! Bah!* She would show that clueless human how vampire fiction was supposed to be written.

After opening a new document, she flexed her fingers and got to work.

A couple of hours later, she paused and reread the last few paragraphs she had written. *Hmm.* Long, flowing hair the color of polished copper, enchanting green eyes, alabaster skin... The vampire's love interest bore a striking resemblance to Alana.

She needed a job, though. Robin took her fingers off the keyboard and started fiddling with a pen. Maybe Alissa, the love interest, was a surgeon. That way, she could provide her lover with blood from the hospital. Every now and then, Robin tried to get her hands on some bags of expired blood from the blood bank too. Heat rose to her skin at the thought. *No! Stop thinking about blood.* Making her a surgeon was not a good idea anyway. Too overdone already. She needed something original, something that fit a person who was as fascinating as Alana. *Alissa! The character's name is Alissa, dammit!*

When she couldn't think of anything, she pulled the business card from her pants pocket and looked at it.

Alana Wadd

Attorney at law

Family law and divorce

A divorce lawyer... A grin formed on her face. Now that was a fun idea!

She stuck the business card to the whiteboard above her desk and started tapping away at her keyboard.

When Robin logged into her e-mail account six days later, she had a response from Fangs and Fur Publishing. "Oh, great!" The publishing house she usually sent her manuscripts to was wonderful, but it took them much longer to read and accept stories, so she had decided to try a small press that was known for a quick turn-around. If all went well, maybe she could publish a longer work with them too. Possibly a novella about her vampire and her divorce lawyer girlfriend. That would help pay for her Synth-O.

She clicked on the e-mail and read it. What? Was she hallucinating? She read it again, heat boiling in her body with every word.

Dear Ms. Caldwell,

Thank you for submitting your short story "Till Death Do Us Part" to Fangs and Fur Publishing.

Your short story submission was highly engaging and your characters well rounded, with believable conflicts. Unfortunately, we feel that your story is not suitable for inclusion in our romance anthology. In our experience, heroines who have careers in that branch of the legal profession don't rate well with our readers.

If you would like to revise your manuscript with that feedback in mind, I would be happy to take another look.

Best regards,
Tina McNealy

Senior Editor
Fangs and Fur Publishing

Robin let her keyboard tray snap back with a resounding thud. *Heroines with careers in that branch of the legal profession don't rate well with our readers...* What the hell was that supposed to mean?

She glanced at the business card on her whiteboard. It had seemed like just the right occupation for her character, but apparently, her target audience didn't think divorce lawyers were sexy. Huffing, Robin got up from her desk. *Pah, what do they know?* Obviously, they had never met Alana.

She stomped to her fridge and opened it. Maybe a pint of blood would help her calm down enough so she could sit down and tweak her story to the editor's liking. While she still believed that divorce lawyer was a perfectly good occupation for a paranormal romance character, she knew she had to swallow her pride and be a professional. Pride wouldn't pay for her Synth-O.

She reached into the fridge, but her hand came away empty. *What the...?* She bent and peeked in.

The fridge was empty except for a few bottles of water that she used to get rid of the rusty-nickel taste in her mouth after guzzling the Synth-O. Apparently, she had finished the last of the synthetic blood on one of her late-night writing binges.

Great. She banged her head against the door of the fridge. Now she had to go out and spend her last dime on a six-pack of that nasty stuff.

Alana threw her pencil on the desk. "So to sum it up, he's as poor as a church mouse and the victim of a conspiracy out to ruin him."

Her client, Mrs. Smith, nodded. "You'd think after almost eight years together, he'd know better than to assume I would believe any of that crap."

Alana sighed. *Crap indeed.* Why on earth had she chosen to become a divorce lawyer? She shook her head. *You know it was the right thing to do.* After being cheated on by Kelly, helping others free themselves from cheating and unloving spouses had appealed to her sense of justice.

Besides, she had kept herself entertained for centuries trying to find loopholes in her masters' wishes, and that had prepared her perfectly for finding loopholes in laws, contracts, and prenuptial agreements. Sometimes, though, she wondered whether there was at least one couple that got their happily ever after. Mrs. Smith and her future ex-husband for sure weren't candidates. "Okay, here's what we'll do: I want you to write down all you can remember about his assets, and I mean every little bit. He won't get away with this." She gestured at the papers on her desk.

Mrs. Smith smiled. "Thank you, Ms. Wadd. I don't know what I'd do without you."

Alana stood and extended her hand. "I'm glad to help."

After Mrs. Smith left, Alana's assistant, Grace, peeked into the room. "Hey, boss."

Smiling, Alana rounded the desk and gave Grace a letter from Mr. Smith's lawyer. "Could you please scan this for the case file?"

Grace entered the office and took the document. "Sure. Anything else?"

"No. Thank you. After that, you can call it a day."

"Okay, boss." Grace grinned like a Cheshire cat. "So Mr. and Mrs. Smith are getting divorced?"

"Yeah." Alana failed to see what was so funny about that.

Grace rolled her eyes. "Come on. Didn't you see the movie?"

If only Grace knew how many movies and TV shows she had watched trying to learn more about the behavior of humans when she'd first started to live as one... Unfortunately, she had quickly discovered that movies and romance novels didn't represent typical human interaction. The shouting matches and ridiculous dramas in the scripted reality TV shows she'd seen had been easy to recognize as fake, but, for a while, she had believed in the happily-ever-after endings portrayed by romance novels and movies. "Yes, I saw that movie."

"Brad Pitt..." Grace sighed, clutching her chest. "Isn't he just dreamy?"

Sometimes, it was hard to believe that Grace was twenty-four and not twelve. But for Grace's sake, she smiled. "Angelina Jolie is more to my liking." She winked.

"Yeah, well, I guess there's a reason the cutest man in the world is in love with her."

A glance at her wristwatch told Alana that the AA meeting would start in less than an hour. Her growling stomach reminded her that she hadn't eaten all day. "I gotta go." She snatched her coat from the coatrack and left her office. In the reception area, a teenage girl of maybe fourteen sat at Grace's desk.

Alana stopped. "Oh. Hi."

Grace hurried after her, Alana's briefcase in hand. "This is my niece Sheryl."

"Hi." The girl flashed her a radiant smile and waved.

"I hope you don't mind that she's here," Grace said. "I told her to meet me here so we can go to a wedding fair right after I finish work."

"Of course not." It was a total mystery to Alana why anyone would want to spend their time at a wedding fair, but she decided not to comment on that.

"Isn't it romantic?" Sheryl asked. "So many people wanting to get married and so many beautiful dresses and…"

Yes, this girl was definitely related to Grace. Had no one ever told her that romance was just an illusion supporting the movie, chocolate, and flower industries? "So many people spending a fortune on a wedding that will be the beginning of a most likely miserable life together," Alana said before she could stop herself.

The girl's smile faded.

Grace stepped closer. "Oh, come on, boss."

"What? We've seen it a thousand times, haven't we? First, the couple is on cloud nine. Then, after a while, little things like leaving the toilet seat up or squeezing the toothpaste from the wrong end become annoying. He starts resenting her for spending too much money on clothes and beauty products that don't make her any more beautiful, while she gets more and more fed up with his increasing lack of devotion in everyday life but especially in bed—which wasn't anything to write home about to begin with. Bickering becomes heated arguments, and before you can say 'marriage counseling,' both demand a divorce, hate each other's guts, and sue each other over the ugly set of tableware that Great-Aunt Agatha gave them for their wedding." Alana gasped for air. Wow, where had that come from?

Grace and her niece stared with their mouths hanging open.

"Um..." Alana took her briefcase from Grace. "Have a nice fair, girls." Before she could make an even bigger fool of herself, she rushed toward the door. "See you Monday."

She stared at herself in the mirrored wall of the elevator. What had just happened? Yes, it had been a long week with a lot of work. But she'd had worse weeks. So what was it that had made her so antsy and moody today? Surely it wasn't the fact that she'd caught herself thinking of Robin once or twice, was it? *Once or twice? More like once or twice an hour!* It didn't matter, because Robin most likely wouldn't show up at the AA meeting tonight anyway. Alana had seen it quite often during the last year and a half. Many newcomers attended just one meeting and then never showed up again. Judging by Robin's hasty retreat the previous week, she was likely one of them. Alana rarely gave those one-timers a second thought, so what was it about this woman that made her think about her all the time? Maybe Robin just reminded her of herself when she started attending the meetings. Yeah, that had to be it.

Alana stepped out of the elevator and waved at the liveried doorman at the desk close to the entrance. "Good night, Jeremy. Have a nice weekend."

"Thanks. Same to you, Ms. Wadd," Jeremy said.

She waved again and left the building. When she got into the car, she decided to drive by her favorite bakery and take some of their calorie bombs to the meeting. Nothing lightened the mood more than nougat-filled pastries. Smiling, Alana started the car.

Julius Prichard didn't sell his wares in dark alleys or shady backrooms, but Robin still felt like a drug addict trolling for her fix as she stopped her car in the driveway of his colonial mansion in Malba.

His assistant let her in and showed her to Julius's office, which overlooked the Whitestone Bridge. Instead of admiring the stunning view, Robin found her gaze drawn to framed diplomas and certificates on the walls. Julius collected academic degrees the way some humans collected stamps. Over the many years of his life, he had earned degrees in biology, chemistry, medicine, economics, and engineering. Robin had met him while doing research for a novel set during the Civil War, a time that Julius, one of the oldest Girahs she knew, had actually lived through. During one of their interview sessions, he had introduced her to his latest invention: synthetic blood.

Julius rose from behind the desk and gave her a nod but didn't reach across to shake her hand. Shaking hands was a human tradition and not necessary when they were among themselves. "Back so soon?" he asked, his thin lips curling into a half-smirk. "I thought you said my invention tastes like dirty nickels?"

Robin gritted her teeth and forced herself not to react to the mocking in his tone. She shrugged as casually as possible. "What can I say? I guess it's an acquired taste." She glanced at the fridge that was hidden behind the wood panels of his office.

"Not so fast. Let's handle the financial transaction first."

Robin forced her gaze away from the wood panel. "Of course." She dug her wallet out of her back pocket and laid five twenty-dollar bills on his desk before turning back to the hidden fridge.

"I'm afraid that's not enough."

She whirled back around. "Not enough?" She glanced at the bills. "A hundred bucks for a six-pack, as usual."

"That was in the past," he said, his voice cool. "Prices have gone up since the last time you were here."

"What? Why?"

He shrugged. "It's simply a question of supply and demand."

Robin stared at him. "Demand? There can't be many of us who want to drink that stuff." Most Girah would laugh at the mere thought of paying even one cent for blood that tasted like crap and, as Girah scientists suspected, reduced your lifespan by a few decades when you could have the real stuff for free.

"You want it," Julius said.

Worse, she needed it, and the old cutthroat knew it, so he could afford to play his stupid Girah power games with her. It was a common form of entertainment for her kind, and Robin hated it. If living to see your three hundredth birthday meant playing with other people's lives just to stave off boredom, maybe it was a good thing she had stopped drinking the fresh blood that prolonged their lives. With her teeth so tightly clenched that her fangs started to ache, she pulled out her wallet again. "How much for a six-pack of Synth-O?"

"For you, just a hundred and fifty." His grin showed a hint of his fangs.

No wonder Julius could afford a mansion like this. Robin opened her wallet and laid her last fifty-dollar bill on the desk.

He put the money in a drawer and pushed a lever behind his desk that opened the secret compartment where the fridge was hidden. "There you go. Excellent vintage, if I do say so myself."

Robin wasn't in the mood for jokes. She took the bottles from him and put five of them in her backpack. The sixth one she opened instantly, both to make sure the quality was worth the price she'd had to pay and to stop the ache in her stomach and her muscles, which set in when she went without blood for too long.

What the...? She nearly spat the sip of synthetic blood back out. Synth-O tasted bad enough, but this brew raised unpalatable to a whole new level. She popped a piece of gum into her mouth to get rid of the horrible taste before glancing at the label of the bottle. Instead of reading *corn syrup*, it indicated that the bottle held cranberry juice, which was Julius's code word for Synth-A. "You gave me the wrong bottles. This is Synth-A, and you know I prefer Synth-O."

"Sorry," he said, not looking sorry at all. "I'm all out of Synth-O. This is all I have. Take it or leave it."

Rage bubbled up in Robin. She wanted to grab him by the neck and smash him against the walls until his diplomas crashed to the floor and he stopped playing his little games with her. For a moment, she allowed herself to imagine how satisfying that would feel. Then reason prevailed. If she harmed even one of the perfectly coiffed hairs on his head, she'd have to go back to biting humans to survive. "Fine," she managed to say before putting the cap back on the bottle, sliding it into her backpack, and stomping off.

In the foyer, she nearly slammed into the cleaning lady, who looked up from dusting an antique vase.

The vase nearly toppled over, and Robin's reflexes kicked in. She grabbed it before it could shatter.

"Oh, thank you." The cleaning lady stared at her through wide eyes, one hand pressed to her chest. Blood rushed to her face, making Robin suddenly aware that she was human.

They stood so close that if Robin bent her head a little, she could press her lips to the woman's neck and—

No! She let go of the vase and ran. One desperate shove and the heavy door flew open, and then she was finally outside, in her car, where she was safe from temptation, at least for the moment. She drove aimlessly, not caring where she ended up. No matter where she went, she couldn't outrun her problems.

CHAPTER 3

CARRYING A BOX OF PASTRIES, Alana hurried through the throng of cars in the church parking lot. Because of the heavy traffic, she still hadn't found the time to eat, and now the delicious scent coming from the box in her hands made her mouth water. Out of the corner of her eye, she saw a dark figure sitting in a light aqua Prius. Wasn't that Robin? Changing her direction, Alana walked toward the car and stopped next to the passenger's side door. It was indeed Robin.

She stared straight ahead.

Alana shifted the box to free one hand and knocked on the window.

Robin jerked and turned her head in her direction.

Without moving, they gazed at each other.

In the light of dusk, Robin's eyes sparkled like sunshine gleaming on the clear surface of the Mediterranean Sea. *She's gorgeous.* Alana blinked. What was she thinking? Robin was here because she needed help, and Alana was her potential sponsor. Besides, Alana wasn't interested in getting involved with a human. Her one experience had been more than enough. She had learned her lesson. And even if she were ready to risk her heart and soul again, she wouldn't risk her sobriety. There was a reason why AA recommended not to start a relationship before being sober for at least two years.

Relationship? She mentally shook her head at herself. She didn't even know Robin. It had to be her low blood sugar that caused these weird thoughts. She plastered a smile on her face and waved. "Hi, Robin."

Robin rolled down the window on the passenger side but made no move to get out of the car. "Um…hi."

Alana gestured to the church entrance. "Don't you want to come in?" She held up the box and grinned. "I've got pastries."

Instead of looking at the box or Alana's face, Robin seemed to squint at something in between. She cleared her throat. "No, thank you."

Did she mean the meeting or the pastries? On closer examination, it seemed as if drops of sweat covered Robin's forehead. *Is she in withdrawal? Or has she been drinking?* Robin was chewing gum, and Alana remembered that she'd done that too when she'd still been drinking so no one would smell alcohol on her breath. A quart of gin and some chewing gum had been her pre-trial ritual. But if Robin was drunk, she was hiding it well. Alana gestured to the passenger seat. "May I sit for a moment?"

Robin blinked a few times as if she needed a minute to process what Alana had asked. Finally, she sighed. "That's not a good idea." She shook her head. "It was a bad idea to come here. I don't know how I ended up here in the first place."

Alana bent to have a better view of Robin's face. "You came here to find people who listen and understand how you feel."

"They don't know a thing about how I feel," Robin mumbled. She fixed Alana with an intense gaze. "Thank you. I know you mean well, but you really can't help me."

Alana had heard these words before from others who had come seeking help but then preferred going back to drinking instead of learning to face their problems sober. "Then who can?"

"Huh?"

"Do you think you can resist the urges you feel right now on your own?"

"I…I don't know." Robin swallowed and again looked at a point somewhere between Alana's face and the pastries. Did she have a hard time looking Alana in the eyes, or was she staring at her breasts?

No. Her gaze was directed at Alana's neck. Maybe she was studying her necklace to keep herself distracted from the urge to drink. Alana had found some interesting ways to distract herself her first few weeks of sobriety too.

Alana's stomach rumbled so loudly that one of Robin's eyebrows shot up. "What was that?"

Alana's cheeks burned. "Um…I haven't eaten since breakfast. That's why I brought pastries for the group."

"I don't want to keep you from going inside."

"You aren't," Alana said. "I was the one who stopped by your car. So, will you come in with me?" What was it that Brian always said to tentative newbies? "We don't bite."

Robin's eyes widened before she avoided her gaze.

"So?" Alana asked when Robin didn't move but scowled down at her own knees. For a few seconds, all Alana heard was her own breathing.

Then Robin asked quietly, "What do you do when the craving becomes too strong?" She looked up.

The lost and vulnerable expression on her face robbed Alana of breath. It took her a few moments to think of an answer. Robin was willing to talk. That was a start. But talking through the open window of a car was no way to have an important conversation like this. "Would it be okay if we talk in your car for a moment?"

After a short hesitation, Robin took the backpack from the passenger seat. The clanging indicated that there were bottles inside.

I'd bet a month's pay that's alcohol. I wonder if she's the bourbon type.

Whatever Robin's beverage of choice, she was here to fight her urges, and Alana had every intention of helping her. She opened the door and climbed into the passenger seat. With the box on her lap, she closed the door. Her stomach chose this moment to rumble again. She pointed at the box. "Do you mind?"

"No, go ahead. I know what it's like to be hungry."

What a strange thing to say. Not having to be told twice, Alana opened the box and took a big bite of a nougat-filled pastry. A moan escaped her lips. "God, I love these." The ability to enjoy food had to be one of the best things about being human. She gestured to the other pastries. "Do you want one?"

Instead of looking at the pastries, Robin stared at Alana with an expression best described as panicked.

"What is it?" She touched Robin's forearm but withdrew when the contact caused an electric shock to course through her body. She peeked at Robin, hoping she hadn't noticed.

Thankfully, Robin seemed lost in thought. Like most humans, she didn't appear to notice the gentle current of energy that happened whenever Alana's skin touched theirs, even though it had been unusually strong with Robin.

Alana breathed a sigh of relief. God, she hated when this happened. She had lost all her powers, so why was her taqa still surrounding her like a force field?

Robin blinked once, then twice. "I'm not hungry. At least not for pastries," she said, more to herself than to Alana.

Alana remembered a time when she had gone days without eating. Alcohol killed her appetite and made her crave just one thing: more alcohol. By now, she had no doubt that Robin was in withdrawal. She finished her pastry before answering Robin's initial question. "When the craving becomes too strong, I go to a meeting, call Brian, my sponsor, or—don't laugh—watch *Buffy, the Vampire Slayer.*"

"Huh?" Robin tilted her head to one side.

"Yeah, you know, the TV show about this blonde teenager hunting vampires."

Robin arched one brow. "Vampires?"

Humans tended to believe creatures like those were superstitions, just silly myths and legends used to scare children.

While Alana knew better, she had to admit that the TV show wasn't exactly realistic. "I know, I know. The show is pretty silly, but that's part of what makes it so entertaining. Watching it makes me laugh and forget about wanting a drink. At least it works sometimes."

Was that a hint of a smile on Robin's lips?

"Yeah, it's ridiculous. The show I mean." Robin gazed at Alana's lips. "Um... you have some..."

"What?"

Robin gestured to her lips. "There's some icing left. From the pastry."

"Where?" Alana wiped at her mouth. "Gone?"

Shaking her head, Robin extended her hand. Hesitantly, she touched the side of Alana's mouth and wiped off the white-powdered sugar with her thumb.

Energy sparked between them. Was it just her imagination, or was it stronger with Robin than with other humans?

Robin averted her gaze. "Gone."

"Thank you."

Robin nodded while fidgeting in the driver's seat.

Now what? Instead of focusing on the attraction between them, she should concentrate on Robin's problem. "May I ask what's in your backpack?"

The fidgeting stopped. "What?"

"Your backpack."

"Nothing. Just some bottles of, um, cranberry juice."

"Cranberry juice?"

Robin lifted her chin. "Yes."

Not the most creative excuse she had ever heard. She closed the box. "Can I see?"

"You want to see my cranberry juice?"

"I like cranberry juice."

"You don't like this brand. Trust me." Now Robin looked into Alana's eyes for the first time, as if willing her to let it go.

So I was right. Alana ignored the intense gaze. "It's something alcoholic, isn't it?"

"What? No!" Robin grabbed the backpack from the backseat, opened it, and got one bottle out. "See? Cranberry juice."

Alana tried to reach for the bottle, but Robin was faster. "No!" She snatched it out of her reach and put it back into the backpack.

Alana stared at her.

After a few seconds of uncomfortable silence, Robin said, "Okay, it is alcohol. Happy?"

Alana took a deep breath. "No, I'm not happy that you're this close to falling off the wagon. But at least you were honest now. Aren't you tired of lying about how much you drink? You can't beat this alone, and you know it." She gestured toward the church. "Why else would you be here?"

Robin averted her gaze and studied her hands instead. Alana could almost feel her inner struggle. Eventually, Robin sighed. "Okay, maybe I do need help, but I don't feel up to coming to the meeting tonight. Maybe next week."

Alana furrowed her brow. "Putting it off won't help. That's like the people whose diet always starts tomorrow."

At the mention of *diet*, Robin winced.

"There's no time like the present, so why don't you take the first step now?"

"Fine," Robin said after a while. "But I'm still not coming to the meeting tonight. My first step is accepting you as my sponsor."

That wasn't what Alana had been after, but she had to let Robin make her own choices. At least she was doing something to get sober. "Thanks. You won't regret it." *I hope.*

Robin said nothing.

"Call me if you need me, okay?" When Robin nodded, Alana opened the door and got out. She turned back and indicated the backpack. "Promise me you'll get rid of it."

Robin bit her lip. "I…"

"Want me to do it for you? Behind the church is a Dumpster. I'll discharge it there."

"No!" Robin clutched the backpack to her chest. "I…I'll do it later."

Alana sighed. "We both know that you won't. Come on. Let me do it. Let me help. Please."

Robin looked back and forth between Alana and the backpack; then she closed her eyes. Her face was a picture of pain. When she opened her eyes again, she looked as if she was about to cry.

Alana leaned through the still-open door and took the backpack from her limp grasp. "Thank you," she whispered. "You made the first step. Try to keep yourself busy with something pleasant during the weekend."

Instead of answering, Robin laughed, but it was bare of any humor. "Good night."

"Good night." Alana closed the door and watched as Robin drove off. A hum of energy still hung in the air. *Great. Now you're her sponsor and can't stay away from her. You're playing with fire.* But if she hadn't searched her out, Robin probably would have gotten drunk instead of accepting a help.

Tucking the pastry box under one arm, Alana looked down at the backpack and then marched to the Dumpster. Not wanting to tempt herself by looking at the bottles too closely, she just opened the backpack and dumped its contents into the large trash container.

The bottles burst with a satisfying crash.

She peeked into the Dumpster and watched the red liquid trickle down the shards of glass. *Ugh. What the heck is she drinking? Bloody Marys?*

For a moment, she stood next to the Dumpster, thinking about Robin's devastated expression when she allowed her to take the backpack. *I'll try my best to help her.* If she made sure to meet Robin only in public places and stick to the role of a sponsor instead of allowing herself to become friendly with Robin, she would be fine.

She took a deep breath, closed the now-empty backpack, and carried her box of pastries toward the church entrance. If she hurried, she would still be on time for the meeting. She would return Robin's backpack when they saw each other the next time. As strange as their conversation had been, she was almost sure there would be a next time.

Robin pulled her car into the parking garage beneath her high-rise condo building, turned off the engine, and then just sat there, staring at the gray concrete wall in front of her. What the hell had just happened? *You let a human take away your blood; that's what happened,* the voice in her head that sounded like Meghan said. *A human who likes Buffy, the Vampire Slayer!*

It was pathetic, really. Why hadn't she just promised to get rid of what Alana thought was alcohol? For some strange reason, she had a hard time lying to Alana and hadn't been able to come up with an excuse fast enough. And what was even stranger was that Robin had used her thrall, but Alana hadn't reacted at all. She had continued questioning Robin about the damn bottles as if nothing had happened.

Were her mind-control skills slipping? Maybe it was an unknown side effect of her abstinence or the Synth-A she had drunk earlier. Robin swallowed, not sure if she was ready to give up so much of her identity. Could she still consider herself a Girah if she stopped drinking blood and couldn't thrall people anymore?

She got out of the car, locked it, and walked into the building as if on autopilot. Maybe it had been just a fluke. She nodded. *Yes, that must be it. Just a fluke.* Still, the hollow feeling in her stomach wouldn't go away.

When she unlocked the door to her condo, steps sounded behind her. Without turning her head, she knew that it was her next-door neighbor, an Indian guy who constantly smelled of turmeric, cardamom, and coriander. She didn't like spicy food, so she'd never been tempted to bite him. She wanted to make a quick escape into her condo before he could decide to exchange some chitchat, but then she stopped and turned.

He stood in front of his own door and looked over at her with a hesitant smile.

Oh, yeah. He'll do for a test run. "Excuse me?"

The key already in the door, he paused. "Uh, yes?"

Hmm, what should she ask of him to test her thrall? For a moment, she considered ordering him to hand over his wallet. Since Alana had tossed her bottles of Synth-A, she needed to buy more, and the next royalty check was still two weeks away. But then she quickly discarded the idea. While she might have almost killed a human on New Year's Eve, she wasn't going to add thievery to her list of crimes. She fixed him with an intense stare, the same one she had used on Alana without any success. "Do twenty-one jumping jacks."

With a glazed-over expression in his eyes, he started jumping up and down, raising and lowering his arms in time with the movement of his legs.

Robin leaned against the wall and watched him with a big grin. She hadn't lost her touch after all. When he finished, she was tempted to have him try a handstand next but then changed her mind. *You tested your thrall. Now let him go, or you'll be no better than Meghan, who thinks nothing of playing with humans.* "Go into your apartment and forget this little stint of gymnastic exercise."

He turned and disappeared into his apartment without a word.

Her thrall was as strong as ever. Why hadn't it worked on Alana? The thrall had snapped back from her as if it had met an invisible barrier, and even increasing the force of her thrall had succeeded only in giving Robin a headache.

The ringing phone from inside of her condo interrupted her before she could come to a conclusion. She hurried to pick it up. With any luck, it might be someone from Fangs & Fur Publishing, calling to accept her revised short story submission.

Instead, Meghan's voice greeted her from the other end of the line. "Hi, Robin. Long time no see. Your parents say you're making yourself rare at clan meetings too."

Robin groaned inwardly. That would teach her to look at the caller ID before picking up the phone. "I have deadlines to meet," she said. "I'm writing practically twenty-four seven."

"Oh, come on. If you stay in, never leaving the apartment, your neighbors will start thinking there's something weird going on—like you being a vampire or something." Meghan chuckled.

Robin thought of her neighbor doing jumping jacks in the hallway and grinned.

"How about leaving your fictional vampires behind for the rest of the night and going out with a real one?" Meghan said, her voice full of promises.

A tingle crept up Robin's spine. Not the same one she felt when Alana had touched her but one that was full of forbidden temptations. "I don't have time to—"

"You've got to eat some time. Let's go grab a bite."

When Meghan said *bite*, she meant exactly that. From the moment they had undergone the rite as teenagers, allowing them to hunt on their own, Meghan had gone out every night, grabbed some unsuspecting passerby from a quiet side street or an alley, and drank from him or her until her hunger was stilled. She wasn't particular about her food sources, male or female, young or old, anyone would do, but she didn't like to eat alone. They had feasted together more often than Robin could count. She pushed the thought of their last meal together out of her mind. "I can't," she said.

"Oh, come on. The literary world won't end just because you're away from the keyboard for an hour or two."

Meghan had never understood how much writing meant to her. She had never understood her, period. "It's not just that. I...I'm trying to change my eating habits."

For a moment, only silence filtered through the line; then Meghan started to laugh. "You're on a diet? I thought you had gotten that crazy idea out of your head by now."

Robin squared her shoulders and gripped the phone more tightly. "It's not crazy, Meghan. That woman on New Year's Eve..." She shuddered as she could again taste the salty-sweet tang of the woman's blood on her tongue. Guilt burned through her.

"What about her?" Meghan asked, clearly not caring.

"I nearly drained her," Robin whispered. "I lost control and...and...I almost...I almost killed her."

"That happened because you hadn't gone out and hunted for so long. It's the way of the Girah, Robin. You're denying your very nature, and it won't work. Come on, have you ever heard of Dracula going on a diet?" Meghan laughed again.

Robin bit her lip until she tasted blood. That delicious copper taste of human blood was missing, though. "I have to go," she said. "The deadlines are looming."

"Call me when you change your mind and want to go out," Meghan said.

Robin hesitated. Should she ask Meghan for money so she could buy more Synth-O or at least Synth-A? No. If she went out to meet her, Meghan would try to get her to hunt with her, and Robin wasn't sure she was strong enough to resist temptation. Not with that nagging hunger ripping at her. So she just said good-bye and hung up.

She went into the kitchen and opened the fridge, hoping she had somehow missed a bottle of Synth-O hidden behind the bottled water.

Nothing. Not a drop of synthetic blood in her fridge.

Without it, she couldn't survive longer than a few more days. Where was she supposed to get the money from? Meghan was out, and so were her parents. She would rather drain Mr. Singh next door than beg her parents for money. Their words when her first vampire novel had come out still rang in her ears.

"You're a disgrace to this clan and our entire race!" her mother had shouted, and her father had thrown the book with her handwritten dedication to them in her face.

Sighing, she stared at the phone. Did she know anyone who could afford to lend her one hundred and fifty bucks?

CHAPTER 4

Panting, Alana reduced the resistance setting on her elliptical trainer. Even after four years, she hadn't gotten used to the amount of maintenance her human body required. She let her thoughts drift while she exercised. *I wonder how Robin is doing.* As confident and independent as Robin might come across, she also seemed to have a fragile side that made Alana's protective instincts flare.

A high-pitched sound that came out of nowhere made Alana flinch. With her leftover abilities, she sensed a ripple in the ethereal currents. A glowing band of color wafted past her TV, and then a figure materialized in the middle of her living room.

Alana lifted the towel from around her shoulders and wiped sweat off her face. "One of these days, you're going to give me a heart attack," she muttered under her breath.

Dahir sprawled across Alana's couch, rested her head on one hand, and smirked at her. "Nah, your human form is not that fragile. In forty or fifty years, though…" She shrugged. "Who knows?"

Alana stepped down from her exercise machine. "With the residual taqa, my lifespan will probably be much longer than that of normal humans. So I don't think I'll age that fast."

Dahir swung her feet up onto the couch. "Probably, but we can't be sure, since you're the only one of us stupid enough to become human." She shook her head. "What's two or three hundred years compared to watching the universe for eternity? I still don't understand why you gave that up."

Alana had heard it all before, and she wasn't in the mood to be scolded for her decision again. Looking back, she couldn't understand her decision either, but it was over and done with, so now she had to make the best of it.

Unfortunately, Dahir wasn't through with her. "Human bodies are so limiting. I'll never understand how you can bear having your senses so blunted." She touched her eyes and ears and then shook her head.

Alana walked over to the couch and sat down beside Dahir's high-heeled feet. "Is there a reason for your visit, or are you just here to give me a hard time?"

"My, my, are we a little moody today?" Dahir inspected her fingernails. "Can't I just visit my dear friend," she fixed her gaze on Alana, "and offer her a wish?"

Alana shook her head. "You know it's against the rules to grant wishes to fellow—"

"You're no longer one of us."

Of course Alana knew that, but Dahir's words stung nevertheless.

As if reading her thoughts, Dahir said, "But you will always be my friend. So, do you have any wishes?" She swirled her finger as if Alana had already answered in the positive.

Alana grunted. "Like I'd tell you. Remember what happened when I asked you to fix the cut in my couch?"

"What's the problem? I fixed it, didn't I?"

Alana rolled her eyes. "Finding loopholes in a wish is one thing, twisting it like you did is something else entirely." She indicated the couch beneath them. "This is not my couch. Giving me a brand-new couch is not exactly the same as fixing a cut, is it?"

Dahir caressed the couch. "What's the matter with this beauty?"

"It's pink. I hate pink. You should know that after all these centuries."

Dahir sighed. "But your old black one was boring. If you have to live your life as a human, at least spice it up a little."

Instead of answering, Alana just glared at her.

Raising her hands in defeat, Dahir said, "Okay, okay. So you want your old couch back?"

"Repaired," Alana said.

Dahir nodded. "As you wish."

Alana held on to the coffee table as the pink monstrosity disappeared beneath her and her old couch took its place. She turned around to inspect it thoroughly, especially the place where the material had been ripped. The long cut in the armrest was gone. "Thank you," she said.

"You're welcome." Dahir kicked off her red five-inch heels and massaged her feet, groaning. "I've kept an eye on humanity for centuries now, but I still can't figure out why they invent things like these." She shook one of the high-heeled shoes. "This isn't a shoe; it's a torture instrument."

Alana snorted. "You chose to wear them, didn't you? Besides, if you think that's torture, try menstrual cramps," she muttered. Other than being cheated on by Kelly, that had been the most unpleasant surprise of her human existence.

Dahir squinted over at her. "Try what?"

"Nothing," Alana said. She wasn't in the mood to discuss anatomy with Dahir. Her best friend already thought Alana had been foolish for giving up her skills and limiting herself to a human body with all its shortcomings. Some days, especially days with cramps, she didn't fully understand it herself.

With a swirl of Dahir's finger, the high-heeled shoes disappeared. A pair of fuzzy, pink slippers took their place. Dahir leaned back with a satisfied grin. "Better. Now tell me how you're doing. Has anything interesting happened in your boring human life?"

Alana folded her arms over her chest. "My life isn't boring. I get plenty of excitement, thank you very much." Since meeting

Robin, at least her thoughts had been heading in an interesting direction. "I'm fine."

"Excitement?" Dahir eyed her skeptically. "When humans want more excitement in their lives, they usually wish for a new car, a trip to an exotic location, or a more passionate love life. I know you still drive the same car, and you haven't gone on vacation, so…"

"I don't have a love life."

"But?"

"No but," Alana said.

Dahir regarded her. "Why don't I believe you?"

"How would I know?" Alana averted her gaze. She didn't want to tell her that her long-lost libido had returned with a vengeance. Dahir would just think that Alana hadn't learned her lesson and was about to ruin her life again by getting involved with a human. Alana stood, walked back to her elliptical trainer, and continued her exercise at maximum speed. "Really, there's nothing to tell."

"Uh-huh." The tone of Dahir's voice indicated that she didn't believe a word.

Alana squirmed under Dahir's intense gaze. "Listen, I don't want to talk about it, okay?"

"So there is something to talk about. Come on, tell your best friend."

Even though *best friend* was the closest equivalent in human culture, it didn't quite manage to describe the nature of their relationship. After all, they had once been connected in a way no human could understand, coexisting on a plane of light, energy, and fire, where it was hard to tell where the natural form of one ended and the other began. *Well, I'm not part of the Great Energy anymore.* "Maybe another t—"

The phone rang.

Dahir smiled like a predator showing its canines. "Is that who you don't want to talk about?"

Again out of breath, Alana stepped off the elliptical trainer. She had obviously put a little too much energy into her exercise. "There's no one I don't want to talk about." She panted, picked up the phone from the coffee table, and looked at the caller ID. *Unknown.* Frowning, she lifted the phone to her ear. "Alana Wadd." She gestured for Dahir to stay quiet.

Heavy breathing was the only answer.

Alana was about to end the call, but then she got the feeling that she was dealing with a woman in distress, not an obscene caller. Maybe it was her leftover taqa giving her an insight that other humans didn't have. Whatever it was, she'd learned to trust her instincts.

Maybe it's Mrs. Phillips. Her newest client had been so devastated this morning in her office that Alana had made an exception, writing down her private number on the back of the card she'd handed her. "Hello?" she asked gently. "Mrs. Phillips, is that you?"

The person at the other end of the line cleared her throat. "No," the woman croaked.

I know this voice. A blush heated Alana's cheeks. Of all the people who could have called while Dahir was looking in on her, it had to be her. "Robin?"

It seemed to take forever before Robin said, "Yeah, it's me. I hope I'm not interrupting. You sound out of breath."

Alana had thought about Robin and the desperation in her blue eyes quite often since their encounter in front of the church three days ago, but she hadn't expected Robin to take her up on the offer to call if she wanted to talk. "No. I was just working out, that's all. Could you give me a minute?"

"Um, sure."

Alana covered the phone with her hand and whispered, "Dahir, would you mind? I need to talk to the woman I'm sponsoring."

"You're her sponsor?" Dahir shook her head. "Didn't you tell me that it's a big no-no in AA to get...," she circled her finger in the air, creating swirls of brilliance that floated over the coffee table for a second before disappearing, "involved with someone you sponsor?"

"What are you talking about?" Even though Alana still had her hand over the phone, she lowered her voice. "It's not like that. Could you now please give us some privacy?"

"Have fun," Dahir said and winked before disappearing with the familiar high-pitched whistle.

Alana sat back on the couch and withdrew her hand from the phone. "I'm sorry. How are you?"

Instead of answering, Robin said, "I didn't want to disturb you. Maybe I should call another ti—"

"It's fine. Really. Now tell me how you're doing. If you drank, you can tell me, you know? I won't judge you." Alana tried to keep her voice as soft as possible.

Robin sighed. "No, I haven't had a drink in what seems like forever, and that's the problem."

"That's not the problem," Alana said. "It's the solution. You should be proud of yourself."

For a while, Robin didn't answer. Then she asked, "Listen, I know we barely know each other, and I really hate to do this, but do you think you could lend me some money? It's just for two weeks; then I'll pay back every cent, I swear."

Alana blinked. Had she heard correctly? Robin had called her to ask for money? Every time she thought she'd seen it all and could no longer be surprised by something a human did, something happened to prove her wrong. It wasn't Alana's job as a sponsor to lend her money. And why did she need money? Was she out of work and behind on rent, or did she need the money for alcohol?

When Alana didn't answer, Robin said, "Ah, forget it. Sorry to have bothered you. Good ni—"

"Wait!" Alana was almost shouting. "Why don't you come over and have dinner with me tonight?" At least this way, Alana could make sure that Robin didn't drink and didn't have to go hungry either.

"Thank you, but I can't." Robin sounded hoarse.

Maybe it was for the best. Alana couldn't do both—keep her distance and help Robin to stay sober. Unfortunately, she doubted that Robin would confide in someone else from AA. She had agreed to be Robin's sponsor, so she was her responsibility now. *I just have to ignore this damn attraction, and everything will be fine.* "Come on. I was about to start cooking, and it's so much more fun if I don't just do it for myself. Do you like lasagna?"

"I really don't think—"

"We could talk." When Robin still hesitated, Alana added, "About the money you need."

Robin exhaled loudly. "Okay."

"Really?" Robin had given in so fast that Alana again wondered why she so desperately needed money. She'd try to find out over dinner. "Um, I mean great." She gave Robin her address.

"I can be there in about half an hour." She sounded wary. "Would that be okay with you?"

"Absolutely."

"Should I...? Can I bring anything? I mean, no wine, apparently, but is there anything else you want me to bring?"

Cute. She's rambling. There was nothing Alana could think of, and Robin probably didn't have the money to buy anything she might have needed anyway. "No, just yourself and a healthy appetite. Drive carefully."

After a moment's hesitation, Robin said, "I will. See you soon."

Alana ended the call and sat back. "You're doing a fantastic job staying away from her," she murmured into the empty apartment. She had promised herself to keep the interaction with Robin all business and to meet with her only in public, where no real intimacy could develop. But now, after just one call from Robin, she seemed to have forgotten all her promises. When she looked down at herself, she became aware of her sweat-soaked clothes and jumped up to take a quick shower.

With the uncanny sense of a born predator, Robin found Alana's apartment building without any difficulties. Of course, having the address helped a lot too. But instead of going in, she sat in her car in front of the building and counted passing cars. *I'm making a habit of this—sitting in front of buildings without going in.* It wasn't that she didn't want to go in and see Alana again; she wanted it way too much, and that was the problem.

Her stomach was all for it too. *Bring a healthy appetite,* Alana had said. She was hungry all right, but she wasn't sure how healthy the ravenous hunger coursing through her body really was. Certainly not healthy for Alana.

A shadow crossed in front of the window on the second floor, and she instinctively knew it was Alana, even though she saw her only for a moment.

Before she knew it, she had gotten out of the car and had crossed the street. *What are you doing? This is like an alcoholic walking into a bar or a liquor store!*

But the siren call was too strong. Besides, she needed the money for the synthetic blood, and Alana was the only person who could lend her a hundred and fifty bucks without asking too many questions. At least a dinner invitation from her didn't involve hunting down humans.

When she rang the doorbell, Alana buzzed her in with a cheerful "come on up. It's apartment 2A, the first door to the left on the second floor."

Alana opened the door, wearing an apron that read *caution: extremely hot.*

True. Robin's appreciative gaze swept over her.

Alana's hair, still damp from a shower, framed her face and clung to her biteable neck. Her cheeks were flushed, which made her even more attractive, especially since it meant the blood was running close to the surface. Just a little prick and she could…

No! Robin shook herself out of her haze. "Uh, h-hi."

Still standing in the doorway, Alana looked her up and down. "Excuse me for being so frank, but you look like shit."

Robin grinned wryly. "That good, huh? That's about how I feel too." After three days with no blood and just a few sips at Julius's house before that, she was starting to feel like a robot whose batteries were running out. Her empty stomach cramped.

Alana ushered her into the apartment and led her to a homey kitchen that smelled of even more spices than that of her neighbor, Mr. Singh. The only scent that held any interest to Robin was Alana's, though.

She swallowed and stayed back, keeping the kitchen island between them. Not that it was a real obstacle to a hungry Girah. She could vault that thing in a single leap.

"What happened?" Alana asked.

"Nothing."

"Didn't anyone ever tell you that we lawyers can smell a lie like a fart in an elevator?"

Robin chuckled at the unexpected choice of words, for a moment distracted from her hunger pangs. "And here I thought that lawyers are the ones who tell the lies."

"Well, that too, but we're not talking about me. Come on, I'm your sponsor. Tell me what's going on with you."

She could tell that Alana wouldn't let it go. The woman was too damn stubborn for her own good. Just in case lawyers—or just this lawyer in particular—could indeed tell when she was lying, she decided to reveal a tiny part of the truth. "I haven't been sleeping very well lately."

"Cravings keeping you up?" Alana asked, her tone and her expression full of compassion.

The mere mention of it made Robin's hunger flare again. She didn't dare look at Alana, at the pulsing carotid in her neck, and— She forced her thoughts to switch direction. "Yeah," she said, her voice hoarse. "That too."

"Did anything happen that made the cravings worse?"

You, Robin wanted to say but, of course, didn't. Instead, she revealed another little piece of the truth. "My job isn't going so well at the moment."

Alana nodded knowingly. "Trust me, I know all about that. I love my job, but some days it makes me crave a Dracula's Kiss."

Was the hunger making her hallucinate? Robin was sure she hadn't heard right. She tried not to think about how much she wanted to give Alana that kind of kiss. "It makes you crave... what?"

"It's a cocktail. Campari, orange juice, black current liqueur, and—"

"Let me guess," Robin said. "Gin."

With a self-deprecating smile, Alana nodded and gestured at a bar stool at the kitchen island. "Take a seat and tell me about it while I start cooking. Oh, by the way, you do eat red meat, don't you? I could make it a vegetarian lasagna if you don't."

"No, that's not necessary. I do eat meat." Robin sat on the stool, which brought her even closer to Alana. She clutched the kitchen island with both hands and focused on not leaning across to take in her scent and her heat. Almost too low for Alana to hear, she added, "The redder, the better." While she could eat Alana's lasagna or any other human food, it wouldn't appease her hunger or give her the nutrients she so urgently needed. Even rare meat or animal blood wouldn't help much. Her food pyramid looked more like a square, and human blood was the one and only thing in it.

"Great." Alana put a skillet on the stove, took a package that smelled like ground beef out of the fridge, and pulled a knife from a drawer. "So, your job isn't going so well. Is that why you need money? Are you self-employed?"

"Something like that," Robin said. She didn't like telling others what exactly it was that she did for a living. The only thing telling other Girahs had earned her were sarcastic comments, turned-up noses, and hostile threats. Even most humans didn't take authors writing in her genre seriously, so she had learned not to reveal her profession unless absolutely necessary.

Alana looked up from peeling an onion. Her luminous green eyes held no judgment, only a silent question and a request for her trust.

Robin sighed. *Oh, what the hell. What she thinks doesn't matter anyway.* "I'm a writer," she said.

"Oh, wow. That's impressive."

"You think so?" Robin couldn't help feeling pleased. "Are you an avid reader?"

Alana started chopping the onion. "I used to be. There was a time when I devoured five novels a week."

At the word *devoured*, Robin reflexively licked her lips. She tried to focus on the conversation. "And now?"

"I don't have time to read anymore," Alana said. She gripped the knife so tightly that her knuckles blanched. Her heartbeat accelerated, making it even harder for Robin to stay on her side of the kitchen island instead of being lured in by the tempting staccato.

Robin watched her closely. "That's not all, though, is it?"

Alana paused in the middle of chopping the onion and looked up with big green eyes. "Uh, what do you mean?"

"You not reading anymore... It's not just because you don't have the time."

Alana glanced at the onion and started chopping again. The knife sliced through the onion with more force than necessary. "The novels I read were just not realistic, so why bother reading them? They just set you up for disappointment if you are stupid enough to believe in all that romance crap."

"You think romance is crap?" Not that Robin's experiences with love had been any better. Other Girah didn't understand her, never had, never would, and if she started a relationship with a human like Alana, she would never be sure whether it was just bloodlust or truly love that drew her to her partner.

"Don't tell me you write romances. How can—ouch! Dammit!" Alana dropped the knife and clutched her hand.

The sweet scent of blood wafted through the kitchen.

Before Robin could stop herself, she stuck her nose in the air and inhaled deeply. Nothing had ever smelled so good. Her head spun, and she felt as if she were getting drunk on the intoxicating fragrance. She had no idea how she had gotten past the kitchen island, but she found herself standing next to Alana in front of the sink. "Let me see." Her voice sounded strange, even to her own ears, and she realized her fangs had protruded. The razor-sharp points dug into her lips from the inside, adding the scent of her own blood to Alana's. It was an enchanting mix.

Slowly, Alana took her other hand away from her finger.

A red haze floated before Robin's eyes, and all she heard was the fast beat of Alana's heart.

A crimson trail of blood ran down Alana's finger, and a few droplets splashed onto the floor. "Shit. I'm bleeding all over the kitchen."

"Come here," Robin said, putting the full force of her thrall into her voice. At the same time, another voice in her head screamed, *No, stay away! Stay far, far away from me, Alana.*

Alana took a step toward her.

Don't do it. She trusts you. But the call of the blood was too strong. Her gaze locked on the bleeding cut, and she couldn't force herself to look away. She imagined the salty-sweet liquid caressing her tongue and rolling smoothly down her throat until it warmed every part of her. Her belly tightened as arousal and hunger crashed over her in one large wave. As if in a trance, she reached for Alana's hand to lift it to her lips. Her mouth watered in expectation of the coppery taste.

When their fingers touched, an electric current seemed to sizzle through her. Dazed, she stumbled back. *What the...?* She blinked as if waking from a dream and stared at Alana.

"It's my sweater," Alana said quickly. "I get zapped whenever I wear it."

Alana's voice sounded muffled, as if it were coming from a great distance. "I'm sorry," Robin said, fighting for every word. "I have to go." Her tongue felt heavy, and her thoughts were sluggish, as if she had lost the ability to think about anything but Alana's blood.

"What? Why?"

Robin fled to the kitchen door, but Alana followed her, still dripping blood. The urge to lunge around and bite her swept through her, and she started to tremble with the effort to resist. "I...I don't do so well with blood."

"Oh. That's all right. You can sit in the living room while I—"

"No, I have to go." Robin jerked the door open, desperate to escape.

"But what about the lasagna? And what about the money you wanted to borrow?"

Robin couldn't stay, not for all the money in the world. If she did, she'd do something stupid within the next three seconds. With a burning throat and a burning heart, she escaped the kitchen.

Stunned, Alana stared after Robin, who rushed down the hallway as if the devil himself or some other creature from human mythology were after her. When she disappeared around the corner, Alana closed the door and leaned against it. What had just happened?

Another drop of her blood splashed onto the hardwood floor, making her aware of the cut again. She hurried back into the kitchen and held her finger under the faucet. She jerked as pain flared. "Ouch, dammit." No matter how long she lived as a human, she would never get used to pain.

She still remembered her first experience with it. It had been just the third time she'd left the Great Energy to take human form. At the side of her master, she had crossed the square in front of the Palace of Versailles, staring up at the imposing north and south wings. It was so different from the plane of light and energy where her kind existed. A carriage clattered through the massive golden gate behind them, the horses' hooves clomping over the marble flagstones. Guardsmen wearing uniforms and powdered wigs paraded over the square.

A beautiful woman smiled down at her from the carriage, probably on her way to the Sun King's court or a stroll through the gardens. Two large emeralds shone in her ears, and a fur-edged coat was draped over her gown that was trimmed with silver and golden lace.

As the carriage passed, she winked at Alana.

"Tout de suite, tout de suite," her master called and tugged on her arm. "Come along."

Alana stumbled over the hem of her frivolous dress and fell. A strange sensation flared through her knee, and it took her a moment to figure out that it was pain.

Dahir had made fun of her for a century, and Alana had refused to leave the ethereal plane and take on human form for decades.

When she glanced back at her finger, she realized that the cut was no longer visible. Her residual taqa had healed the wound. Her fingertips still tingled, though.

The spark of energy when she had touched Robin had been unusually strong. Normally, humans didn't seem to notice, but Robin had definitely felt it too. That probably wasn't the reason why Robin had fled her apartment, though. She'd seemed sick, and Alana sensed that it wasn't just the sight of blood making her queasy. *Something is wrong with her.* Maybe she was going through alcohol withdrawal. Alana knew firsthand what strange things that could do to a human body. *She shouldn't be alone now.*

But as much as she wanted to help Robin, how could she? She had no address, not even a phone number.

Maybe Robin was still close by and could be talked into coming back. Alana hurried to the window and searched the street for Robin. *There she is.*

Swaying, Robin caught herself against her car with both hands.

Alana threw her apron on the kitchen counter, grabbed her keys, and rushed out of her apartment.

When Alana left the apartment building, Robin was still leaning against her car as if her legs could no longer support her. "Robin!"

Groaning, Robin looked up. Her eyes were bloodshot and... Was she trembling?

For a moment, Alana's steps faltered. Alcohol withdrawal was no laughing matter. Twice, she had seen people hallucinate and have seizures. But even though Robin's shakiness and her apparent confusion fit the symptoms of withdrawal, Alana had this nagging feeling that she was dealing with something entirely different. *Whatever it is, she needs your help. Everything else can wait.* There would be time later to ask Robin if she was addicted to other substances as well. She quickly crossed the street and joined Robin next to her car.

"I...I'm fine. Go back inside," Robin whispered, staring into Alana's eyes as if willing her to do what she said.

"No. You're miserable," Alana said. "I won't let you suffer alone. I'm your sponsor."

Robin blinked. "Did you just say no?"

Despite the situation, Alana couldn't help smiling. The disbelief in Robin's voice was almost comical. "That's right." She reached out to take Robin's arm and to help her inside but then withdrew at the last moment. If she caused another spark of energy, it would frighten Robin even more. So instead of touching her, Alana pointed to the building's entrance. "Can you make it back inside?"

"I'm going home."

"You're in no condition to drive. Remember the story I shared with the group at your first AA meeting?" The memory made her shiver. "I know you don't want to risk getting in an accident like that."

Robin squeezed her eyes shut. "No," she murmured, her voice low. "I never want to hurt anyone again."

Again? Alana sensed the pain behind her words, but this wasn't the time to ask questions. "Then come on."

Robin still didn't move.

Knowing she had no other choice, Alana took Robin's arm and pulled her toward the building. The spark of energy made them both jerk, but Alana kept her grip on Robin's arm. Eventually, the burst of energy subsided and transformed into a pleasant tingle. It reminded her of an arousal she hadn't felt since... *Cut it out! You're her sponsor. She needs your help, not a crazy infatuation.* "Come on." She tugged on Robin's arm again.

"Your finger." Open-mouthed, Robin gaped at her healed finger.

Oh, shit! "Um, the cut wasn't deep, just a little scratch." She forced a smile. "Can you imagine my surprise when I held the finger under water and pulled it back looking like this?" Without waiting for an answer, Alana tugged Robin away from the car. "Anyway, let's get you upstairs."

Instead of following along, Robin tried to free herself from Alana's grip.

It took all of Alana's strength to hold on and not let her pull away. *Wow, she is amazingly strong for someone going through alcohol withdrawal.* After a few seconds of a silent tug-of-war, Alana gave up her attempts to pull her inside. "Either you're coming with me, or I'm calling an ambulance. Going cold turkey can be life threatening if you're doing it all alone."

With narrowed eyes, Robin didn't move an inch. She half turned to her car, as if battling with her decision. Eventually, she sighed, turned back around, and followed Alana. "Just give me the money, and I'll be on my way. No reason to worry."

"So you can buy alcohol or drugs?" Alana shook her head. "Forget it."

"What? No, I won't use the money for that. I need it for, um…for medicine."

"Sure. I know that kind of medicine all too well, trust me." She linked her arm through Robin's and flinched at the strong spark of energy. *You'd think I would finally get it through my thick head that touching her is not a good idea.* "It won't help you in the long run."

Robin took a step away from her.

No wonder. She had to be petrified from all these little electroshocks.

Robin shook her head. "No, I swear, it's a kind of medicine."

"If that's true, then tell me what kind of sickness you have."

"Um…"

Alana sighed. "Come on, Robin. Aren't you sick of all the lies? Why are you so stubborn? Come in, and let me help you."

"I'm not stubborn, and I don't need your help. What I need is the money and to go home." When they reached the apartment, Robin tore herself loose from Alana's grip and stumbled away from her, landing on the couch with a thump. She pressed both hands to her thighs and breathed deeply as if trying to gather the strength to get back up. Her skin was unnaturally pale, and even though it was cool in the apartment, sweat dripped from her temples and her forehead. Finally, she gave up her attempts to get up and sank against the back of the couch.

Alana watched her with a growing feeling of helplessness. Oh, how she wished she had her skills back for just a moment, so she could help Robin with the swirl of a finger. But maybe Robin was like her. Back when Alana had been sweating and trembling on her first day without gin, she had declined Dahir's offer of help. Being human meant having to cope with the good and bad things life threw your way, without being able to manipulate the ethereal streams. How could she learn from her mistakes if she didn't have to suffer the consequences? *The same is true for Robin.* She needed someone to offer guidance and teach her how to help herself, not to take the easy way out with the snap of her fingers. "Stay here and try to relax. I'll make some coffee, okay?"

A reserved smile and a slight nod was Robin's only answer.

Alana went to the kitchen. While loading the coffee machine, she listened for the slightest noise from the living room indicating that Robin was trying to run, but everything was quiet—almost suspiciously quiet.

She peeked over the kitchen counter into the living room. *Oh no.* Robin was nowhere to be seen. What if she left the apartment and got behind the wheel in this condition? What if she had an accident? Pictures of her own accident eighteen months ago flashed before her mind's eye.

She rushed out of the kitchen and stopped abruptly when she faced the front of the couch.

Robin had slid down on the couch and was now fast asleep, her head lolling against the backrest. To make sure that Robin was okay, Alana felt for the pulse in her neck. Thankfully, neither the touch nor the spark it caused woke Robin. *If that didn't wake her up, she really needs to sleep.*

Her skin was unusually cool, but at least she wasn't running a fever. Her pulse was fast, but not dangerously so.

It's best to just let her rest. With a little luck, she would have forgotten about the miracle healing of Alana's finger by the time she woke up or would blame it on hallucinations.

Alana got a blanket from the hall closet and covered Robin with it. Careful not to wake her, she sat at the other end of the couch and looked at the sleeping woman. *She looks so vulnerable. And so beautiful.* Before she could stop herself, she trailed her fingertips over Robin's soft cheek. Instead of the expected spark, a tingle spread through her body. Alana tore her hand away and tried to push aside her attraction. *It wouldn't matter if she were Angelina Jolie. Starting anything with her would still be a bad idea.* She had promised herself not to fall for a human ever again. This infatuation would pass. It had to.

CHAPTER 5

A PIERCING SCREAM STARTLED ROBIN AWAKE. The taste of blood still lingered in her mouth, and she could still feel the woman in her arms as she drained her. Her heart hammered against her rib cage. But she wasn't outside, hunting with Meghan, and her stomach was as empty as a grain silo after a drought. Had it all just been a hunger-induced dream or a hallucination?

Her memory was hazy, and she could hardly tell what was real and what wasn't. Had she really gone to Alana's apartment? Shards of memories flashed through her mind—Alana wearing a cute apron, Alana touching her, setting off a spark of electricity between them, Alana coming after her because she didn't want her to suffer alone. The most vivid image was that of a crimson droplet splashing onto the kitchen floor.

Blood. The scent still hung in the air. *Oh, no. What did I do?* Her gaze darted around.

She was in a living room that, after several seconds, she recognized as Alana's. Someone was sitting on the couch beside her. *Alana.* Her eyes were closed, and her head tilted against the backrest in a way that exposed her neck.

Oh, no. No, no, no, no! Please tell me I didn't drain her! She tried to calm her racing pulse so she could hear whether Alana's heart was still beating, but to no avail. Her heartbeat sped up even more.

Finally, Alana's chest rose under a calm breath.

Robin fell back against the couch as relief weakened her muscles. Her shoulder brushed Alana's, sending a tingle down her arm and into her fingertips. Maybe it was just her imagination, but the light contact seemed to chase away the haze of sleep, hunger, and exhaustion. For a moment, the red veil lifted and the pain stopped.

Then her gaze fell on Alana's bare neck, the soft skin exposed to her eyes—and her fangs. Her hunger returned with a vengeance, raging through her belly until she bent over and clutched herself in pain. Even from her doubled-over position, she couldn't help peering up, lusting after that ivory skin and the blood vessels lying beneath it.

Just one bite and a little suck. It won't hurt her. The endorphins that her fangs injected into the wound would take care of it, and other substances as well as the use of thrall would wipe her memory. Robin forced herself into an upright position and slowly lowered her head until her lips were just an inch away from Alana's carotid. Her blood smelled better than anything Robin had ever encountered in her sixty-seven years.

Her eyes fluttered shut as she opened her mouth and—

At the last second, a hum of energy stopped her forward motion and brought her to her senses.

No. Don't. Not her. Despite her muscles screaming in pain, she jumped up and ran—out of the living room, through the hall, and down the stairs, as fast as her weak legs would allow. She stumbled down the last steps and, about to jerk the door open, crashed into a human, a young blonde who had just entered the building, carrying two grocery bags.

Oranges went flying as they both went down. Robin landed on top of the woman, her already protruded fangs just inches away from the human's neck. She groaned as she breathed in the woman's scent. She smelled of the life pulsing through her blood vessels.

"Sorry," the woman said from beneath her. "I didn't see—"

"Don't scream," Robin said hoarsely and put the full force of her thrall into her voice. "You won't remember a thing."

"Scream? Why would I—?"

Robin sank her fangs into her neck. The woman wasn't Alana, nor was she O negative, but beggars couldn't be choosers. The pain in her muscles faded away as she gulped down big mouthfuls of blood.

The woman moaned, more in pleasure than in pain.

Oh, yeah. This is good. So good. Robin sucked more strongly. *More, more, more.* A feeding frenzy threatened to take over.

An image of the last woman she had fed from flashed before her—lying on the cold pavement, pale as a corpse, as the paramedics struggled to save her life.

Robin wrenched her fangs out of the woman's neck and gave the soft neck an extra lick that would close the two puncture wounds almost instantly due to a substance in Robin's saliva. The last drops of blood hit her tongue. The taste almost made her go back for more. *No! You'll kill her if you take more.* In her famished state, she didn't have the self-control to take just a pint of blood and then let the human go without doing any true harm.

The woman blinked up at her.

Robin allowed herself to rest on top of the stranger for a few seconds longer, until she felt the strength return to her muscles. Power pulsed through her, and she jumped up, feeling truly alive for the first time in weeks. She reached for the woman and lifted her to her feet without even having to strain herself. "Are you okay?"

The woman nodded dazedly. "I think so. What happened?"

"We crashed into each other, and you went down hard."

"I just remember opening the door and..." The woman frowned. "Then nothing."

Robin still held on to her, steadying her. "Maybe you hit your head on the way down. You might have a little concussion.

You'd better take it easy for a few days." She put a bit of thrall in her voice, making sure the woman would take care of herself.

"Thanks, I will." The woman bent to pick up the fallen grocery bags and then swayed.

Quickly, Robin grasped her elbow. Now her belly cramped with guilt instead of pain. *Shit. I took too much. A little more and she would have...* She didn't want to even think about it. "Let me do this." She gathered the oranges, put them on top of the other groceries, and hefted the two bags onto her right arm. "Where do you live?"

The woman pointed upstairs. "Second floor. Apartment 2B."

Damn. Robin grimaced. Just her luck. The woman was Alana's next-door neighbor, and now she would have to go back up, right past the place that was more dangerous to her than a bar full of gin was for Alana. *Well, you already fell off the wagon. It's not like things can get much worse.* Sighing, she wrapped her free arm around the young woman. "Come on. I'll help you to your apartment."

With the woman clinging to her, they made their way to the elevator.

Alana gazed deeply into Robin's twinkling eyes.

As if in slow motion, Robin came closer and licked her lips.

Is she going to kiss me? Alana trembled in expectation.

Robin's full lips were slightly open and formed an enchanting smile. But instead of capturing Alana's lips in a passionate kiss, she lowered her mouth to her neck.

As if under a spell, Alana tilted her head back to give Robin easy access. Her whole body tingled when she felt Robin's hot breath on her sensitive skin.

Finally, Robin touched Alana's neck with her lips.

Instead of an initial spark, there was just this incredibly pleasant tingling. Alana groaned.

A loud noise jerked her awake. She blinked a few times and realized she must have fallen asleep sitting up on the couch. Dammit! Why hadn't the dream lasted at least a few seconds longer? She glanced to her right and sucked in a breath.

Robin was gone.

How could she have fallen asleep while Robin needed her to look after her? The wall clock indicated that about half an hour had passed since she had first sat down on the couch.

Maybe she's just using the bathroom. Alana stood, walked to the closed bathroom door, and knocked. "Robin?"

Silence was the only answer.

Alana's heart thudded against her ribs. What if Robin had collapsed and hit her head and was now lying on the bathroom floor, totally helpless? "Robin? Can you hear me? I'm coming in!" Before she could talk herself out of it, she opened the door.

The bathroom was dark and empty. Robin wasn't in there.

"Shit!" She should have kept an eye on her instead of taking a nap and dreaming of making out with her. She hurried to the window in the living room, hoping she hadn't totally fucked up and that Robin's car was still there.

The aqua Prius was still parked in front of her house.

Alana breathed a sigh of relief and turned around. Where else could Robin be? After searching the rest of the apartment, Alana went to the door. Maybe she was lying in the hallway or the elevator, too weak to get to her car or to come back.

Just as Alana stepped out of her apartment, the elevator at the end of the hall opened with a quiet *ping*.

Please, please, please, let it be her! Alana's hand clenched around her keys until her fingers started to hurt. Time seemed to slow, and it appeared to take hours until the elevator doors were fully open and a woman stepped out.

Alana recognized her neighbor, the yoga instructor.

Kenison wasn't alone. She clung to another woman in an intimate embrace.

Isn't that...? Robin!

Alana's jaw dropped at the sight before her. A surge of jealousy rushed through her. She had to hold on to the door frame to keep her balance. *What the heck is she doing?*

One arm wrapped around Kenison while juggling two grocery bags with the other, Robin led Kenison out of the elevator and looked down at her with an almost tender expression.

Unlike thirty minutes ago, Robin looked as fresh as a daisy. The beads of sweat had disappeared from her forehead; shadows no longer lurked beneath her eyes, and her cheeks had a healthy flush. She moved with the elegance and power of a panther.

How is that possible? Alana had never seen anyone recover from acute alcohol withdrawal that quickly. There was no time to think about it now, because while Robin looked fine, Kenison seemed a little pale. "Kenison?"

"Oh, hi, Alana. This is…um…" Kenison looked up to Robin with a dreamy expression.

Alana pressed her lips together.

"We know each other," Robin said in a quiet and resigned tone.

It reminded Alana of a child called into the principal's office—or a lover who'd been caught cheating.

Alana walked over and took the paper bags from Robin. "What happened?"

Robin averted her gaze.

"We ran into each other—literally," Kenison said and fumbled for her keys when they reached her apartment door. Her hand trembled.

What the hell is going on here? Nothing made any sense. Just bumping into someone, even someone as attractive as Robin, didn't normally leave women breathless and weak-kneed. Had Kenison hurt herself?

When Kenison couldn't get the key into the lock, Alana stepped forward. "Give me the key. I'll help you inside."

Robin blocked her way. "That's not necessary. I'll help her. You can go back to your apartment."

"That's ridiculous," Alana said. "You don't even know—"

Kenison pitched forward and hung limply in Robin's grip. "Oh my God, Kenison."

In one smooth move, Robin lifted Kenison into her arms.

Awed at that display of strength, Alana gaped at her for a second before returning her attention to Kenison. "Should we call an ambulance?"

"No," Robin said with authority. "All she needs is some rest. I'll bring her to bed."

Worry about Kenison and another surge of jealousy battled for control. With one glance at poor Kenison, Alana shoved the absurd feeling aside. She had no right to feel jealous anyway, and Robin probably wasn't even gay. She took the keys that her neighbor had dropped, unlocked the door, and held it open for Robin to enter. "If the layout of the apartment is the same as mine, the bedroom should be the second door on the left," she said and placed the paper bags on the kitchen counter. She put away the groceries as fast as possible before following Robin and Kenison into the bedroom.

Kenison lay on her bed, passed out.

Robin sat beside her, regarding Kenison with a worried and almost guilty expression.

"We should call a doctor," Alana said, coming closer. "What if she has a concussion?"

Wide-eyed, Robin shook her head. "She didn't hit her head. I think she said something about a recently diagnosed anemia or something like that. A little rest and she'll be as good as new. You can go back to your apartment if you want."

Alana crossed her arms over her chest. "I'm not going anywhere." Was it just her imagination, or was Robin trying to keep her away from her neighbor? What was going on?

"Okay, if you insist on staying, could you keep an eye on her?" Robin asked. "I...um, have to go."

When Robin got up and tried to squeeze past her, Alana grabbed her arm. She ignored the spark of energy and held on, even as the sensation turned into a much-too-pleasant tingling. "Not so fast. You owe me an explanation."

Robin looked down at the hand on her arm but didn't try to break free. "Let me go. Please."

"No." Alana took a deep breath. "I fell asleep for just thirty minutes, and in that time you managed to leave the apartment, have a quickie with Kenison or something that leaves her entirely exhausted, and come back looking as if you weren't passed out on my couch just half an hour ago."

"Quickie? What?" Robin vehemently shook her head. "No, I—"

Kenison stirred and sat up. She blinked up at them. "What happened?"

"That's what I was just asking her." Alana let go of Robin, sat on the edge of the bed, and studied Kenison's face, which was finally regaining some color. "You passed out right in front of us."

"Oh, wow." Kenison rubbed her face. "That's never happened to me before."

Robin stepped behind Alana and peered over her shoulder to look at Kenison too. "How do you feel?" Robin asked.

"Better, but still weak as a kitten," Kenison said.

"Do you want me to call anyone?" Alana asked.

Kenison shook her head. "I'm sure I'll be fine."

"Stay put, okay?" Alana told her. "Try to get some sleep. I'll check on you later and bring you something to eat. That might help."

Kenison leaned back against the headboard and nodded. "Thank you."

When Alana got up from the bed, something on Robin's collar caught her attention. Was that...? She took another step toward Robin and lifted her hand to point at the stain. "What's this?"

Robin looked down at herself but didn't see anything. "Where?"

"On your collar." Alana touched Robin's shirt and accidentally brushed the bare skin of her neck, setting off another spark.

Every part of Robin's body started to tingle, not necessarily in an unpleasant way. "We really have to get you out of that sweater," she said with a shake of her head and then froze when she realized what she'd just said. "I didn't mean it the way it sounded. I just meant you shouldn't wear it if it produces such static electricity."

Alana laughed. "I didn't take it the wrong way. But we should really get you out of that shirt. You've got an ugly red stain on your collar."

Robin tugged on her collar so she could see it. *Oh, shit.* Apparently, she'd been a messy eater. Some of Kenison's blood had splashed onto her collar. "Uh, it's nothing."

"That's not nothing," Alana said. "It looks like…blood."

Hot and cold waves of dread swept through Robin as she searched for a halfway believable excuse. Her gaze darted from Kenison, who was watching them, to Alana. "Must have happened when you cut your finger."

"Oh." Alana blushed. "How did that happen?"

Robin shrugged as casually as possible. "No idea. Maybe you accidentally touched my collar."

"I'm sorry. I didn't mean to bleed all over you."

I wouldn't mind. Robin pushed the mental image aside and forced down her rising hunger. *You just ate. You can't be hungry again so soon.* But despite her admonishment, her mouth watered every time she glanced at Alana. She cleared her throat. "It's okay. I'll just put it in the washing machine when I get home."

Alana shook her head. "Let me soak it, or you'll never get the stain out. Blood is hard to get out."

Oh, trust me, I know.

"Try to get some rest," Alana said to Kenison. "We'll check on you a little later."

Another wave of electricity flowed through Robin as Alana grabbed her arm and pulled her out of Kenison's bedroom, leaving the door ajar. She dragged Robin to her apartment.

Now that she was satiated and no longer close to losing control, Robin allowed herself to step back into Alana's home. She still needed the money, because she'd be hungry again tomorrow, and she couldn't allow herself to get used to the sweet taste of fresh blood again. She needed to go back to Julius and buy more synthetic blood.

Alana dragged her into the kitchen and urged her toward a stool. "Have a seat and take that shirt off."

"But ..."

"No buts," Alana said in a tone that surely made her opposing counsels hunch their shoulders and agree to everything she wanted. "I can turn around if you want."

Robin snorted. She wasn't shy about her body. Even though she was wearing just a bra beneath, she unbuttoned her shirt and shrugged out of it.

Alana's gaze swept over her torso, setting off more little sparks all over Robin's body. The flow of energy between them was almost palpable.

"Here." Robin's voice sounded hoarse. It had been ages since she'd last been so affected by a woman's closeness—literally. The last time she'd found herself so fascinated by a woman had been right before the Cuban Missile Crisis, when she had gone through the Girah equivalent of puberty. She handed over her shirt, careful not to let their fingers brush.

Alana took the shirt—and promptly dropped it. She bent to pick it up, drawing Robin's attention to her cleavage. "I'll just wash it out and then put it in the dryer." Her voice sounded a little husky too. "Be right back."

When she returned a few minutes later, the hair at her temples was damp, as if she had splashed some water on her face. She handed Robin an oversized *Buffy, the Vampire Slayer* sweatshirt.

Robin eyed the wooden stake in the fictional character's hand and raised a brow at Alana.

"You're taller than me," Alana said, almost apologetically. "It's the only thing in my closet that'll fit you."

Without comment, Robin put on the sweatshirt. *Good thing the clan can't see me now. They wouldn't let me live it down for the next century.* At least the damn thing smelled faintly of Alana.

Alana looked down at the abandoned ingredients for the lasagna. "Are you still in the mood for lasagna? Or do you want me to order pizza?"

Robin had never understood why humans were so fond of that piece of cheese-dripping bread with a random assortment of leftover food on top. "No, thanks."

Ignoring her protests, Alana rummaged through a drawer, searching either for food or for takeout menus. "You need to eat something. You seem to be a lot better now, but half an hour ago, you looked so weak that I debated calling an ambulance."

"I'm fine. I…grabbed a bite while I was out." Robin's own choice of words almost made her laugh, but then she remembered her momentary loss of control. In the past, she had always tried not to take more than humans would lose while donating blood to a hospital or blood bank, leaving them a little dazed, but otherwise fine.

If Alana's neighbor hadn't been as healthy or if Robin hadn't reined herself in before losing the remainders of her self-control… She forced herself to face reality and finish the thought. *I could have become a murderer. That's twice now.* It might not have been a big deal for most Girah, but as far as Robin was concerned, it was two times too many.

Alana gave up her search and sat on a stool across from Robin. She regarded her across the kitchen island, her green eyes serious and intense. "While you were out," she repeated. "Care to tell me what you were doing?"

"I just needed…" *Blood.* "Some fresh air."

Alana's gaze never wavered.

For once, Robin felt as if she were the one being put under thrall. Not that her attempts to thrall Alana had ever worked.

"Please don't lie to me, Robin."

"I'm not lying. I—"

Alana sighed. "I'm not stupid. I've been in your shoes once. Fresh air can't cure acute alcohol withdrawal. We both know that. Tell me what's going on."

For someone who made her living making up stories, Robin found herself strangely at a loss for words. "I...uh..." She tugged on the borrowed sweatshirt. The vampire slayer's grinning image seemed to taunt her. Finally, she took refuge in the only explanation that Alana would accept. "I had a relapse." That, at least, was not a lie.

Alana studied her through narrowed eyes. "You don't seem drunk."

"I've always held my liquor well." Robin struggled not to look away from Alana's intense gaze.

"You don't smell drunk either."

"You can't smell vodka," Robin said. At least she'd heard humans insist that vodka was odorless, even though she didn't agree.

"Where did you even get hold of booze that fast?" Alana asked with a shake of her head.

"There's a bar right around the corner." Robin waved her hand in a vague gesture, since she had no idea where the nearest bar actually was. But this was New York, so there had to be a bar somewhere, right?

Alana sighed and then frowned. "I thought you don't have any money?"

Gosh. She must be a great lawyer. Her questions made Robin sweat. "Um, your neighbor bought me a drink. Or two."

"Hmm." Alana rubbed her bottom lip, drawing Robin's gaze to her luscious mouth. "Kenison is an attractive woman."

Was that jealousy in her voice, or was it just wishful thinking? Robin grinned. "Maybe, but she's not my type."

"Sorry, I didn't mean to assume that you'd be attracted to a woman."

Robin tilted her head in a vague gesture, neither denying nor confirming that she was a lesbian. "I'm not attracted to blondes. I'm a sucker for redheads."

In a gesture that looked entirely unconscious, Alana ran her fingers through her long, copper hair and then shook her head as if trying to clear it. "Back to the topic at hand. If you want to get sober and stay sober, you really need to try harder. You need to go to a meeting every day, not just every once in a while. And you need to start doing your step work. Like we say in AA, it only works if you work it."

"I'm willing to do whatever it takes to avoid another relapse," Robin said, meaning it.

"Good." Alana lifted her hand as if about to pat Robin's arm but then seemed to change her mind. "You're not alone in this, okay? I'm here to help. If you want, we can meet twice a week to work on your twelve steps."

Robin groaned inwardly. Just what she needed. More time with the tempting Alana. But after what had happened earlier, she freely admitted that she needed help. Somehow, Alana had managed to fight her own compulsion, so maybe she was the right person to help her do the same—even if she was temptation personified. Suppressing a sigh, Robin glanced down at the sweatshirt. *How about that stake through the heart now, vampire slayer?*

CHAPTER 6

CLOSING THE DOOR WITH MORE force than necessary, Alana threw her briefcase on the low table to her left, opened it, and got Robin's book out. After almost three weeks as Robin's sponsor, she'd finally given in to her curiosity and had stopped by a bookstore on the way home to buy one of Robin's novels.

After a quick trip to the bathroom, where she changed out of her business suit and into something more comfortable, she got herself a glass of apple juice. Dinner could wait. Curiosity won out over everything else.

She carried the book to the couch and gazed at the author's photo on the back cover. Robin's alluring, electric blue eyes seemed to look back at her. Before she knew what she was doing, she trailed her finger over the picture. *Would you look at yourself? Now you're fondling a book! That must be what humans go through during puberty.* Shaking her head at herself, she turned the book around and took a closer look at the cover. A female vampire stared at the reader with a seductive gaze. Ivory fangs glinted against cherry-red lips. Alana chuckled. *I guess sex sells. I wonder how much influence Robin has on the covers of her books.* Well, at least there was no bare-chested vampire slayer on the cover, displaying his muscles as he swung a stake.

She sprawled on the couch and opened the book. Knowing she wouldn't have enough time to finish the book before she had to leave for the AA meeting, she skipped ahead, eager to find out how Robin had handled the romance. She picked a chapter in the middle and started to read. Her mouth fell open as if in slow motion.

Sarah couldn't stop looking at Christy. Strangely, it wasn't just her elegant neck with its pounding artery that fascinated her. Everything about Christy drew her in—her full lips, her cute nose, and the humor sparkling in her beautiful green eyes. It didn't make any sense. She had never been attracted to a human. Not that way at least. Confused, she turned away. "I need to go," she croaked.

Christy touched her arm. "Why?"

Because I can't stand being close to you for much longer, or I'll kiss or bite you or both, Sarah thought. But what she said was, "I forgot an important appointment with my supervisor." Before Christy could react, Sarah hurried down the steps as fast as her legs would carry her.

The vampire's love interest was a human named Christy, not Chris, as Alana had first thought when she had skimmed the back cover description in the bookstore. Robin wasn't just writing romances. She was writing lesbian romances.

Wow. Robin is a lesbian. She shook her head and tried to calm her thumping heartbeat. *Maybe she's just trying out writing in another genre. There are probably plenty of straight women writing lesbian fiction.* But her instincts told her that Robin wasn't one of them. *I should have known.* But she had convinced herself that she was only imagining the sexual tension between them and the flirting undertones of their interactions. Alana tried to swallow around the lump in her throat. Why did she have to sponsor another lesbian, of all people—and one she was strongly attracted to? Falling in love with a human woman had led her down a very dark, lonely road, so she was determined not to go there again. Besides, Robin had just started on the road to recovery, so she had good reasons to stay away from relationships too. Whatever attraction she felt toward Robin didn't matter. Nothing would ever happen between them. "Right," Alana said into her empty living room, willing herself to believe it. She leaned back on her couch and continued to read.

Sarah's breathing came in ragged gasps. She buried her face in her hands and squeezed her eyes shut, but she couldn't block out the reality of what she'd almost done. She didn't know what would have been worse: kissing Christy or biting her. She had restrained herself for so long, but now Christy was breaking through all her defenses, weakening her self-control in the process. For other vampires, humans were just food, but for Sarah, Christy was so much more.

Alana turned the page to start a new chapter, which had Sarah interacting with other vampires. Because Sarah considered the draining of humans immoral, she was an outsider with her own people. Sarah was trapped between two worlds without ever fully belonging to either, lost and alone, longing for the love and acceptance she would never get from her own kind, but at the same time afraid to let any human close.

Alana could empathize with that. Some days, she felt entirely human, but at other times, she felt as if no human could ever fully understand her and love her for who she was—and who she had once been. Even if she ever trusted another human enough to fall in love with her, she'd have to watch her lover age and die long before she did, just as Robin's vampire would have to witness her beloved's death.

Alana continued reading, ignoring the surge of various emotions she couldn't name. Instead, she concentrated on the story. *She's good.*

Robin's writing was compelling and witty—so different from the romances Alana had read years ago, when she'd still been studying love between humans. She was eager to find out what would happen to the characters, and her gaze sped over the words. Would Robin let them have their happy ending, or would their circumstances and differences keep them apart?

Sarah's fangs flashed in the slowly setting sun. "Don't say I didn't warn you," she said and bent down to Christy's neck.

"Enough with the disclaimer already. What are you so afraid of?"

Feisty. Alana grinned. *Is that how Robin likes her women?* She shoved the thought away and reread the last line she'd read to get back into the story.

"Enough with the disclaimer already. What are you so afraid of?"

"Love," Sarah whispered.

Then her fangs pierced Christy's skin. Instead of pain, arousal surged through Christy. She groaned. She had waited for what seemed like an eternity for this moment. "God, yes!"

The ringing of her cell phone pulled Alana out of the story. "God, no. Not now." *Just when it's getting interesting.* She sighed and stood. On the fourth ring, she snatched the cell phone from her briefcase and looked at the caller ID. "Hi, Brian," she said. "What's up?"

"Well, you said you wanted to come earlier today to help us set up."

"I will. Anything else you need me to do?"

"Uh, no, but the meeting starts in twenty minutes, so..."

"What?" Her gaze searched and found the clock on the wall. *Oh, shit!* While reading, she'd lost track of time. Her stomach chose that moment to protest its neglect and made her realize she hadn't eaten in hours. "Oh, Brian, I'm so sorry, I..."

"Are you all right?"

His concern warmed her. "Yes, I'm fine. I just got engrossed in a good book."

Brian's laughter vibrated through the phone. "There are worse things, you know? I'm glad you're getting back into reading. It's been a while, hasn't it?"

"Yeah." Alana had to smile. He was right.

"What's the book about? Something I might be interested in?"

Heat rushed to Alana's face. "Um, I don't think so. It's..." She cleared her throat. "It's a romance."

"I had no idea you were into that."

"I'm not. I'm just reading it because it's Ro—" She stopped herself. Robin probably wouldn't want others from AA to know about her career. "It's lesbian fiction, so you probably wouldn't enjoy it. Listen, I really need to leave now if I'm going to make it on time."

"Oh, yeah, sure. See you in a bit."

Alana put a bookmark between the pages and, with one last glance of regret, left the book behind. No time to grab something to eat from the kitchen. Well, maybe she and Robin would go out for dinner after the meeting again, as had become their norm. It wasn't just her growling stomach that made her look forward to it.

She grabbed her keys and wallet, dashed down the stairs, and got into her car.

It was still a complete mystery to her how she could have lost track of time, reading Robin's novel. But the story had been so damn distracting. *Just like Robin.* She wondered whether Robin put a lot of herself into her characters.

Alana shook her head and rolled her eyes at herself. *What, you think she's a vampire afraid of love?* Grinning, she turned on the radio.

Christina Aguilera's "Genie in a Bottle" reverberated through the car.

"Argh." That damn song had to be the dumbest thing in the history of music. Alana switched to another station and listened to Frank Sinatra singing "I've Got You Under My Skin." Not much better, considering how much Robin had gotten under her skin. She turned off the radio and focused on traffic, driving in silence.

Alana wolfed down her burger, barely pausing to chew. The meeting today had lasted forever. At least her stomach had thought so. She snatched a couple of french fries from her plate but paused when she felt Robin's gaze on her.

Robin smirked. "Hungry?"

Heat rushed to Alana's cheeks. After swallowing, she said, "I missed lunch and didn't have time to grab a snack at home either."

"How come?"

Around a mouthful of french fries, Alana mumbled, "Too busy." She wasn't sure why, but she was hesitant to admit that it had been Robin's novel that had kept her too busy to eat.

"You're awfully quiet today," Robin said. "Are you okay?"

"Sure. Just got, um, a lot of things on my mind." The way Robin's full lips closed around her straw as she sucked on her strawberry milkshake, for example. Alana licked her suddenly dry lips and forced her gaze away from Robin's mouth. "What about you? How are you holding up?"

"I'm doing okay, I guess. No more relapses." After hesitating for a moment, she added, "You're a big help."

"Really?" Since Robin's relapse, they had met two or three times a week to talk about how to cope with addiction, but Alana didn't feel as if she'd been much help to Robin, maybe because sponsoring Robin was so different from her relationship with Brian. And it wasn't just because she was the sponsor instead of the one being sponsored now. With Robin, laughter, banter, and interesting conversations filled most of their time. Forming a friendship with the person you sponsored wasn't against the rules, but anything more was.

Unfortunately, Alana had to admit that her attraction to Robin couldn't be denied any longer, especially now that she knew for sure Robin was a lesbian too. Each time they went out for coffee or a milkshake, it felt more and more like a date. She shoved the thought away.

"Really. I truly appreciate your help and all the time you spend with me." Robin's electric blue eyes seemed to reflect sincerity. Still, a *but* lingered between them.

"But?" Alana prompted.

Robin looked down, inspecting her fidgeting hands.

"Come on. Talk to me. You know I won't judge you." At times, Robin still seemed to think that her addiction was different from everyone else's and that no one could really understand her.

Instead of answering, Robin unfolded and refolded her napkin.

Alana covered Robin's hand with her own and squeezed it gently.

At the little surge, Robin looked up but didn't withdraw her hand.

Alana stared at their hands on the table. Was it just her imagination, or were the little electroshocks her taqa caused no longer painful? The spark of energy was still there with every touch, but instead of hurting, it just made her tingle all over—in a very good way. It had been the same way with Kelly after they'd known each other for a while, just not as strong as the tingles she felt now. Apparently, her taqa assumed that things were heading in the same direction with Robin. *Proves that not even the Great Energy knows everything.*

Robin sighed. "I really thought it would get easier. That going to the meetings and talking to you would help. But the craving..." She avoided her gaze and cleared her throat. "Don't get me wrong, you are fantastic. I mean... Well, I know you're doing what you can to help me. But it just doesn't seem to get easier."

Very aware of the fact that neither of them had withdrawn her hand, Alana had problems focusing. But as much as she knew it would have been the right thing to do, she couldn't end their contact. *Get a grip!* "Do you...?" She swallowed heavily. "Do you think having another sponsor would help? Maybe Brian could take you o—"

"No!" Robin turned her hand and clutched Alana's fingers, causing the current between them to grow stronger. Her eyes glowed with intensity. "I mean, I'm sure Brian is great, but I don't want him as my sponsor."

Against her will, relief washed over Alana. "Okay." Her voice sounded strange to her own ears. "So, let's see what else we could do to make things easier on you. You are going to a meeting every day, not just to the one I'm going to, right?"

Robin nodded. "I'm going to a different one every night."

"Good. Are you staying away from temptations? Bars, parties, hanging out with the wrong people..."

Again, Robin averted her gaze and stirred the remainders of her milkshake. "Um, well, for the most part. I'm staying away from old friends because I know they'll want me to go out for a drink with them."

"Good. Very good. But even then it will be hard to resist the temptations around you."

Robin gazed from Alana's face to a point below.

Is she staring at my neck? Alana mentally shook her head at herself. That's what she got for reading Robin's vampire novel. Just a few chapters into the book and she was already beginning to imagine things.

"Resist temptation." Robin sighed. "Yeah. It's hard." She looked up and again fixed Alana with her intense gaze.

Alana blinked. She had heard the words but needed a minute to grasp their meaning. Robin's luminous eyes, her soft voice, her touch that made her tingle all over... Why did she have to be so damn distracting? *Focus!* She cleared her throat. "So, what do you do instead?"

"Huh?"

Was Robin having the same difficulties staying focused?

"Yeah, instead of going out with your friends."

"You mean hobbies?" Without waiting for a reply, Robin said, "I write. That's all I do. Writing, going to the meetings, and going out with you." She froze and let go of Alana's hand. "Uh, I didn't mean going out as in dating or anything. Just going out like..." She gestured helplessly.

"Friends," Alana said. Part of her was relieved that they were finally setting some boundaries, but another, maybe even bigger part was disappointed that she'd never get to date Robin.

Robin's head bobbed up and down. "Yeah. Exactly. Friends."

Well, being friends with a woman like her isn't so bad either, is it? She had a feeling that Robin didn't have many friends, or she wouldn't have borrowed money from Alana.

Silence spread between them.

When she couldn't stand it any longer, Alana said, "If you hide at home, you're up for disaster when you go out again."

Robin frowned. "Are you saying I should go out with my friends?" Her eyes sparkled. "Or that I should spend more time with you?"

Yes! But what Alana said was, "I mean you should try to make new friends."

She looked down at her fidgeting hands and shrugged. "I thought that's what I was doing?"

Alana tried to ignore the butterflies in her stomach. She reached for Robin's hand again and gave it a squeeze. "You are." After several moments, she added, "You'll get through this."

Robin looked thoughtful and smoothed her thumb over the back of Alana's hand, probably not even aware of what she was doing. "You think so?"

Alana's heartbeat tripled, and everything but Robin seemed to disappear around her. The energy field she had been part of for many centuries had felt almost the same, like a mix of a relaxing hum and an exciting surge. How could such a simple touch by a human cause this familiar feeling? *More!* "Um, yeah," she croaked. "So, um, Brian asked me if I thought you were ready to speak to the group soon."

"What did you tell him?"

"That I wasn't sure. What do you think? Why don't you give it a try?"

Robin closed her eyes for a moment. When she opened them again, she said, "A try." She stared at Alana's necklace and licked her lips. "Sure."

What's up with her strange obsession with my necklace? Or is it my neck she keeps staring at? Heat crept up her chest under Robin's intense gaze. She rubbed her cheek with her free hand. "Good. Just say what's on your mind. I know it's scary, but it really helped me feel like I could give something back to the newer members of the group. You don't have to go up on the podium. Just say a few words the next time Brian opens the discussion."

Hesitantly, Robin nodded. "I will." After a moment, she added, "Thank you."

"You're welcome. I know you can do it."

Their gazes met.

Alana had to swallow. Before she got lost in Robin's beautiful blue eyes, she looked away. Her hand stayed where it was, though. It was wrong, but it just felt so damn good. She had never been a very touchy-feely person, but this tingling was almost addicting. *Yeah, and that's why you need to cut it out. Don't replace one addiction with another.*

Robin didn't seem to mind; she didn't move her hand away either.

Say something. Anything. "I started reading one of your books."

Robin blinked. "Oh yeah? I thought you don't read romances anymore?"

Smiling, Alana said, "I made an exception for yours."

"Really? Um, I mean which one?"

Alana's lips parted when she looked into Robin's eyes, which had darkened to a rich azure color. "*Bite Me.*" She grinned and winked.

Robin croaked, "W-what?"

What are you doing? Stop flirting. You're her sponsor! And she had promised herself to never start anything with a human again. Alana wrenched her hand away, instantly missing the contact and the gentle buzz humming through her hand. "Your vampire novel, *Bite Me.* That's the one I'm reading."

Robin looked down at her hand. "Oh, yeah. Of course." She leaned back in a pose that was probably supposed to look casual but seemed forced. When she looked up again, curiosity and something else Alana couldn't fathom gleamed in her eyes. "So? What did you think?"

That you're very talented. And very beautiful. Alana blinked at that thought. Where had that come from? "It's..." She wasn't sure how to describe what she'd felt when she had read some chapters of Robin's book. "Really interesting."

"Interesting?" Robin arched one brow. "If it's not your cup of tea, just say so. I know a lot of people find novels about vampires a bit...silly." She looked at Alana warily, hurt and fear of judgment lurking in her eyes. "They say they just can't identify with creatures that don't exist."

That wasn't the reason why Alana hadn't picked up a paranormal romance novel for years. It was the romance she didn't believe in, not the vampires. Not that she'd ever met one in person. The older entities kept her away from the more challenging species, since it was much harder to fulfill their wishes and still stick to the complex rules and code of ethics that bound Alana's kind. So Alana, Dahir, and the other individuals who hadn't yet lived for a full millennium had been stuck dealing with humans. Humankind was bigger in numbers anyway, and they never seemed to lack for wishes, so they alone could have kept Alana busy for all eternity, without her ever working with nonhuman creatures. But since she'd connected to others of her kind in the Great Energy, she'd been aware of the existence of beings that humans dismissed as superstition.

Some of them drank blood to survive; others could shift shape and transform into animals. She'd even heard of beings who drained others of their energy. The thought made her shiver. Compared to that, bloodsuckers seemed like downright pleasant company.

"They don't know what they're missing," Alana said with a reassuring smile. "A good book is a good book, no matter the outer trappings of the main characters. And your book is one of the good ones. Your vampires are really convincing."

A grin inched across Robin's face. "They should be. Uh, I mean, I did a lot of research into the genre. So you liked my vampires?"

Alana nodded. "I know they are just characters in a book, but I really bonded with your main characters, especially Sarah. She's fascinating. How did you come up with the idea to give your vampire an obsession with numbers? I loved how she started counting things whenever she was stressed or nervous."

Robin shrugged, but again it didn't seem casual at all. "I have no idea where that came from. Writers' brains work in strange ways, you know?"

"I wouldn't know. You're the first writer I've ever met."

"I hope I'm not a disappointment, then." Robin's voice sounded almost like a purr.

Great. Now we're back to flirting. Alana tried to sound matter-of-fact when she said, "Uh, no. I wasn't sure I'd enjoy a vampire romance, but I did. It's the first one I ever read."

"I thought you're a *Buffy* fan?"

Alana rubbed her heated cheeks. "Not because of the vampires. I started watching because of the lesbian relationship. That's another reason why I liked your novel. No bare-chested alpha males."

Robin's mouth dropped open. "Y-you…" She stared at Alana for several seconds as if Alana had hit her with an electric shock again. "You're gay?"

If her sexual orientation was that much of a surprise to Robin, Alana had apparently been hiding her attraction better than she thought she had. "You couldn't tell?"

Robin shook her head. "I thought it was just wishfu…" She coughed. "What I meant to say was that I wasn't sure."

Did Robin almost say what Alana thought she wanted to say? So the attraction she felt definitely wasn't one-sided. *It doesn't matter. You're here to sponsor her, not seduce her.* She forced herself to focus on the conversation about Robin's novel. "Their sexual orientation was probably part of why I could relate to your characters. There was just one thing I didn't get."

Robin tilted her head. "What was it?"

"Why does Sarah bite Christy even though it could be dangerous for her? She seems to really care about her, so it doesn't make much sense to me."

Robin licked her lips and gazed at Alana's neck as if imitating her vampire characters. "Lust," she whispered after a while as if she was afraid to say it out loud.

Even though they weren't touching, a tingling sensation swept through Alana's body, making her feel light-headed. She forced her attention back to the topic of Robin's writing. "Do all of your books have a human/vampire couple?"

"Most of them. It's a seductive combination." The hoarse timbre of Robin's voice made Alana shiver. "The thrill of biting someone is pretty erotic. Um, at least that's how I imagine it must be for a vampire."

A woman stopped next to their table and smirked at Robin. "My, my, my. If it isn't Robin Caldwell, out and about, enjoying…" Her gaze swept over Alana. "Dinner."

Alana frowned at the stranger, who was wearing a short leather skirt and a red silk blouse that showed a bit too much cleavage. But her perfect hair, her expensive earrings, and an aristocratic British accent indicated that she wasn't a hooker. *Who's she?*

Before Robin could answer, the woman bent down, took Alana's hand, and kissed it. "It's a pleasure to meet you."

The touch sent a strong electric shock through Alana. Unlike the gentle tingling that Robin's touches caused, this one was as painful as whiplash, as if her taqa wanted to keep the stranger at a distance. Alana wrenched her hand away and rubbed her fingers beneath the table. They still felt as if she'd just put them in a socket. She glanced at Robin, who had visibly paled.

———————

Robin squeezed her eyes shut. *Great.* Things like this never happened to one of the characters in her novels. Her fictional vampires' friends never set foot in a diner, so what was Meghan doing here of all places? She wasn't here for milkshakes and french fries; that was for sure.

"You don't mind if I sit with you, do you?" Meghan asked and slid into the booth next to Alana without waiting for a reply. She sent a toothy grin across the table at Robin and ogled Alana's vulnerable neck out of the corner of her eye. "I really miss having dinner with you, Robin."

Robin's fangs unsheathed in an instant, and she barely held herself back from hissing at Meghan. *No! Stay away from her!* She glared at her, but unlike humans, Girahs weren't prey and couldn't be thralled, so Meghan kept eyeing Alana's neck as if it were the most delicious item on the menu.

Another wave of protectiveness swept through Robin. She jumped up and grabbed Meghan's shoulder, not bothering to be gentle. "Excuse us for a minute, please," she said and tried not to wince as she cut her tongue on her fangs. "I need to talk to my friend."

Meghan waved and winked at Alana as Robin dragged her away from the table. "I'll be back for dessert."

"No, you won't." Robin shoved her out of the diner. "If you touch her, I swear I'll—"

"What's going on with you? You never minded sharing."

Robin dragged her into the empty alley behind the diner. "I'm not sharing her. Stay away!" She flashed her fangs and stared into Meghan's eyes, letting her know that she wasn't afraid to fight for Alana tooth and nail. Okay, maybe not nail, but she would use her fangs to defend Alana.

Meghan lifted her hands and smirked. "Ooh, so you haven't gone entirely soft. Good to know. I thought you'd lost your bite when I saw you with that milkshake." She spat out the last word as if it was something disgusting.

Truth be told, Robin didn't much care for milkshakes either, but she liked the sucking involved. And she liked spending time with Alana. Not bothering with an answer, she continued to stare Meghan down.

Unfortunately, Meghan wasn't easily impressed. "I know you've got a thing for O negative, but don't you think you're going a little far? Going to all that trouble just to get a snack?"

Heat shot through Robin. She hissed at Meghan. "She's not a snack!"

"Oh, no?" Meghan leaned against the wall. "I saw how you were looking at her. What are you doing with a human? Didn't your parents teach you not to play with your food?"

"I... It's not about that. Can't I just like her?"

"Oh, come on. Can you honestly look me in the eyes and tell me that you wouldn't like to sink your fangs into that slender, succulent neck and then suck, slowly, until you taste that smooth, copper ambrosia, feel it trickle down your throat and—"

"Shut up!" Meghan's words caused vivid images to flash through Robin's mind until the hints of strawberry milkshake on her tongue started to taste like O negative.

"Why? We both know you want it. Just think about—"

She grabbed Meghan by the lapels and shoved her against the wall. "Stop it!" She wasn't sure who she was screaming at—Meghan or her own imagination that was taunting her with images of tasting Alana's blood. "Not everything has to be about bloodlust. Who's to say I can't care for her just because of who she is, not because of her blood type?"

Meghan broke Robin's grip on her lapels with one powerful jerk of her arms.

Robin stumbled back, ready to jump forward again and fight.

But Meghan didn't seem to be in the mood for a fight. Instead of baring her fangs, she tilted her head and studied Robin. The taunting expression faded from her face and was replaced with something that looked almost like pity. "You're young and idealistic. Once you're older, you'll understand that humans aren't meant to be anything but prey to us."

Robin snorted. "I'm sixty-seven." She hated being treated like the baby of the clan. "And so are you, so don't even try to sound like one of the elders."

"Why not? Unlike you, I've spent enough time with the elders to know what they would say. If you think that sixty-seven is old enough to understand how the universe works, you've been hanging out with humans for too long."

"I'm old enough to know that this isn't how I want to live my life."

"This?" Meghan repeated.

"Yeah. Always on the edge of killing someone."

"Humans," Meghan said, waving her hand dismissively. "That hardly counts."

Robin shook her head. "I don't know why I even bother talking to you. You'll never understand me." No Girah would.

"You think she will?" Meghan pointed at the entrance of the alley, where footsteps now sounded.

A quick sniff told Robin who was approaching seconds before Alana rounded the corner.

Instead of stopping at a safe distance, Alana shouldered between Robin and Meghan. "Everything okay?" She sent Robin a worried glance.

Robin nodded and tried to edge past Alana to put herself between her and Meghan. "My friend was just leaving."

"Actually..." Meghan took a step forward, but Alana didn't back away. Inches from touching her, Meghan stopped. Electric static hummed like a cattle prod being charged. "I was. Your family invited me to dinner, Robin."

Of course they did. Since Meghan's parents had died in a car accident when Meghan had been a teenager, Robin's parents had practically adopted Meghan, who—unlike Robin—was the perfect Girah, sticking to tradition and going out to hunt.

"That's why I'm here," Meghan said. "I thought I'd get some takeout. Something...fatty. I'll tell your parents I met you tonight." Before Robin could think of something to say, Meghan strolled past them, out of the alley.

Alana stared after her before turning toward Robin. "What was that?" She frowned and squinted. "Is that...lipstick?"

"What?"

Alana gestured at the corner of her mouth.

Robin reached up and touched her lip. Pain shot through her. Her night vision pierced the shadows in the alley, and she discovered a few drops of blood on her fingertips. *Damn.* Apparently, one of her fangs had pierced her lip when she'd been screaming at Meghan. "Uh, no, it's nothing."

Alana looked back and forth between Robin and the corner of the alley, where Meghan had disappeared. "Who was she?"

"That was Meghan," Robin mumbled. She pressed a tissue to her lip, to wipe away the blood and also to hide any hint of her fangs while she talked.

"One of the friends you're trying to avoid?"

"Yeah. Something like that."

"An ex?" Alana asked.

Was that a hint of jealousy in her tone? Robin wasn't sure. She shook her head. "No. Not really. We went on one date, but she wasn't my type."

Alana grinned. "Ah. I forgot. You're a sucker for redheads, and she's a brunette."

Robin couldn't help laughing. Fortunately, her fangs had receded. She winced as the laughter pulled on her still tender lip.

Alana instantly sobered. "Did that bitch hit you?"

"No."

"Well, then what happened to your lip?" Alana asked.

Robin couldn't very well tell her that she'd pierced her lip with one of her razor-sharp fangs. "Um, I guess I accidentally bit my lip when Meghan and I... We had an argument."

"So there is some bad blood between you?"

Robin grimaced at her choice of words. "You could say that."

"Want to tell me about it?"

"Not particularly." Meghan's words echoed through her mind: *You think she will?* "You wouldn't understand."

Alana looked her in the eyes. "Try me."

Robin was tempted. So tempted. And that scared her. *Are you crazy? She's human. You can't tell her who you are. What you are.* She sighed. "Maybe another time."

"Okay." Alana gently gripped her elbow, causing a gentle tingling to run up her arm and down the rest of her body. "Come on. Let's go back inside. My fries are getting cold."

The pain in her lip instantly disappeared, as if Alana had healed her with her touch. *Man, now I'm really losing it. Maybe it's not just bloodlust after all. I'm really seeing her through rose-colored glasses. Next thing I'll think she can cure the blind and walk on water.* Shaking her head at herself, she followed Alana from the alley.

***

Back at their table, where the light was better than in the alley, Alana took a closer look at Robin's lip. Her eyes widened.

The bleeding had stopped. The lip wasn't even swollen. Nothing indicated that it had ever been hurt, as if it had magically healed.

Was it possible…? *Bullshit.* Alana mentally shook her head. Yes, she had touched Robin, but her residual taqa couldn't heal others. Or could it?

"What's wrong?" Robin fingered her lip. "It's not that bad, is it? It doesn't even hurt anymore."

Alana's thoughts were still racing. *Impossible.* She couldn't heal humans. Not that she had ever tried. "Um, no, it looks fine."

As if she wasn't aware she was doing it, Robin's tongue moved over the formerly pierced lip and paused. Gulping audibly, she hid her mouth behind a napkin. "You know what? I'm not hungry anymore. Do you mind if we leave?"

Alana searched Robin's face. "Are you okay?"

Dabbing her lip as if it were still bleeding, Robin nodded. "Yes, it was just a long day."

Alana's mind was brimming over with questions. What had Meghan and Robin talked about in the alley? Had Robin really just bit her lip? And what the heck was going on with her taqa? Was she gaining new abilities, even though she was human now, or was Robin special somehow, so the sudden healing skills were restricted to her?

Knowing she wouldn't get any answers today, Alana suppressed a sigh and put a few bills on the table, since it was her turn to pay. She left a big tip, thanking the waitress for keeping an eye on their table while she'd gone after Robin. "Okay, then let's go."

CHAPTER 7

"Come on. Get in," Alana said when they reached her car. "I'll drive you home."

The last thing Robin needed was to be even closer to her. "No. I'm parked over there." She pointed over her shoulder. "And I live all the way in Manhattan. I don't want you to drive that far. I'm sure it was a long day for you."

"I don't mind. You seem a bit…shaky after meeting your friend. I'm not letting you drive or go home alone like this. We can come back tomorrow to get your car."

Letting me? Robin arched one brow. After a lifetime of being able to thrall humans into doing what she wanted, meeting a human who could stand up to her and even order her around was an entirely new experience. Strangely, she found that she liked it.

Alana unlocked the car and gently pushed her toward the passenger's side door.

An electric current passed between them. By now, Robin was used to it, and it didn't hurt anymore. Quite the opposite, actually. *Why isn't she getting rid of that sweater? Hey, wait a minute.* With one hand on the passenger's side door, she stopped and turned. "Your sweater."

Alana looked down at her unbuttoned coat and the sweater she wore beneath it. "What about it?"

"It's not the one you said makes you get zapped."

Alana's eyes widened. "Oh? It's not? Uh, yeah, right. Well, I guess it wasn't the sweater after all. Must be my shoes, then."

Robin glanced down at Alana's sensible leather shoes. "I don't think so. They don't have rubber soles."

For a moment, Alana looked around helplessly. "Then… then…" A small smile curved her lips. "I guess there's just a spark between us."

Robin looked into her eyes and got lost in their green depths. Knowing that Alana was feeling that strong pull between them too made her head spin. Or was Alana just joking around? She searched her face.

Abruptly, Alana turned away and circled the car. "Let's get going. It's getting late."

The tension between them made it hard to breathe in the confines of the car. The drive to Robin's condo seemed to take forever.

Robin breathed a sigh of relief when her condo building finally came into view. "Just let me out here." She pointed.

"No, I'm parking," Alana said. "I want to make sure you're okay before I go."

Robin shook her head. "You don't need to do that. I'm fine."

"Humor me. Please?"

Damn. Garlic and holy water couldn't harm her, and bright sunlight caused only mild skin irritations, but one simple *please* from Alana broke through all of her defenses. Robin's chest constricted. She had never let a human into her home. *No big deal,* she tried to tell herself. She would let Alana in for just a minute and then pretend to be tired or something. It wasn't as if anything in her condo gave away the fact that she was what Alana would call a vampire. She slept in a bed, not a coffin. Not that Alana would see her bedroom anyway.

After guiding Alana to a guest parking spot in front of the towering building, she led her to the elevator. She shuffled her feet as she unlocked the door to her condo on the eighteenth floor. "Don't look around. I didn't have time to clean up my mess before I left for AA."

But when Alana stepped into the living room, she didn't look at the piles of paper on the coffee table. She was staring wide-eyed at the small, glassed-in balcony overlooking Central Park. "Wow. Great view. Rent must be a bitch. I can see why you needed to borrow some money."

"I don't rent," Robin said before she could censor herself. "The condo is mine."

Alana whistled through her teeth. "Your books must sell like crazy, then."

"They do okay." Truth be told, she wouldn't have been able to buy a condo like this nowadays, but in the seventies, it had been more affordable. She couldn't say that, though, because Alana thought she hadn't even been born back then. "I inherited the condo from...an aunt who bought it back when you didn't have to sell a kidney to buy a condo in this neighborhood."

Alana stepped over to the bookshelf that took up an entire wall of the spacious living room. "May I?"

Her gaze clinging to Alana's firm backside, Robin cleared her throat. "Go ahead."

Alana pulled a book from the shelf and looked at the cover before putting it back. As she leaned forward to look at another book, her faded jeans tightened over her ass, making Robin's body temperature skyrocket. "These are all yours?" Alana asked. "I mean you wrote them?"

"All the ones on the top shelf, yes."

Another whistle came from Alana. "You have an impressive body of work."

Robin was more interested in Alana's body, which she found pretty impressive too. Despite knowing that she should stay away, she walked over to join Alana next to the bookcase. "Well, I—"

The intercom buzzed.

What now? Robin strode to the door and pressed the button for the intercom. "What?"

"That's no way to talk to your parents," her father's strict baritone sounded through the intercom.

Oh, Zeus on a bike! Robin's gaze darted back and forth between the intercom and Alana, who still stood next to the bookcase but was looking at her with a curious expression. "W-what are you doing here?"

"Can't we just visit our only child?"

Girah were allowed to have only one child per century. It kept their numbers small so they could avoid killing off their prey too fast and lowered their risk of being detected. Maybe that was part of why her parents were so frustrated with their wayward daughter.

"Uh, now's not a good time."

"Buzz us in," her father said.

"But I'm not…"

"Buzz us in," her father said. His tone brooked no argument. "Don't make me tell you a third time, Robin!"

Shit, shit, shit. Robin pressed the buzzer and whirled around to face Alana. She needed to get her out of the condo, or her parents would take her presence as an invitation to stay for dinner. "I'm sorry, but you have to leave. Now."

Alana blinked. "Uh…"

Thoughts racing, Robin searched for a halfway believable explanation. "They don't know I'm a lesbian."

"But…but we're not doing anything…lesbian."

Unfortunately. Robin shoved the thought away. No time for that now. "I know. Still… I think my father already suspects, and if they find you here this late in the evening…"

"Just tell them I'm your sponsor."

Robin rubbed her temples. Why did this woman have to be so stubborn? "They don't know I'm in AA either. Please. I want to tell them in my own time, not have them find out like this." She sent Alana a pleading gaze. "Please," she repeated, hoping it would have the same effect on Alana as it had on her when Alana had uttered that word.

"Didn't your friend Meghan say she wanted to have dinner with your par...? Never mind." Alana sighed. "All right. I'm going."

"Thanks." Robin ushered her toward the door.

Alana stepped out of the condo but then turned back around. "You really should come out to them and tell them you're an alcoholic. Hiding who you are is not good for the soul."

Robin sighed. Some days, she wasn't even sure she had one, and hiding who she was had long since become second nature.

"Trust me," Alana said, now more softly. "I learned that lesson firsthand."

Their gazes met, and the deep understanding in Alana's eyes calmed Robin's pounding heart for a moment.

Then the elevator pinged open, revealing her parents and Meghan, who had one arm wrapped around a human woman with the glazed-over expression of someone under thrall.

Shit. Now there were two humans Robin had to save from being drained.

"We brought dinner," Meghan said cheerfully. "I see there'll be dessert too."

Alana sent her a confused gaze, because Meghan was holding neither dinner nor dessert—at least not anything a human would have eaten.

Robin's fangs made another appearance. She pressed her lips together so they wouldn't be visible. Glaring at Meghan until she moved out of the way, she tried to lead Alana past them.

But, apparently, Alana had other plans. "Hi," she said with a bright smile and held out her hand to Robin's father. "I'm Alana, Robin's...editor."

Robin's father stared at her, ignoring her hand. To him, shaking hands with a human was akin to exchanging pleasantries with a plateful of ham and eggs. "Leave," he said, using the full force of his thrall.

Any other human would have probably broken a speed record dashing into the elevator, but Alana continued to stand there, holding out her hand. "Nice to meet you too," she said dryly, but with that pleasant grin still on her lips.

Robin nearly fell over. Withstanding her thrall was one thing, but resisting her father, one of the most powerful Girah on the East Coast, was unheard of. Over the years, she had seen hundreds of humans buckle under the force of his thrall.

Her father stared at Alana as if he'd swallowed his fangs.

Quickly, Robin urged Alana into the elevator before their shock could wear off. She pressed the down button.

Alana gave her a nod. "Call me when you...want to talk about that scene that has been giving you trouble."

The elevator doors slid closed just as her father's fangs erupted and he let out a long hiss. "What was that? That human...she..."

Robin shrugged as casually as possible. "Editors. You know how they are. As long as they have a red pen in their pocket, they're pretty fearless."

They followed Robin into the condo, the woman Meghan had apparently picked up at the diner in tow. Getting her out of here was going to be much harder.

Robin closed the door and leaned against it, folding her arms over her chest. "What's going on?"

"We're staging an intervention; that's what's going on," her mother said. She took a step closer. "We're worried about you, Robin. You never call us anymore. You don't come to clan meetings, and Meghan says you're not drinking."

Robin pushed away from the door and walked past her. "I am drinking."

Before Robin could stop her, her mother went to the kitchen and opened the fridge. "That's not drinking, Robin. That's... that's...despicable. That stuff isn't good for you."

Just like losing two quarts of blood isn't good for humans, Robin thought but knew better than to say it out loud. Her parents didn't care. She strode over, took the bottle of Synth-O out of her mother's hands, and put it back in the fridge. The fridge door slammed shut.

Her father joined them, the human woman following him like a puppy. "Here." He shoved the woman at Robin as if she were a box of chocolates they had brought as a gift. "Have something healthy."

Robin caught the woman before she could fall. "Mom, Dad, please..."

"Offer her your neck, human," her father said, the thrall strong in his voice.

The human did as she was told, baring her neck.

Robin stared at the pale skin. Two small puncture marks indicated that Meghan had already sampled dinner and then hadn't bothered to heal the marks. Robin could sense the blood rushing through the woman's carotid. *O negative.* So Meghan had remembered. She knew that Robin always had trouble resisting the lure of her favorite drink.

But to her surprise, the pull wasn't as strong as expected. Sure, she felt the undercurrent of bloodlust pulling at her, but instead of the raging torrent she was used to, it was more of a gentle tug that was relatively easy to resist.

"Come on, take a bite," Meghan said from where she was leaning against the door frame, keeping a respectful distance from Robin's parents. "I brought your favorite. She's delicious."

I bet she is. But it was as if being offered a sip of water when all you wanted was a glass of Dom Perignon. *I won't hurt her. I don't want her.*

"Get it over with, girl," her father said. "We want to have our turns too."

Oh, no, you won't. Sneaking glances at her parents out of the corner of her eye, Robin slowly lowered her head and pretended to search for the best place to bite. *Don't be scared,* she mentally told the woman. *I'm not going to hurt you. I want to help.*

The woman stood still, not appearing scared at all under the strong thrall.

Now that she was this close to the pounding carotid, Robin's gums started to ache and her fangs threatened to make a reappearance. But after weeks of resisting the most irresistible thing in the universe—Alana—Robin's self-control had increased. Ignoring the singsong of *bite, bite, bite* in her head, she stuck out her tongue and licked the woman's neck before pulling back.

The two puncture marks closed instantly.

There. Robin directed a defiant grin at Meghan. Then the grin dropped off her face as a bit of half-dried blood melted on her tongue, whetting her appetite. *Oh shit. Not your brightest idea.* Her attempt to show Meghan and her parents that she had better self-control now and didn't need their gifts had backfired. She took two panicked steps away from temptation. Clutching the kitchen counter, she squeezed her eyes shut and said, "Go home and rest. Forget that you were ever here."

When the door fell shut, she opened her eyes.

The woman was gone.

Robin blew out a breath and sank against the counter.

"Why did you do that?" her father asked. A deep line was carved into his forehead as he gave her a disapproving glare.

Robin rubbed her eyes. He wouldn't understand. "I'm not hungry."

"Not hungry?" her father sputtered. "You are a Girah. We are always hungry."

Her mother stepped between them and cupped Robin's cheek. "What's going on with you? This isn't still about what happened on New Year's Eve, is it?"

As memories of that night resurfaced, Robin pressed a hand to the spot over her heart. "Yes," was all she could get out. "Yes, it is."

"Oh, child." Her mother stroked her cheek. "Why are you taking this so hard? It was just a human."

"Just a human..." Robin abruptly pulled away. "Have you ever considered that they are living, breathing beings with feelings and dreams, just like all of us?" She thought of Alana, the way her eyes sparkled when she laughed. The thought that she could die in the blink of an eye, just because one of her kind was in the mood for a midnight snack, nearly made her double over.

Her father shook his head at her. "Who put that nonsense into your head? It sure isn't what we or the elders taught you." He grabbed her shoulders and shook her roughly. "Come to your senses, or—"

Robin tried to shake off his hands, but he was much stronger. "Or?"

His anger seemed to deflate, and he let his hands drop to his sides. "Or I will stand by as the elders declare your ties to the clan cut forever," he said, his voice hollow.

Robin stared at him. A lump in her throat prevented her from speaking. Not that she knew what to say anyway. Cutting clan ties... It was unthinkable. While she had distanced herself from her family since New Year's Eve, she couldn't imagine being clanless.

Her mother gasped. "Oh, no, Thomas. You can't do that. Not that."

"I don't want to," her father said, still looking Robin in the eyes. "But I've tried everything else to reach her, and it didn't work. This is for her own good."

My own good? He had no idea what that was, and she wasn't so sure either.

"Come on," he said. "We said what needed to be said. Let's go."

Her mother wrapped her arms around Robin as if she never wanted to let go and kissed her cheeks. "Please, please, Robin," she whispered.

Robin nodded, just to calm her mother down, not knowing what she was saying yes to. Numbly, she watched them leave. She just hoped the human woman was far enough away by now that they wouldn't hunt her down, just to teach Robin a lesson.

Shaking her head, Alana walked to her car. What a strange encounter. No wonder Robin had wanted her to leave. Her father didn't even know her and had nevertheless been incredibly rude to her. And why had Meghan talked about dinner, even though she'd shown up empty-handed? Had she been talking about a liquid dinner, a bottle of alcohol hidden in her coat pocket, or worse, drugs? The young woman at her side had indeed looked as if she'd been heavily drugged.

But if Meghan wanted to party with Robin, why had she brought her parents with her? And why did Robin's parents look much too young to have a daughter who was Robin's age? Either they had fantastic genes, or they had adopted Robin.

"None of this makes any sense," she mumbled while she opened the driver's side door and climbed behind the wheel. Alana had barely closed the door when a familiar high-pitched sound reverberated through the car.

Dahir materialized beside her on the passenger seat. "That was quick. I thought with your residual taqa, you had more stamina."

"What? No, we're not... We weren't..." Alana rubbed her burning cheeks with both hands.

"Yeah, I know. But you want to."

"I'm her sponsor. And she's a human, a closeted one with weird friends and parents, to make things worse."

"A human in the closet?" Dahir laughed. "Is that like a genie in a bottle?"

Alana scowled. "Very funny. You know what I mean. She's a lesbian, but..."

Dahir dismissed her with a wave of her hand. "Doesn't matter. You want her. Don't bother denying it. If I learned one thing about humans, it's how to tell when they want something. And you—want—her."

"Even if I did, there's no way..." Out of the corner of her eye, she saw the door to Robin's condo building open.

The woman who had been with Meghan and Robin's parents stumbled outside, looking around as if she had no idea where she was or what she was doing.

"Excuse me," Alana said and got out of the car without waiting for a reply. Curiosity and concern for the woman urged her on. "Hi," she said when she stood beside the slightly overweight brunette.

Startled, the woman met her gaze. "Hi."

"You seem a little... Are you okay?"

The woman blinked a few times as if she didn't know how to answer that question. "I..."

She's drugged. Had Meghan given her the drugs? And were Robin's parents in on it too? While they hadn't seemed like the friendliest of people, Alana couldn't imagine that they would bring Meghan to their daughter's home if they knew she was a drug dealer. What kind of parents would do that? *But then again, what do I know about parents?* Her kind grew up surrounded by the Great Energy, without specific individuals taking care of them. If Robin's parents were involved in something illegal, Robin's panicked behavior would make sense. *She doesn't want me to know about it.*

The brunette looked around. "Where am I?" As if just realizing that she was speaking to a stranger, she asked, "And who are you?"

"My name is Alana," she said but didn't extend her hand. After being zapped when Meghan had touched her earlier, she didn't want to risk setting off another electric spark.

"I'm Brittany. Sorry, your name doesn't ring a bell, but you do seem...I don't know...familiar. Do we know each other?"

"I wouldn't say that, but we just met upstairs." Alana pointed at the apartment building. "Don't you remember? You were with Meghan and Robin's parents."

"Meghan? Robin?" Clearly, Brittany didn't know either of these names.

Alana frowned. "What's the last thing you remember?"

"I, uh…" Brittany rubbed her forehead as if that would clear her mind. "I was on my way to have dinner with friends and then…" She shook her head. "I don't remember anything else."

Alana bit the inside of her cheek. Maybe Brittany's friends had taken her out for a wild night of partying after dinner, and she had taken some drug that made her black out the rest of the evening. "I think we should call an ambulance."

"Ambulance? No, I…I'm fine. I think."

The door of the apartment building opened again, and Robin's parents, followed by the obnoxious Meghan, stepped out. They stared in her direction.

Not giving herself time to hesitate, Alana marched toward them and stepped up to Meghan. "What the hell did you give her?" She pointed over her shoulder at Brittany.

"Give her? I didn't give her anything." Meghan laughed. "I took something from her; that's all."

"What's that supposed to mean? Just look at her. A blind man could see that she's on something." Alana half turned and looked at the trembling woman.

Meghan followed her gaze and stared at Brittany, whose eyes widened. Her gaze lost its focus as if she'd just swallowed another dose of whatever drug she'd taken. Without another word, she hurried down the street, away from the building and Meghan as if her ass were on fire.

She's scared. Alana turned back to Meghan. She certainly looked as if she could scare the hell out of a person. Alana couldn't quite put her finger on it, but there was an aura of danger surrounding her… Earlier, in the diner when Meghan had shown up and then in the alley, Robin had also seemed kind of scared. A surge of protectiveness ran through Alana. She straightened up to her full five-foot-four-and-a-half and glared at Meghan. "I don't care who you are and how you know Robin. Stay away from her."

Meghan stared at her before laughing out loud. She pointed to Alana and tried to say something, but her laughter shook her so hard she was unable to form words.

Alana's hands clenched to fists. "Do you think that's a joke?"

Meghan continued laughing, sounding like a hyena on speed.

Looking at Robin's parents, Alana said through gritted teeth, "If you care at all about your daughter, you should keep Meghan away from her."

Robin's father looked as if he wanted to swat her away like an aggravating fly buzzing around him.

Meghan stopped laughing and took another step toward her. "Are you trying to threaten me, little girl? You don't know who you're dealing with, you useless—"

Robin's father shut her up by raising his hand. "Let me deal with her." He fixed Alana with an intense stare.

The fine hairs on Alana's arms stood on end under his gaze, but she refused to back off. If even her parents didn't take Robin's side, she would be the one to defend her.

"Are you the one who put all that nonsense into my daughter's head?" Robin's father asked, his voice a threatening growl.

"Nonsense? What nonsense? I don't know what you're talking about. You are the one who gives Robin dangerous ideas, bringing her here." She pointed at Meghan.

He stepped closer until the energy field surrounding Alana started to buzz like a swarm of angry hornets. "You will stay away from her."

Alana felt as if her stomach had shriveled into the size of a walnut. She put her hands on her hips in a useless attempt to make herself look bigger. Her pulse thudded high in her neck, but she didn't back down. "I will do no such thing. It's up to Robin, not you, to decide who she wants to socialize with."

A deep line carved itself into his forehead as he continued to keep the intense eye contact, as if willing her to give in.

The warning crackle between them grew louder.

"You will stay away from my daughter if you know what's good for you, or I will—"

"Alana!" Dahir called, hurrying toward them.

Alana's mouth fell open. Dahir usually avoided showing herself to humans, unless they were her master or mistress. Why hadn't she stayed in the car or transferred herself back to the ethereal plane?

Dahir grabbed Alana's arm and pulled, nearly making Alana crash into her. "Honey, did you forget our, um, date? We're going to be late." Looking up, she added, "Please excuse us. We're really late." Before any of them could answer, Dahir had dragged Alana back to the car. "Drive," she said as soon as they had both climbed in.

"But Robin—"

"Drive!" Dahir glanced over her shoulder until Alana went left at the next intersection. "What in the name of taqa did you think you were doing?" Dahir shook her head. "Couldn't you feel it? Those people are dangerous. It was obvious, even with my senses being dulled while I'm in human form. Their energy signatures are weird, almost like—"

"I know." It was probably the drugs that had messed with their bodies and dimmed their life energies. Her nineteen months in AA had taught her to stay away from people like that.

"Then why did you get in their way? Remember, your body is fragile now."

Alana shrugged. "I just wanted them to stay away from Robin."

"Robin knows them?"

"The man and the older woman are her parents."

"Her parents?" Dahir squinted. "Are you sure?"

"I didn't ask for her birth record or anything, but yeah."

Dahir fluffed her hair. "I always said human evolution went horribly wrong somewhere." She sighed and squeezed Alana's knee, making her jump. "Maybe in that case you should stay away from Robin too."

Alana shook her head. "I'm her sponsor. She needs me."

"Okay, okay. What kind of influence do they have on Robin?"

Alana circled around the block, just to make sure Meghan and Robin's parents were getting in their car and weren't heading back up to Robin. "I have no idea." But she would find out. Soon.

CHAPTER 8

Robin was up and in her office before dawn the next morning. She stared at the flashing cursor on the blank page. *Forty-eight, forty-nine, fifty.* When she realized she was counting cursor flashes instead of thinking about the scene she wanted to write, she shoved the keyboard tray away and got up. The words just wouldn't come today, mostly because she kept thinking about Alana.

After their run-in with Meghan and her parents the night before, Robin wouldn't have been surprised if Alana wanted nothing to do with her anymore. *Maybe it's better that way.* But she couldn't quite make herself believe it.

Her cell phone chirped.

She took it from her desk and glanced at the display. Her heartbeat sped up. It was a text message from Alana.

You awake? Want me to come over before work to get your car?

Robin hesitated. Her first thought was an enthusiastic yes; she was glad Alana wasn't avoiding her. But Alana would ask questions and demand explanations that Robin couldn't give. Finally, she typed a quick reply.

You don't need to do that. I can take a cab.

Alana's answer came within a few seconds: *You aren't avoiding me, are you?*

Robin sighed. If she tried to stay away, Alana would think she'd relapsed and come over anyway, intent on rescuing her from falling even more deeply into a bottle. *One intervention was enough for this week, thank you very much.*

I wouldn't dream of it, she replied. *Come on over whenever you want.*

The intercom buzzed not even two minutes later.

"Where were you when you sent me those text messages?" Robin asked when she let Alana in. "Parked in front of my building?"

"Yeah. I couldn't sleep, so I thought I might as well see if you're up too." Alana slid her gaze up and down Robin's body.

Was it because she wanted to make sure Robin was all right after last night or because she was wearing sweats and a tank top?

Maybe it was both. Alana's gaze lingered on Robin's bare arms.

A tingling sensation worked its way down to the pit of Robin's stomach, even though they weren't touching. At the thought of touching her, she instantly wanted to reach out and establish some kind of contact between them. *Don't even think about it.* She fiddled with the strings of her sweatpants to keep her hands occupied. *Come on. You resisted your hunger for blood yesterday. You can resist your hunger for Alana too.* "Uh, let me change out of my work uniform."

She hurried to her bedroom and closed the door. While she changed into jeans and a sweatshirt, it occurred to her that humans would normally offer their guests something to drink while they waited, but her fridge held just water and Synth-O. If she kept hanging out with Alana, she'd need to buy a couple of sodas.

She shoved her feet into her sneakers and stepped back into the hall. "Ready to go?"

Alana didn't move toward the door. "Can I ask you something?"

Nervous sweat broke out on Robin's back. She couldn't very well say no, no matter how much she wanted to, so she nodded reluctantly.

"What's wrong with your parents?"

Robin looked down and dragged one foot over the tiles. "Um, what do you mean?"

"A blind man could see that this Meghan isn't good for you," Alana said, her green eyes blazing with an angry fire. "Why would they bring her—and a woman who was high as a kite—to your condo? What kind of parents would do something like that?"

Girah parents. Robin sighed. She couldn't answer that question. "It's a long story." She walked past Alana toward the door. "Come on, let's—"

Alana grabbed Robin's sleeve and pulled her back around. Energy sparked between them. "I've got time, so let's hear that long story."

Robin dragged her heels. "Don't you have to go to work?"

"I don't have court or any pressing appointments today. Let's talk."

Damn. Alana was like a bulldog that had bitten down on something and wouldn't let go.

Still holding on to Robin's sleeve, Alana pulled her into the living room and sat next to her on the couch. "So?"

Robin's thoughts raced. What could she tell Alana to explain the situation without giving away her parents' true identity? "Uh, well, I don't know what to tell you."

Alana let go of her sleeve and rubbed Robin's knee, sending tingles of excitement through every part of her body. "Take your time. I know this must be hard."

When she couldn't stand Alana's touch anymore, Robin jumped up and walked toward the window, looking down at Central Park eighteen floors below, wishing she were down there instead of being trapped in her condo. "My parents...they're not like other parents."

"No kidding," Alana muttered and then said, "Sorry. Go on."

Robin turned and looked into Alana's eyes. Finally, she decided to tell the truth—or as much of the truth as she could reveal. "They are heavy drinkers. Always have been. Everyone in my family drinks a lot—my parents, my grandparents, and their parents before them. My friends too. I grew up with it, so I never questioned it. I always thought it was normal."

"Oh, Robin. That's no way for a child to grow up." Alana slowly shook her head.

Robin shrugged. "It wasn't that bad. The parents of my friends were the same."

"Meghan's too?"

"Yeah. They all drink."

"That's not all, is it?"

Robin frowned. Did Alana sense that she wasn't telling her the whole truth? "Uh, what do you mean?"

"Meghan isn't just into alcohol. She also takes drugs, or at least she deals with them."

Sometimes, the human mind came up with creative explanations for things like thrall. If it meant keeping her identity hidden, Robin was happy to let Alana believe what she wanted. "I guess so."

"What about you? Did you ever...?" Alana gestured.

"Take drugs?" Robin vehemently shook her head. She didn't want Alana to think that about her. "No. I have a drinking problem, but I never touched any drug."

A small smile ghosted across Alana's face. She seemed to take Robin's word at face value. "I'm glad. So, what changed?"

"Hmm?"

"You said you always considered it normal to drink. What happened that made you want to stop?"

Robin turned back toward the window. Part of her longed to come clean and tell Alana everything about that horrible night, but she knew she couldn't. If she did, Alana would either suggest she see a psychiatrist or run screaming into the night, never to be heard of again.

A soft touch to her shoulder made her flinch. She hadn't heard Alana get up and approach. *What a fine Girah you are! You're supposed to have the senses of a predator.*

"Hey." Alana rubbed Robin's shoulder, making her entire body sing with that pleasant buzz. "Are you okay?"

"Yeah, but I'd rather not get into it now. My deadlines are looming, so I need to get back to my writing."

Alana gave her shoulder one last squeeze before letting go and stepping back. "Of course. But I'm always here if you want to talk, okay?"

Robin nodded.

"Come on. Let's go get your car."

Neither of them said anything as they got into the elevator and made their way to Alana's car.

Alana opened the passenger's side door for Robin, but instead of stepping back so Robin could climb in, she paused and looked into Robin's eyes from just a few inches away.

Robin's breath caught. *What is she…?*

"I don't mean to intrude into family affairs, but have you ever thought about cutting your parents out of your life?"

Robin stared at her. She might not have much contact with her parents, but cutting clan ties was unthinkable for any Girah. "I can't do that."

"Then, please, at least be careful. I don't want them to drag you down with them." Concern darkened Alana's irises to a rich pine-green color.

Warmth flowed through Robin, and this time, it had nothing to do with the spark of electricity between them or the anticipation of tasting Alana's blood. It simply felt good to have someone worry about her well-being. She gave Alana a grateful smile. "Don't worry. I'll be careful."

They stood looking into each other's eyes for several moments longer; then Alana cleared her throat and moved around the car. "Let's get going before your Prius thinks you abandoned it for a newer model." She opened the driver's side door.

"Alana?" Robin said just before she could climb behind the wheel.

Alana turned her head, and their gazes met across the roof of the car.

"Thank you."

CHAPTER 9

Two weeks later, Alana followed Robin home after the AA meeting they had attended together.

"Do you want a Coke?" Robin asked when they entered her condo.

"Yes, please." Alana took off her jacket and gave it to Robin. She strolled into the living room, which was familiar territory by now, and sat down on one end of the couch. "My throat is pretty dry after talking so much today."

Robin followed her with two cans of soda and handed her one. She plopped down onto the other end of the couch. "You were great." She leaned toward Alana and nudged her with one of the pillows. "I can't believe how openly you speak about yourself. Patrick never would have spoken up without you opening up first."

Alana averted her gaze when she felt her cheeks grow hot. "He would have. Eventually."

The can hissed as Robin opened it. "He wouldn't." Before Alana could respond, Robin added, "I wouldn't."

During the meeting earlier, Alana had had difficulty keeping her gaze off Robin. As much as she tried to tell herself that it was just to make sure she was okay, deep down Alana knew better. At least to herself she could admit that she had a crush on the enigmatic author. She shook herself out of her haze. "You will. Whenever you are ready."

Robin shifted her weight on the couch. "I know I said I'd try, but I'm not sure sharing my story with the group is the right thing for me. I have no problem at all getting up in front of hundreds of people to read from one of my books, but talking about myself..." She shook her head.

"You do all right with me."

"Yeah, but you're...special."

Silence spread between them.

Eventually, Alana took a deep breath and tried to keep her voice steady as she said, "We're here to talk about the twelve steps. They will help you. Once you have completed the twelfth step, you won't have a problem telling your story anymore."

"I'd better get a pad from the office, so I can write everything down." She jumped up.

"Robin?"

"Yeah?"

"May I...?" By now, she'd been in Robin's condo about a dozen times, but she had yet to see her office. She hesitated, not wanting to be intrusive.

Robin smiled, but Alana detected a hint of insecurity. "What is it?"

"It might sound strange, but... Do you think it would be possible for me to see your writing cave?"

Robin stood frozen. "Uh, you mean my office?"

Alana nodded.

"Well, you know, it's nothing special."

"I'm not expecting the Taj Mahal, it's just... I admit I'm really curious about the place where you write your novels."

Rubbing her chin, Robin seemed to weigh her options.

"I'd understand if you'd rather not, I just thought..."

Robin shifted her weight from one foot to the other and fixed her gaze on the bookshelf against one wall. Just when Alana wanted to tell her to forget it, Robin said, "Sure. Come on."

"Thank you." Grinning, Alana bounded after her.

Robin opened a door and swept her arm in a gesture that encompassed the entire room. "Like I said, nothing special. Just a room with a desk and a computer."

Alana nudged her gently, setting off the familiar tingling sensation again. "And here I was expecting golden typewriters and covers of your books used as wallpaper." She stopped in the doorway and blinked a few times.

Robin's L-shaped desk took up two walls, reminding Alana a bit of the control centers of spaceships she'd seen on TV. The large whiteboard above one side of the desk caught her attention. Index cards and sheets of paper were stuck to it. Alana did a double take when she saw what was pinned to the board below the floor plan of a house—a printout of her photo from the law firm's website hung next to her business card.

"Um, Robin?"

Robin, who was rummaging through a drawer, paused. "Yeah?" She half turned.

"Why do you have my photo on your whiteboard?" Should she feel flattered or scared?

"I...it's not what you think. It's... I based a character in one of my short stories on you."

Alana reached up and scratched her neck, not sure how to feel about that.

"I hope you don't mind. Maybe I should have asked, but we barely knew each other when I wrote that story."

"If you wrote the story that long ago, why do you still have my picture up on the whiteboard?" Alana asked.

"Uh, I...I guess I forgot to take it down."

Alana finally turned away from the whiteboard. *Come on, it's no big deal.* "It's okay. I just... I thought I left those unrealistic love stories behind, and now I'm a character in one of them."

"No. I mean... Alissa, my character, isn't you. The editor had me make her a police officer. She said divorce lawyers don't make for sexy main characters."

Alana sent her a challenging grin. "Oh, yeah?"

"Hey, it's not like I agreed with her." Robin turned around and took a notebook and a pen from the drawer. "Okay, let's get to the step work before I embarrass myself even more."

Half an hour later, Robin furrowed her brow at the third step of the program. "I'm sorry, but I don't believe in God."

Alana tapped her index finger on the brochure they were reading. "It says 'God as we understand Him.' God can be anything, you know?"

Robin ran her fingers through her hair. "What do you mean?"

"Do you believe that there's a higher power?"

"No."

Alana suppressed a sigh. "Okay, who created you?"

"Um, my parents?"

Alana chuckled. "Well, there's that."

Robin moved closer on the couch, but not close enough to touch her. "I don't believe in a higher being creating us, like an author creating characters in a novel."

Alana grinned. "That's because you just use people you know in real life."

Robin flashed her a beaming smile. "Didn't you ever see me wear my *careful or you'll end up in my novel* T-shirt?"

"I didn't, but good to know that you come with a warning label." Alana returned the smile. Their eye contact caused a tingling sensation similar to the one she felt when they touched. She forced her gaze back to the brochure. "I admit I struggled with that step too."

"You did?"

Alana nodded, already regretting that she'd told Robin. That topic was best avoided when she was around humans.

"So you don't believe in the existence of a higher power either?"

What could she say to that? There was no believing about it. She knew that higher beings existed. Hell, she'd *been* one of those higher beings. Not a god, of course. Her kind was neither all-knowing nor did they have unlimited powers. Still, her kind came pretty close to what humans would think of as a higher power. "Actually, I do," she said after a moment's hesitation. "But my beliefs are a little unconventional and don't fit most religions' understanding of God."

Robin tilted her head. Curiosity sparked in her eyes. "How so?"

Alana glanced around, searching for a way out of this conversation. But if she wanted Robin to open up and work on the twelve steps with her, she needed to set a good example and not clam up. "I don't believe in a god who created everything. I believe in the universe and in energy that never dies. It only transforms."

Robin lifted one eyebrow. "Does that mean you believe in life after death?"

Alana shrugged. "Don't you?"

A shadow darted across Robin's face. "No. I've seen too many people die to believe that. There's just blood and death and then…nothing."

There was so much regret in Robin's eyes that Alana reached out and laid her hand on Robin's arm. Instead of the almost painful spark her touch had caused in the beginning, the energy that flowed between them now felt healing. If that was true, she certainly hoped it would heal Robin's emotional wounds, just as it had healed the cut on her lip. She studied her. Why had Robin seen people die? Had she served in the military or something like that?

Before she could ask, Robin refolded the AA brochure and stood.

Robin walked over to the picture window and looked down at Central Park. She pressed the Coke that she had opened just for appearance's sake to her forehead. For a moment, she wished it were blood swishing around in the can, but then she pushed the dark images, memories from past hunts with other Girah, from her mind.

"Robin?"

She more felt than heard Alana approach behind her. Lowering her hand with the can, she turned around. "I'm fine. Can we skip the higher-power steps for now?"

Alana visibly hesitated. "It doesn't work like that, Robin. If you want to stay sober, you can't skip any of the steps. Come on, let's sit back down and approach this another way."

"What other way?" Robin asked but followed Alana back to the couch. "You either believe in God, or you don't."

"There are agnostics and atheists in AA, you know?"

No, Robin hadn't known. Otherwise, she might have attended a group like that. *But then you wouldn't have met Alana.* She mentally rolled her eyes at herself. *Sentimental fool.*

"I think they take the third step to mean that you should give up playing God and entrust your life to people who have dealt with the same problem and found a way to become sober," Alana said.

Robin folded her arms across her chest. "Playing God? I'm not doing that."

"Oh, no?" Alana quirked a gentle smile. "Think about it for a second."

Robin didn't want to. She'd had enough of step work for the day. But Alana's pleading gaze kept her on the couch. She thought back at the events of the last few months since meeting Alana. When had she played God? With one exception, she had stopped biting humans and playing Russian roulette with their lives, as if she had a right to decide who lived and who died. Compared to other Girah, she had a downright humble attitude and didn't view herself as a superior being who could play with humans at will. *Oh yeah?* An image of her neighbor, Mr. Singh, doing jumping jacks popped into her mind. Could using thrall to force humans to do her bidding be considered playing God?

For the first time, she realized that while she'd tried to abstain from biting humans, she had never considered thralling them as wrong. At least she had never thralled Alana. *Not for lack of trying,* her conscience was quick to remind her. *Damn. She's right. I have been playing God.*

When Robin remained silent, Alana said, "I remember meeting a woman named Robin who didn't want anyone's help because she thought she could handle it herself."

Ah, that's what she means. Robin relaxed against the back of the couch. "That was six weeks ago."

Alana smiled. "That's not very long."

"I wouldn't say that. A lot can happen in six weeks."

Their gazes met and held.

Alana looked away first and took a big gulp of her Coke. "What happened for you in those six weeks?"

I struggled with my obsession with O negative and instead became obsessed with you. But, of course, she didn't say that. "I admitted I need help, attended thirty-one AA meetings, and got myself a wonderful sponsor."

A big grin spread over Alana's face. "Wonderful, hmm?"

Robin took a swig of Coke and barely resisted spitting it back out. It hadn't gotten any better since the last time she'd tried it. "Yeah. So I think we can put a check mark next to step three."

Alana took the brochure and a pen off the coffee table and did just that. "There."

They grinned at each other.

"That was easy," Robin said.

"Yes. Especially compared to how long it took me to finish that step." Alana rolled her eyes at herself. "Practically eternity."

"So you were playing God too?" Alana seemed to trust the AA process so much that it was hard to imagine.

Alana laughed. "Oh, yeah. It took me months to stop thinking of myself as superior to the rest of humankind, a better kind of addict than the rest."

Robin knew exactly what she meant. Sometimes, she caught herself looking down on the other members of the group, unable to understand how they could crave alcohol when the only thing she lusted for was blood. Well, blood and Alana. "But you don't think like that anymore."

"No. My arrogance made me relapse. After being sober for a few weeks, I started thinking I could control it. Have a drink after a stressful day, then stop. No problem, right?"

Robin shook her head. She sensed what was coming.

"Next thing I know, I'm waking up on my living room floor in a puddle of gin." Alana gave her a wry grin. "Nothing like having to admit to all your friends in AA how stupid you were to cure any thoughts of omnipotence and teach you a little humbleness."

"Wow." Robin didn't know what to say, but Alana seemed at peace with her road to sobriety and the obstacles she had encountered. Robin rubbed her hands. "Okay, what's next?" With her success spurring her on, she found to her surprise that she wanted to continue. Now that she'd mastered the first three steps, maybe the others wouldn't be as bad.

Alana showed her the next step in the brochure. "You've got some homework to do. Take an honest look at your life and make a moral inventory of who you really are, good and bad."

A long groan escaped Robin. "Is that really necessary?"

"Yes. How will you ever beat your addiction if you don't understand yourself and what drives you to drink?"

Robin already knew what drove her to drink—an age-old biological imperative—but she couldn't very well tell Alana that, so she just nodded in defeat. "And after that?" She was almost afraid to ask. "What's the fifth step?"

Alana crumpled her empty can in her fist. "That's when you tell me all about your life and the wrongdoings on your list."

Panic sent hot and cold shivers down Robin's spine. After keeping secrets and hiding her true self all her life, she couldn't take down all the masks and facades and tell Alana everything. While Alana might feel like her only ally in the world, she was still a human. "I... Alana, I can't."

"I know it's hard."

Robin shook her head. "You don't understand."

Alana let go of the crumpled can and put her hand on Robin's. Her touch sent tingles through Robin's body that soothed the rough edges of her panic. "Do you trust me?"

"Yes," Robin said before she could think about it.

"Then we'll see each other next week." Alana squeezed Robin's hand before letting go and getting up. When she reached the door, she looked back and said, "Don't forget to bring the inventory."

The door closed behind her.

Cursing, Robin hurled Alana's empty can across the room.

CHAPTER 10

ROBIN STABBED THE BACKSPACE KEY repeatedly, deleting the only two sentences she had managed to write in the last hour. She hadn't been able to write more than a sentence or two all week. The scenes that she usually saw in her head were gone. Instead, images of New Year's Eve flashed through her mind, mixed with impressions from her nightmares in which Meghan and her parents hunted down Alana and drained her.

She closed the document, finally giving up on writing for the day, and trudged into the living room, where she stared at Central Park below. Maybe going out, getting some air, would help clear her head. If she finally got up the courage, she could even go to the AA meeting, talk to Alana, and come clean—at least as clean as she could. She had dodged Alana's calls and evaded questions about what was going on when Alana sent her text messages. She knew she couldn't avoid a serious conversation forever, though. By now, Alana probably suspected that Robin was avoiding her so she wouldn't have to talk about the inventory of her wrongdoings.

She grabbed her coat and keys on the way out, pressed the down button that called the elevator, and counted the seconds until it arrived at her floor.

When the elevator doors opened, Mr. Singh stepped out and squeezed past her with a mumbled *hi*.

Robin returned the greeting and fled into the elevator, glad when the doors closed between them. Every time she saw her neighbor now, she had to think of Alana's words about playing God and she couldn't look him in the eye.

Deep in thought, she stepped out of the elevator and left the building.

Cold air and the smell of exhaust fumes, garbage, and roasted chestnuts hit her. Movement to her left caught her eye.

Robin's head jerked around.

A man stood at the corner of the building, staring at her. When he realized she'd seen him, he whirled and ran.

Robin's predatory instincts came alive. Adrenaline pumped through her system as she sprinted after him, dashing around honking cabs and past cursing street vendors. Even though she was running all out, she couldn't close the distance between them. *Dammit!* Either he was a world-class sprinter, or she'd slowed down since she'd stopped drinking fresh blood. Still, if he could outrun her, he clearly wasn't human.

Her muscles were burning, but she refused to give up. Gritting her teeth, she tried to speed up even more.

Ahead of her, the guy crashed into a group of pedestrians, losing valuable seconds.

Yes! This was her chance. *Come on, come on. Just a few more yards...*

Her lungs screamed as she tried to bridge the remaining distance between them. She lunged and gripped the back of the man's coat. *Got you!*

He stumbled but tore himself free with a powerful jerk.

Robin nearly fell when her fingers lost their grip on the coat.

The man skidded around a corner and disappeared into a side street.

Speeding up, she followed. She growled, and her fangs protruded.

By the time she rounded the corner, he'd managed to gain several yards on her. He ran right toward a wall that separated the street from someone's backyard.

No! If he climbed that wall, she would lose him.

He jumped, pulled himself up, and managed to get one leg over the wall.

Gathering every last bit of strength, Robin pounced. Her fingers closed around his other leg, and she jerked him back with all her might.

They landed on the rough pavement, the guy on top of her. Her head hit the ground. Lights sparked behind her eyes. His weight pressed the air from Robin's lungs. Pebbles dug into her palm, tearing her skin. Dazed and breathing hard, she lay still for a moment.

Seemingly unhurt, the man jumped to his feet.

Grunting, Robin rolled around and caught his ankle.

He went down hard, landing on his belly.

Not giving him another chance to escape, Robin tackled him. She grabbed his coat and shook him so hard that his teeth rattled. "Who are you?" She growled into his ear from behind. "Why are you spying on me?"

Instead of an answer, he bucked beneath her.

Robin tried to hang on, but he was too strong. Within seconds, she found herself under him.

He stared down at her from inches away, his fangs gleaming, a dangerous glint in his eyes.

Oh, shit. She struggled against his grip.

He pressed her shoulders to the ground and trailed his index finger down her neck. "Too bad you're not human. All that running made me hungry." He grinned, again revealing his fangs.

Robin growled and spat at him.

That wiped the grin off his face. He let go of her with one hand to dab at his cheek.

Robin drove her knee between his legs and jumped up.

His face the color of a cooked lobster, he got to his feet. "But then again," he said, gasping, "maybe you are human. You certainly fight like one. Maybe if you drank blood, like any

Girah with two brain cells, you wouldn't have so much trouble keeping up."

"What I drink or don't drink is none of your business," Robin said through gritted teeth.

He snorted. "I couldn't care less."

But someone did care enough to send him to spy on her. "The elders sent you to keep an eye on me, didn't they?"

He said nothing. He didn't need to.

"Tell them to keep their lapdogs out of my neighborhood."

He smirked. "Or else?"

Robin clenched her hands into fists until her knuckles turned white. The elders held all the power in Girah society. Without the support of her parents, she couldn't defy them, and as long as she didn't drink fresh blood, she stood no chance in a fight against their spies.

"That's what I thought." He pushed past her and ambled down the street without giving her another glance.

Robin hurled a curse after him. She knew the clan elders kept an eye on their wayward sons and daughters. In the past, she hadn't cared. Other than being a bit weird by Girah standards, she'd had nothing to hide. But now she did.

Steaming, she marched back to her condo.

Even if she wanted to, she couldn't go to the AA meeting now. While she had chased off one of the spies, there might be others. If she went to see Alana now, she would lead them right to her. That would give the elders and her parents the impression that Alana was to blame for Robin's refusal to drink fresh blood and make them think that they only needed to kill Alana to get Robin back on the straight and narrow.

The thought made her fangs sharpen even more. She wouldn't allow that to happen.

As soon as she reached her condo, she slammed the door behind her and grabbed the phone. She realized she had to rely on speed dial, no longer knowing her parents' phone number by heart. Maybe she should have called them a little more often;

then they wouldn't have found it necessary to tell the elders to keep an eye on her. Too late for regrets now.

Her mother picked up the phone. "Oh, Robin. I'm so glad you called. I knew you'd come to your senses and—"

"I'm not calling to say that I came to my senses," Robin said. "I'm calling to tell you to call off the babysitters."

"Babysitters?"

Was her mother really clueless? Had her father acted on his own? Robin realized that she didn't know her parents well enough to be sure. "The elders have someone watching me."

"They're just concerned, Robin. Just as we are."

"There's no need for concern. I'm drinking synthetic blood several times a week, so it's not like I'm going to die."

"But, honey, it's not natural. There's nothing evil about us hunting humans, taking some of their blood."

Robin shook her head, even though her mother couldn't see it. "I doubt humans would share that view."

"They do the same thing with animals. They even kill them, while we don't seriously harm humans. Of course, sometimes, accidents happen, but—"

"Accidents?" Had she ever thought like that too? "Mom, if you slip in the shower and hit your head, that's an accident. Taking a bit more blood than usual because you're hungry, not caring whether your prey lives or dies, that's a choice."

Her mother sighed. "It's no choice. Drinking blood is a biological imperative for us. Can't you feel the call of the blood every time you're near one of them?"

Robin squeezed her eyes shut. Oh, yes, she could, especially now that she was hungry and furious. She started counting the stacks of paper on her coffee table to get rid of the images in her head. "I don't want to feel it," she whispered.

Her mother was silent for several seconds. "Where did we go wrong?" she finally asked, her voice mournful. "Is it because we allowed you to eat human food so you would fit in at school?"

"No, Mom." Robin sighed. How could she make her mother understand? "It has nothing to do with what you did or didn't do. It's just that I—"

"It's that woman, isn't it? The one we saw when we came to your apartment. I have a bad feeling about her, Robin. She's not like other humans."

No, she wasn't. And that was part of what Robin loved—she shook her head at herself—what she liked about Alana. "It has nothing to do with her either. I'm an adult. I can make my own decisions."

"Then make the right ones, please," her mother said. "Your father talked to the elders. They're giving you one sapte luin to straighten up."

Robin didn't need to ask what would happen if she didn't *straighten up* within these forty-nine days. They would cut her clan ties, making her a persona non grata who couldn't rely on help, no matter how badly she needed it. No one within the clan would be allowed to even speak to her anymore. She would cease to exist for them.

"That…that's blackmail," she finally managed to get out.

"No. It's like you just said—you have a choice. Make the right one, and everything will be all right." For the first time in her life, her mother hung up on her.

Robin threw the phone on the couch. What was she supposed to do now?

When the AA meeting ended, Alana headed for the door instead of hanging around for coffee and conversation, as she normally did.

"Alana?" Brian called. "Do you have a minute?"

"Um, sure." She hoped it wouldn't take long, because she was itching to get out of here and check on Robin.

"How are you doing?" Brian asked. "You haven't talked to me in a while. Is everything okay?"

Alana bit her lip. It was true. For the last two months, she'd left right after the meetings to have dinner with Robin or to help her with her step work. "Sorry. I didn't mean to worry you. I'm fine. Really." She looked him in the eyes because that's what humans did if they wanted to convey sincerity. "It's just that sponsoring Robin takes up a lot of my time."

"Where is she today?" Brian asked.

Alana swallowed against the lump in her throat, while she watched some of the other members file out of the room. "I don't know." This morning, they had exchanged text messages, as usual. Well, not really as usual. Since Alana had left her with the moral inventory homework two days ago, Robin took her time answering or didn't answer at all. She also didn't pick up the phone. Alana hated to admit it, even to herself, but she missed Robin.

Brian took a seat in the last row and let his gaze roam over the nearly empty basement. "Do you think she had a—?"

"No," Alana hurried to say. "I have an idea what the problem is." She gestured at the door. "I'll call her from the car, and if she doesn't pick up, I'll drive over to her place to see how she's doing."

Brian rubbed his beard, a gesture that usually indicated that he had something to say but was hesitant to come right out with it.

"What?"

Brow furrowed, Brian sent her an imploring gaze. "Is there something going on between the two of you?"

Her first impulse was to deny it, but—with the exception of who she'd been in the past—she had never lied to Brian and didn't want to start now. But what could she say? "We're friends." Not a lie. Not the entire truth either.

"I know. But there's more, isn't it?"

JAE & ALISON GREY

Was it that obvious? A sigh escaped Alana's throat. "It's complicated." She searched Brian's face. There was no judgment. There never was.

"You know why it's not a good idea to get involved with her."

"Yes, I know." She plopped down on a chair next to Brian. "I can't even tell you what this is between us. She is so...and I'm..." How could she explain it to Brian when she didn't even understand it herself? She had sworn she wouldn't fall for a human again, and as Robin's sponsor, she had to protect her from getting into a relationship too soon, yet she couldn't deny the growing attraction between them. And it wasn't just physical desire that drew her to Robin.

And Robin? One moment, her eyes revealed the same attraction and growing fondness Alana felt, but at other times, she seemed to withdraw. *She's hiding something. Maybe that's why she's avoiding me instead of coming over to talk about her moral inventory.* Whatever it was, Alana would help Robin to deal with it and try to take away the pain so visible in Robin's eyes. Alana turned to her sponsor and friend. "I'm sorry, Brian. I have to go."

"To her?"

Alana nodded without looking at him. "I have to."

Brian stood and laid his hand on her shoulder. "You don't need me to tell you what's right or wrong. Just be careful. Friendship can be dangerous enough in this situation. More..." He shook his head but didn't finish his sentence.

Alana covered the hand on her shoulder with her own. The spark of electricity was so weak that even she barely felt it, and there was no accompanying tingle of pleasure. "Don't worry." She wouldn't let it come to more than friendship, no matter how much her body and her heart yearned for it. Without waiting for an answer, she jumped up and dashed out of the room.

Sitting in her car in the church parking lot, she dialed Robin's number. By now, she had her on speed dial, another indicator of how important Robin had become to her. But she didn't want to think about it right now.

When Robin's voice mail picked up, Alana ended the call. Doubts and worries started to gnaw at her. What if Brian was right and Robin really had relapsed? Maybe her parents or that Meghan person had visited her again, and now she was hiding away in her condo, either drinking or too ashamed to come to the meeting, face Alana and the other members, and admit that she'd fallen off the wagon.

Alana was determined not to let her withdraw completely. Whatever had happened, Robin wouldn't have to go through it alone. Alana would stay at her side and help her. As a friend.

She started the car and drove as fast as the speed limit allowed to Robin's condo building. She parked in the visitor parking spot, hoping she wouldn't get towed, rushed to the main entrance, and pressed the button for Robin's condo.

No reaction.

After trying a second time to no avail, she stepped back and looked up at the building. She counted at least three times to make sure she was looking at the correct window on the correct floor. As far as Alana could tell, the lights were on in Robin's condo.

A noise from the main entrance brought her attention back to the door.

A middle-aged woman stepped out.

Alana opened her purse as if searching for her key, smiled at the woman, and slipped past her into the building. *Ha!*

Less than two minutes later, she stood in front of Robin's door and knocked. For long seconds, there was no reaction, so Alana knocked again. "Robin? I know you're home. Open the door. Please. I'm worried about you."

Footsteps approached, and then the door swung open. Robin stood in the doorway, but instead of inviting Alana in, she blocked the way into the condo with her body.

Alana let her gaze roam over Robin.

Her hair was disheveled as if she had run her hands through it several times. She was wearing a baggy pair of sweatpants and a T-shirt that was wrinkled and had stains of something brown. A few drops of...maybe syrup? At least Alana couldn't smell alcohol. *But who knows? When she bolted from my apartment in January and then showed up later with my neighbor, I couldn't smell anything either.*

Robin cleared her throat, and Alana's gaze snapped to Robin's face. Dark circles under her eyes indicated that she wasn't sleeping well. "What are you doing here?" Robin's voice sounded strange. Hoarse.

Alana straightened. "I'm your friend; what do you think?" Even though it was almost painful to look into Robin's hollow eyes, Alana didn't avert her gaze.

"Did anyone see you enter my building?" Robin asked, looking past Alana at the empty hallway behind her.

"Uh, I slipped in when one of your neighbors left. Why?" What was up with the sudden paranoia?

"Alana, I...I can't. Please, can you just..."

"Five minutes. Then I'll be on my way, if you still want me to go."

Sighing, Robin let her in, closed the door with a quiet click, and plodded into the living room. Without looking back to see whether Alana followed, Robin sank onto one end of the couch. "Five minutes."

Alana took a seat at the other end of the couch.

Robin folded her hands in her lap und peered at the hardwood floor as if there were something fascinating about it.

After taking a deep breath, Alana asked, "What's going on?"

"Nothing," Robin mumbled without looking up.

"Sure, and I'm Jeanne D'Arc."

A hesitant smile crept upon Robin's lips, and she looked at her. "Nice to meet you, Jeanne."

Smiling as well, Alana moved closer but didn't touch Robin. "Remember what we talked about last time we saw each other? About playing God and not admitting you need help? Maybe we shouldn't have been so quick to check off that step."

Robin's smile vanished as fast as a shot of gin had in Alana's past. "I'm not playing God, and I don't need help. Everything's fine."

"Then why are you avoiding me?"

"I'm not avoiding you," Robin said but couldn't look her in the eyes. "I'm just busy writing."

"We're friends, aren't we?"

Robin stared at her hands and didn't answer.

An icy ball formed in Alana's stomach. Did Robin want to give up their friendship and the progress she'd made so far? *No, no, no!* Fighting against threatening tears, Alana pulled one of Robin's hands out of her lap to take it in her own. The spark between them was...different. Even more intense than usual and not nearly as pleasant. But Alana didn't let go, and as the seconds ticked by, the sensation changed, turning into an intense buzz, as if energy flowed through both of them, melding them together. For a moment, Alana couldn't move. Her eyes fell shut. The feeling was overwhelming.

"What's happening here?" Robin's voice trembled, but she didn't withdraw her hand.

Alana opened her eyes and met Robin's gaze.

The same confusion Alana felt showed in Robin's electric blue eyes.

"You feel it too, don't you?" Alana whispered.

Robin swallowed audibly and nodded.

"There's a connection between us, so please don't run away from me or lie to me. Tell me what's going on." The flow of energy between them was distracting but energizing as well. *Focus!* "It's about what you've done in the past, isn't it? That's why you're avoiding me and why you didn't show up for the meeting earlier."

Robin squeezed her eyes shut. "Alana, I can't!"

"Whatever you did while you were drunk, we can talk about it."

Robin jumped up and took the few steps to her floor-to-ceiling window, looking down at the darkness of Central Park. She wrapped both arms around herself. "I don't want you to…"

Alana stood and took a step toward her. "What? What don't you want me to do?" She was prepared to do whatever Robin needed.

Robin took a deep breath as if preparing to say something but then remained silent.

"What are you so afraid of?" Alana asked.

"I don't want you to think I'm a monster," Robin whispered, still facing the window.

"Oh, Robin." After a moment's hesitation, she enfolded Robin in a tender embrace. "I would never think that about you," she whispered as if speaking louder would make Robin bolt.

Robin trembled in her arms but didn't answer or turn around.

"Remember what I did? I killed a dog. I nearly killed a woman and her baby." Whatever Robin had done, it couldn't be worse than that, could it?

Robin freed herself from Alana's embrace, even though a part of her wanted to stay in her arms forever. She couldn't allow herself to think like that. Alana shouldn't even be here. If the elders were still having her building watched and they found out Alana had been here…

Alana regarded her with a concerned expression. "Whatever you did, don't you think you'd feel better once you got it off your chest?"

By now, Robin knew her well enough to realize Alana was in her overprotective mama-bear mode and wouldn't budge. She had to tell her something and then escort her to her car as fast as possible. "What you said about taking an inventory of my life… It brought up a lot of unpleasant memories."

"Do you want to talk about it?" Alana asked gently.

How could she? She couldn't very well tell Alana she had pierced a woman's carotid with her fangs and then nearly drained her.

"Come on. Let's sit down." Alana took her hand and pulled her toward the couch.

Robin flinched, not because of the tingle of electricity but because of the abrasions on her palm.

Alana instantly let go. She stared at the Band-Aids on Robin's hand. "How did I not notice this when I held your hand earlier?"

"It was the other hand. It's nothing, really, so don't worry about it."

"What happened?"

Since Robin couldn't tell her she'd fallen when chasing down the spy the elders had sent, she said the first thing that came to mind. "Just a couple of paper cuts." When Alana continued to stare at her, she shrugged and said, "Occupational hazard."

They sat down on the couch.

Alana reached for her injured hand and lightly stroked the back of Robin's hand with her thumb. The burning pain in Robin's palm instantly lessened. "I can't leave you alone, can I?"

You should. You should stay far, far away. Robin couldn't bring herself to say it.

Finally, Alana cleared her throat. "So? Want to tell me what's been on your mind the last few days?"

Robin pulled back her hand. She didn't deserve Alana's tender caresses. Not while she told this story. "I already told you that I've been drinking practically all my life."

"You didn't, but please go on." Alana gave her an encouraging nod.

"I drank with my parents and, when I got older, I headed out with my friends several times a week. They all drank, and I just went with the flow. I…I admit I enjoyed it."

"You were a teenager," Alana said softly. "You didn't know any better."

Accepting that excuse was tempting, just as tempting as the blood running through Alana, but Robin was determined not to indulge in either. "I knew," she whispered. "I knew that sometimes, bad things happened when we drank."

"Bad things? What kind of bad things?"

Robin didn't answer, already lost in memories.

On New Year's Eve, Robin and Meghan had lurked in the shadows of a quiet side street. Meghan had smashed the nearby streetlights, so the area was shrouded in darkness.

Robin didn't need the light. Her eyes pierced the darkness, and her mouth watered as a human stepped out of an all-night pharmacy.

The woman's steps faltered as she approached the car they were hiding behind, parked against the curb. "Hello?" the woman called, her voice trembling. "Is someone there?"

"She's scared," Meghan whispered, her breath hot in Robin's ear. "Isn't it sweet?"

Robin nodded halfheartedly. Unlike Meghan, she didn't enjoy drawing it out. "Let's just pounce, eat, and get out of here. I want to get back to my writing."

Meghan's grip on her arm held her back. "Not yet. It's New Year's Eve, and you haven't been out hunting with me in weeks, so let's live a little. Let her come to us."

The woman slowly came closer, her fingers clenched around her keys. That improvised weapon wouldn't help her against the danger lurking in the darkness.

When the human reached the car, Meghan sprang up from her crouched position. "Good evening, lovely," she said conversationally.

The woman jumped and pressed a hand to her chest. "Oh my God! You scared me half to death!" Apparently, she thought because she was facing two women, she wasn't in any danger.

She couldn't have been more wrong.

Robin bit her lip. She tugged on Meghan's arm, trying to drag her away. "Come on, Meghan, let's just…"

"Hey, lady," someone shouted.

They all stared at the man who left the pharmacy, waving something. "You forgot your credit card."

Meghan grinned as he approached. "Ooh, I didn't know this was a two-for-the-price-of-one eatery!"

"What?" The man frowned at her. "I run a pharmacy, not a—"

Meghan pounced. She grabbed him with her superior strength, tilted his head back, and licked her lips. Her fangs flashed in the moonlight and then pierced his carotid.

The woman screamed.

Meghan wrenched her fangs out of the man's neck long enough to say, "Get her!"

Still screaming, the woman tried to get her car door open, but Robin was faster. She wrenched her back, at first intending only to keep her from fleeing and calling the police. But once she felt the woman's warmth against her, the hectic pounding of her heart, her hunger flared.

As the scent of fresh blood drifted over from the man, her fangs unsheathed.

Robin hesitated, struggling against her rising need. But it was a losing battle. She hadn't eaten in days, making her hunger overwhelming.

"Why are you fighting it?" Meghan asked. Blood dripped from her fangs. "You can't change who you are. Bite her."

Just a sip. She'd take just a sip and then send the woman on her way, unharmed.

"Hold still," she whispered, using her thrall. "It won't hurt."

The woman went slack in her arms.

Before Robin was even aware that she'd sunk her fangs into the woman's neck, her mouth flooded with the taste of copper. *So good. So, so good. Just a little more.* A hazy red veil seemed to cover her, and the world around her retreated as she drank.

Seconds or maybe minutes later—she'd lost track of time—movement from the corner of the street startled her from the haze of bloodlust.

Squeaking, a rat darted out of an overturned trash can at the street corner.

Otherwise, everything around her had gone silent.

Meghan withdrew her fangs from the man's neck and dropped him like an empty can of soda. "Are you finished with yours too?"

Robin looked down at the woman hanging limply in her arms. She wasn't moving. At first, Robin thought it was because she'd ordered her to stay still, but then she realized how pale the woman was. Her fangs retracted instantly. *Oh, no. No, no, no. How much did I take?* She'd gone into a feeding frenzy, so she couldn't tell. With shaking fingers, she felt for the woman's pulse.

Sirens wailed in the distance, quickly coming closer.

"Shit." Meghan tugged on her arm. "Someone heard the screams and called the cops. Let's go."

Robin licked the woman's neck, desperately trying to get the bleeding to stop. "We can't just leave them like this. We have to—"

"We have to what? Get caught by the police? Run, Robin! Now!"

The sirens were very close now.

Softly, Robin settled the woman on the ground and ran, not after Meghan, just away—away from it all.

When she doubled back minutes later and peeked around the corner, EMTs were crouched over the two humans, working in a flurry of activity to save their lives. On shaky legs, she leaned against a wall. In decades of hunting humans and drinking blood, she'd never hurt someone so badly. A couple of times, she'd seen other Girah drain humans, not caring if they lived or died. While she'd never liked their careless drinking, it had never hit her like this.

"Hey." A touch to her arm brought Robin back to the present. Alana regarded her, her green eyes filled with concern. "What were you remembering? You've been staring off into space for a long time."

"I almost killed someone. I couldn't stop. Couldn't stop drinking." The words poured out without volition.

Thankfully, Alana didn't ask for details. She just sat next to Robin and held her hand while Robin kept talking.

Once she had started, she couldn't stop. She barely knew what she was saying and could only hope she wasn't revealing what kind of drinking she'd really been doing. She told Alana about everything else—her daily struggles not to drink, the loneliness she sometimes felt not fitting in anywhere, discovering her parents were having her watched, and her fear of losing her family if she remained abstinent.

Finally, no more words would come. She felt as drained as a human after a couple of Girah had feasted on her. Her muscles trembled as if she'd just run a marathon. She slumped against Alana, who wrapped her arms around her, holding her.

Peace settled over her as she closed her eyes and laid her head on Alana's shoulder.

Holding Robin brought a peace Alana had never known outside of the Great Energy. At the same time, she was feeling for Robin. Suffering with her, even. The pain so visible on Robin's face, her body language, even her breathing was hard to stand.

Robin's confessions whirled through Alana's mind. Robin had been drinking even as a child? What kind of parents would give alcohol to their innocent offspring or any other child for that matter? And what had Robin meant when she'd said she'd been on the hunt with Meghan on New Year's Eve? She'd mentioned a woman she'd badly hurt while drinking. Was Robin one of the people who became aggressive under the influence of alcohol and started fistfights when she'd been drinking? Or had she hit someone with her car too?

It doesn't matter. For now. Robin needed help and reassurance, not more questions. Keeping her voice soft, Alana said, "Thank you for sharing this with me. I'm sure it wasn't easy. If you want to talk about it some more, know that I'm always here to listen."

Robin gazed down at their joined hands. "Thank you. For now, I'm all talked out." She swallowed. "Does it ever get easier?"

"You mean the urge to drink?"

"No. I mean this feeling of guilt. Does it ever go away?"

Alana shook her head. "No. I don't think it's supposed to. But I'm able to live with it now."

"How? How did you get there?"

Alana caressed the back of Robin's hand. "I think that's a step for another day." Robin was clearly emotionally exhausted.

But Robin didn't let it go. She was just as eager to get rid of the pain and guilt as Alana had been. "What step?"

"Step nine of the program. Making amends to the people you hurt during your drinking days. Once I had apologized to the woman whose dog I hit, it became easier to forgive myself. I hope you'll one day be able to do that too."

"I can't," Robin croaked.

"Forgive yourself?"

"No, apologize. I can't apologize to the woman I hurt."

"I know it's hard." Alana took a deep breath. Maybe it would help Robin if she told her a little about her own experience. "I know it's not easy. It took me a while to get up the courage to face the woman. Because she was suing me for compensation back then, it was easy to get her address."

Now Robin gazed at her. "You visited her at home? Just like that?"

The admiration in Robin's voice brought a smile to Alana's face. "Well, I wouldn't call it just like that, but yes, I went."

"And? Did she talk to you?"

Alana remembered the stony expression on the young woman's face as she stood in the entrance of her small house. "I wouldn't exactly call it talking. At first, she just stared at me, then she started screaming. Her words, the tears in her eyes... It was horrible."

"What did she say?"

"It doesn't matter. At least she didn't smash the door into my face. When she'd calmed down enough to listen, I apologized for..." Tears welled in her eyes, and she blinked a few times to clear her vision. "For killing her dog and endangering her and her son." She cleared her raw throat. "I tried to explain how much that afternoon still haunted me and that I was working hard to make sure I wouldn't do something like that ever again."

Without her noticing, Robin had taken Alana's hand between both of hers. "Did she try to understand?"

"She tried. First, I thought she'd tell me I'd rot in hell, but instead she thanked me for coming and wished me good luck with my recovery."

"Wow, that couldn't have been easy for her to say."

"Yeah. I'm not sure I could have been so forgiving if I were in her shoes." After taking a deep breath, Alana added, "I felt so much better afterwards, just for having faced her and no longer running away from my fears. I hope it'll be the same for you."

She took Robin's chin between thumb and index finger and raised it.

Their gazes met and held.

It felt as if Robin touched something deep inside her. "I know you feel awful right now, like the worst human being on earth, but believe me, it does get better. I was able to close this chapter of my life and start anew. I can't change the past. But I can learn from it and do better in the future. And you can do it too."

Robin still looked doubtful.

She needs more time. That's okay. Alana was willing to be patient.

CHAPTER 11

THE TIRES OF ROBIN'S CAR crunched over snow as she parked against the curb. Heavy snowfall—probably the last one of the season—had hit the city overnight, and since it was Sunday, the few cars roaming the streets hadn't yet managed to turn the snow into gray slush. The world around her looked new and clean, so unlike Robin's dark thoughts of the past.

She didn't get out but sat in the car, looking across the street at the two-family brownstone with the number eighteen. When the woman she had hurt on New Year's Eve had been released from the hospital, Robin had followed her home, needing to see with her own eyes that she was okay, but she hadn't been here since.

After sitting in the car for countless minutes, she shook her head at herself. *This is really becoming a habit.* She climbed out of the car. *Now what?*

Part of her longed to do what Alana had done—march over and apologize to the woman she'd harmed, but she couldn't do that without getting herself in trouble. Another part was glad that she didn't have to face the woman. Still, after what Alana had told her about step nine of AA last week, she'd felt compelled to come here, to the place where she'd last seen the woman she'd hurt.

When her cheeks started to feel frozen, she reached out to open the car door and return home. Just when she was about to climb behind the wheel, movement caught her eye.

The door to number eighteen opened.

Robin held her breath and ducked behind the car, even though she knew that other people lived in the house too.

A woman stepped out.

Even with the woolen cap pulled low over the woman's forehead, Robin instantly recognized her. *It's her!* Robin's heart drummed against her rib cage.

The woman climbed down the three steps leading to the small lawn in front of the house. Two children rushed out behind her. Bundled up in winter coats, scarfs, and gloves, they romped through the snow.

A fist seemed to hit Robin in the gut, making her double over. *Oh, shit. She's got kids.* Maybe that was why she'd been in the all-night pharmacy on New Year's Eve. One of the kids might have been sick. *And thanks to you, she never made it home with the medicine.*

Robin sank onto one knee, ignoring the cold and the snow drenching her jeans. *If I had killed her, the kids would have to grow up without a mother.* The thought made her stomach churn.

Through the car's side windows, she watched as the little boy and his bigger sister bombarded their mother with snowballs.

The woman laughed and screamed.

For a moment, Robin flashed back to New Year's Eve, to the woman's terrified screams.

The two children started to build a snowman in the yard. Finally, their mother helped them lift the snowman's head onto the torso. The girl created a nose and eyes, using sticks and stones, and stole her brother's scarf to wrap it around the snowman's neck.

A gust of wind tugged the scarf out of her hands and blew it across the street and over Robin's car.

As it flew by, Robin grabbed it reflexively. She knelt, frozen, and stared at the orange scarf. It smelled of cinnamon and strawberry-scented children's shampoo.

Snow crunched, and then the little boy came running around her car. He slid to a stop when he saw her kneeling in the snow with his scarf.

They stared at each other, Robin just as startled as the boy.

For a moment, Robin considered thralling him and making a quick escape, but then she mentally shook her head. *No. No more playing God for selfish reasons.*

The boy took a careful step toward her and pointed at the scarf. "Thanks for saving my scarf."

"Uh, you're welcome. Here." Right as she was about to hand over the scarf, the woman ran over.

She eyed Robin warily. "Come here, Jackson."

"But she's got my scarf, Mom."

"You can have mine." The woman unwrapped her own scarf, handed it to Jackson, and sent him back to his sister.

Robin slowly rose from her kneeling position. She couldn't look away from the woman's now bare neck—not because she was tempted to bite her again, but because she was glad to see no scars or other signs of what had happened on New Year's Eve. The woman's cheeks held a healthy flush from the cold, not the sickly pallor from less than three months ago. "I didn't mean to scare him—or you."

"You didn't. It's just..." The woman shrugged and smiled apologetically. "I'm a bit wary of strangers lurking behind cars."

And with good reason. Guilt knifed through Robin, nearly making her double over again. She didn't know what to say, so she just held out the scarf.

"Thank you." The woman stepped closer and reached for the scarf. Before taking it, she paused and tilted her head. "Do I know you from somewhere?"

Oh, shit. She couldn't remember, could she? Not with the thrall and with how much blood she'd lost. It was impossible, but every muscle in Robin's body tightened all the same. "No. I don't think so."

But the woman kept regarding her with an imploring gaze. "I know you from somewhere. I'm sure of it."

Robin squirmed, the snow crunching beneath her shuffling feet. "I, uh, have to go." She pressed the scarf into the woman's hand and turned to pull the car door open.

The woman's voice stopped her. "Oh, now I remember!"

With her heart in her throat, Robin turned around.

"You're an author, right? I've got one of your books on my bedside table."

Robin's knees went weak, and she had to catch herself against the car. She nodded numbly.

"Can you wait here for a second while I get it? I'd love to have you autograph it."

"Uh, sure." Feeling as if she were trapped in a very surreal novel, Robin waited until the woman returned with *Bite Me.* If she was reading novels about vampires, she apparently didn't remember having her own neck pierced by one. Robin, though, remembered only too well. Her hand shook as she took the pen the woman held out to her.

"Can you make it out to Emily?"

Robin nodded since her vocal chords still didn't work. Now she had a name to add to the face she saw in her nightmares. She wanted to write, *Stay away from vampires*, but instead settled on *Take good care of yourself, Emily.*

Emily beamed at her as she took back the signed book.

That grateful smile was harder to take than a slap to the face. She felt as if she had attacked Emily a second time. Mumbling something about having to go back to her writing, she climbed into her car and drove off.

When she glanced into the rearview mirror, Emily and her kids were standing there, waving.

Without being aware of having driven in that direction, Robin found herself in front of Alana's apartment building. The only thing she could think of was wanting to be in Alana's arms and to again feel the peace that had settled over her after she'd told her about New Year's Eve. She could only hope that the elders' spies hadn't followed her. Very likely, she and Alana would be safe, at least until the ultimatum ran out.

She got out of the car and locked it with jerky movements. Cars honked as she stumbled across the street without looking left or right.

Her hand trembled as she pressed the buzzer.

No answer came.

Oh, no. Robin rubbed her cold cheeks with both hands. *Be home. Please, be home.* She didn't know where else to go.

She pressed the buzzer again, this time more urgently, but again, no one answered.

Alana jerked when the familiar high-pitched sound rang in her ears.

"Hi, girlfriend." Dahir appeared beside her on the couch and glanced at the file Alana was reading. "Working again on a Sunday?"

"Guess it happens to us humans since we're so slow." She didn't mention that she hadn't been able to focus on work all week since thoughts of Robin had intruded time and again. The dark-haired beauty seemed to be all she could think of these days.

Dahir leaned back and shook her head at Alana. "Work, work, work. Is that all there is to you?" She circled her index finger through the air, and a tall glass decorated with cherries, pineapples, and a little pink umbrella appeared on Alana's coffee table. "Here, drink that. It's a Brazilian fruit cocktail."

"You know I don't drink anymore."

Dahir nudged the glass closer to Alana. "It's alcohol-free, stupid."

Ignoring the orange drink on her coffee table, Alana closed the file and placed it next to the cocktail. She had a nagging feeling that Dahir hadn't just shown up to serve her an alcohol-free cocktail. She wanted something, and Alana wasn't sure she'd like whatever it was. "No, thank you."

Dahir shrugged. "Suit yourself." She took the little cocktail umbrella and rolled it between thumb and forefinger before draining the glass and making it disappear with a snap of her fingers.

"Don't get me wrong, it's nice to see you, but is there a special reason for your visit?"

For a while, Dahir studied her silently. Then, as if coming to a decision, she said, "I've been thinking."

"About?"

Dahir crossed her legs. "Don't you miss it?"

She didn't need to specify; Alana knew what Dahir was talking about. "No. I'm human now, and I don't waste time looking back. I like the person I've become."

"Really?"

Alana stared at Dahir with folded arms. "Really."

Dahir held up one hand, and Alana's bottle appeared in it. She trailed her fingers over the curve of the blue glass and the golden stopper, caressing it in a sensual gesture.

Alana pointed at the locked oak cabinet, where she usually kept the bottle, hidden behind a chocolate fondue set a colleague had given her last Christmas.

"Would you please put it back?"

"If you don't miss being a djinn, why did you keep your bottle?"

Alana took it out of Dahir's hand and felt the cool glass under her fingers. She tenderly stroked the wavy edges of the stopper. Memories of her free-flowing energy and the soothing limitations of the bottle, like a caring embrace, flooded her mind. Before she could stop it, a sigh escaped her lips. "Maybe I do miss it a little. But talking about it won't—"

"What do you miss the most?"

Alana closed her eyes. "Feeling the taqa," she whispered. She could still sense the threads of light and energy that held the universe together when she touched other people, especially with Robin. But compared to what she had felt when she'd possessed all of her skills, it was like seeing a firefly when she'd been blinded before by the brilliance of a sun. Only when it had gotten to be too much had she crawled into her bottle to isolate herself from the Great Energy for a while.

"Mmh, yeah, that's nice," Dahir said. "I can't even imagine how it would be to live without it. Isn't it depressing?"

"Sometimes," Alana said. Looking back, she'd battled depression in the past, even though she hadn't known it at the time. Lately, though, she'd begun to enjoy her life as a human more fully.

"I would be scared to death...no pun intended. But with your body being so vulnerable and taking so incredibly long to heal... And the pain every time you hurt yourself..." Dahir shook her head. "Horrible."

"So far, my residual taqa protected me from any serious injuries and helped me heal. Once, I think it even healed Rob—" She bit her lip. She'd better not mention that.

"It healed...what?"

"It's nothing, really."

"Let me be the judge of that."

Alana suppressed a groan. "I'm not even sure, but I think a little cut on Robin's lip healed when I touched her."

Both of Dahir's brows shot up. "Really?"

Shrugging, Alana averted her gaze. "Maybe I'm just imagining things."

"Maybe. Maybe not. You know that when you decided to leave and become human, the others weren't thrilled to say the least. But we care about you. We never stopped caring."

"What does that have to do with Robin's lip and my healing abilities?"

"The others didn't take away all of your skills. They left you with just enough of your djinn taqa to protect you. At least that's what I hear when I'm hanging out in the Great Energy. Maybe your residual taqa is stronger than expected." The expression on Dahir's face was unusually serious. "Please be careful. You know how dangerous our taqa can be when dealing with vulnerable humans. If you have enough power left to heal, you could also hurt someone."

The thought of hurting Robin made Alana's heart rate accelerate.

Dahir studied her fingernails. "On the other hand, it might be totally irrelevant anyway if..."

Alana knew that Dahir was baiting her with her dramatic pause, but she couldn't resist asking anyway. "If what?"

Dahir lowered her hand and looked at Alana. "You've been mastering your life as a human for years now, and you've been sober for...what? Twenty months? Granted, that's an incredibly short time for one of us, well, me, but for a human, that's a long time. Long enough to prove yourself, if that's what you were trying to do."

"I'm not trying to prove anything," Alana said but admitted to herself that it wasn't entirely true. After practically throwing her powers at the older entities' feet like an old rag that she no longer wanted, she'd been too embarrassed to face them again when her relationship with Kelly failed. Not without proving first that she could make it on her own, without any special powers.

"Good," Dahir said.

"What's that supposed to mean?" Why did she have to worm every word out of Dahir? "Just tell me why you're here, okay?"

"My, my, aren't we impatient?" Before Alana could say something, Dahir continued, "What if I told you that you might be able to get your old life back?"

Alana's mouth dropped open. Dahir couldn't be serious. When she had decided to become human for good, the older entities had left no doubt about the fact that it would be a final, irreversible decision. A whirlwind of emotions rushed through her, too intense and too complex to identify. "N-no. It's not possible...is it?"

Dahir nodded. "Yes, it is. At least I think you stand a good chance of convincing them. While some of us seem to think looking in on your life as a human every now and then is a great form of entertainment, others think it's time for you to come home."

Alana clutched the couch's armrest with both hands, feeling as if the world had tilted on its axis. Home. She could go home. *Wait.* "You said 'others.' So not everyone wants me back."

"No. Not yet. Maybe if you..."

The doorbell rang.

She wasn't expecting anybody. For a moment, she considered ignoring the visitor, but then a worrying thought intruded. *What if it's Robin? Maybe she needs me.* She looked back and forth between Dahir and the door. "You need to go. We'll talk about it later."

"Later? Alana, we're talking about you coming back home. What could be more important?"

Robin, her mind—or maybe her heart—screamed. Alana blinked. Where had that come from?

The doorbell rang again.

"Dahir, please."

Sighing, Dahir got up. "All right, already. Don't get your panties in a bunch. I'm going." She disappeared in a histrionic pink cloud, leaving behind only the little cocktail umbrella on the coffee table.

Alana rushed to the door.

Robin's shoulders hunched when Alana didn't answer. Just when she was about to get out her cell phone and call Alana, the intercom crackled to life.

"Yes?" Alana said from upstairs.

"It's me. I..." How could she explain what had happened and why she was here? "I went to see her. Alana, she's got kids."

The buzzer sounded immediately. "Come on up," Alana said.

Robin burst into the building and bobbed up and down on the balls of her feet while she waited for the elevator. When it finally arrived, she counted the seconds, willing it to move faster.

Alana greeted her at the door. "Come in. You look like hell." She reached for Robin's hand and pulled her into the apartment.

Energy seemed to flow through Robin, clearing her head of its dark thoughts a little. She clung to Alana's hand on the way to the living room, not even letting go as they settled next to each other on the couch.

"Tell me what happened," Alana said with a gentle caress to her arm.

Robin took a deep breath and tried to sort her jumbled thoughts and figure out where to start her tale. Her gaze fell on the coffee table. Her mouth, already opened to tell Alana everything, snapped shut.

On the coffee table, next to the remote control, stood a bottle. It was blue, with the pleasing curves of a woman, and had a golden stopper. Robin had seen a similar bottle once, when Meghan had dragged her to a Chinese restaurant to try the Asian cuisine—or rather, the people working there. The bottle had held a liqueur called Baijiu. The stuff had bitten into Robin's nose, indicating that it was as strong as vodka. *Or as gin.*

She stared at the bottle on the coffee table. Next to it lay one of the little umbrellas that usually came with a fruity cocktail. *She's been drinking.* After almost two years of sobriety, Alana had relapsed and thrown away everything she'd worked for. Shocked helplessness gripped Robin and then, without warning, turned into anger. She let go of Alana's hand and jumped up. Before

Alana could stop her, she snatched the bottle off the table and stormed into the kitchen.

Alana ran after her. "What are you doing?"

"Throwing this shit away!" Long since familiar with Alana's kitchen, she pulled open the cabinet that held the garbage can.

"No!" Alana grabbed Robin's arm with both hands, sending a zing of electricity through her entire body.

Doggedly, Robin held on. They struggled for a few moments, fighting for the bottle. Robin was stronger, but Alana stubbornly hung on, as if her life depended on saving the bottle. Finally, Robin's superior Girah strength won out. She freed herself from Alana's grip and hurled the bottle into the garbage can.

Glass splintered with a satisfying crash.

Alana stared at the blue shards. She whirled around, getting right into Robin's face, and shoved her against the kitchen counter. "How dare you! You had no right to do that."

"No right? I had every right to help you! I care about you, dammit!"

They paused and stared at each other from only inches apart, both breathing hard. Alana's cheeks were flushed, and Robin just wanted to pull her into her arms—and kiss her. *What the fuck...? Not now. Not ever.*

After several moments, Alana shook her head. "No, you don't. If you really cared, you wouldn't have destroyed my bottle."

"I threw it away because I care." With growing helplessness, Robin watched as tears filled Alana's eyes and ran down her cheeks. Why was she so upset about a stupid bottle? It dawned on her that this might be about more than just the desperate urge to drink.

Alana sank to her knees in front of the garbage can and started pulling the blue shards out of the garbage.

"Don't!" Robin knelt next to her and gently took one of the shards out of her hands. "You'll hurt yourself." She didn't want to even think about what would happen if Alana cut herself now, while Robin was so agitated and close to losing control.

Alana struggled against her grip. "Let me go! I need to put it back together."

Robin held her gently, but firmly. "I can't, Alana. Please. I can't let you hurt yourself."

Finally, Alana gave up her struggles and sank against Robin's shoulder. "Why did you do that?" she whispered. Her voice trembled, as if she barely held herself back from either shouting or sobbing.

"I'm trying to protect you." Robin caressed Alana's hair, relieved when the touch wasn't rejected. "I know how strong the urge to drink can get sometimes, but I can't let you—"

"The urge to drink? What are you talki—?" Alana lifted her head off Robin's shoulder and peered past her at the blue shards. Paling, she gazed up into Robin's face. "You thought I was drinking?"

The disbelief in Alana's eyes couldn't be fake, could it? Robin held her more tightly. "You weren't?"

"No!"

"But...but..." Robin shook her head to clear it. "Then what were you doing with that bottle?"

"There's no alcohol in it. There never was."

Robin wanted to believe her. She really did. At the same time, she was afraid to let it go too easily and let Alana spiral into a relapse. "So you just happen to have an empty bottle lying around in your living room, next to a little cocktail umbrella?"

Alana pulled out of Robin's arms. New tears glittered in her eyes as she reached out and carefully touched the blue shard Robin was still holding on to. "A friend came over for a surprise visit earlier. She left the umbrella behind. The bottle is something from my past." Alana sighed. "I guess I've been holding on to it for sentimental reasons. It reminds me of my...my family and of the life I once had, so I was really attached to it. I couldn't throw it away, but it had nothing to do with my alcoholism."

Robin continued to look into her eyes, searching for the truth in the swirling green depths. At the sight of the tears welling in Alana's eyes, her own eyes started to burn. "I believe you." Her relief was so strong that she nearly collapsed face-first onto the kitchen floor. Instead, she pulled Alana into her arms.

Alana flung her arms around her and held her tightly.

"I'm so, so sorry about your bottle," Robin whispered. "I really thought you'd relapsed, and I didn't want that bottle anywhere near you. What can I do to make this right?"

Alana's lips compressed into a tight line. "I don't think there's anything you can do."

"I'm sorry," Robin said again, around the big lump in her throat. She'd wanted to protect Alana and had ended up hurting her. Was that her destiny—hurting people?

"It's okay," Alana said after a moment. "You didn't know. How could you? I never told you about the bottle. Maybe it was time to let go of it anyway." The grief in her voice said that she hadn't been ready to let go. She ended their embrace, stood, and gently closed the door to the kitchen cabinet that held the garbage can.

Still kneeling, Robin looked up at her, waiting for some sign that she'd really been forgiven.

Alana pulled her up and back into her arms.

A long breath escaped Robin, and the tension drained from her body. For a few moments, she just rested against Alana, enjoying the peace of being in her arms after everything that had happened today. Then she became aware of the little thrills of excitement their full-body contact sent through every fiber of her being. A current ran through her, almost as exciting as tasting blood. She realized that she'd bent down and put her head on Alana's shoulder, a move that put her mouth at level with Alana's neck. Alana's carotid pounded just two inches away from her lips. The steady beat pulsed through Robin until her entire body seemed to resonate with the rhythm of Alana's heartbeat.

Hunger rose swiftly. Knowing she'd drive over to the house of the woman she'd harmed, she hadn't been able to drink any of the Synth-O this morning. Her stomach had been too upset, but now the only thing she felt was roaring hunger.

She moved even closer and sniffed Alana's neck. *Heavenly.* Her mouth watered. She'd never smelled anything so good. She wanted to devour every inch of her, kiss her, lick her, bite her. Her jaw ached, warning her that her fangs had protruded. Groaning, she gave in to her need and lowered her head the rest of the way.

"Um, what are you doing?"

Alana's voice, laced with confusion, was like a bucket of ice-cold water being poured over her head. Her fangs instantly retracted. "Uh, I..." Caught with her mouth just a fraction of an inch away from Alana's neck, Robin couldn't think of a good excuse. She couldn't think at all, so she did the first thing that came to mind. She kissed Alana's neck.

A moan rippled through Alana. She swayed and clutched Robin's shoulders, for a moment just holding on as if she wasn't sure whether to push her back or pull her closer. Then her grip tightened, and she pulled up Robin's head. Her eyes had darkened to a forest-green color.

Robin's gaze darted to her red lips. She leaned in, following the siren's call—but this time, it wasn't the call of Alana's blood. She realized that she craved kissing her as much, if not more, than biting her.

———— •••• ————

The look Robin gave her was hungry. She watched as Robin licked her lips. That was all it took. Alana surged forward and pressed their lips together. Before her mind could form any coherent thought, her lips parted and her tongue demanded entry into Robin's mouth, which was immediately granted. Her whole body came alive, tingling all over in a kiss unlike any Alana had ever experienced before. She clutched Robin's back to keep her balance and to press her even closer.

Robin's muted moan crashed over Alana like a wave, robbing her of breath. *What are you doing?* Panting, she pulled back and stared into Robin's eyes, which mirrored the passion she felt. "This is a bad idea," she whispered, still struggling to think coherently. None of Kelly's kisses had ever left her so dazed and breathless.

"Doesn't feel like it," Robin murmured and brought their lips together again.

No, it didn't. All thought left Alana for good at the sensation of Robin's hot, exploring tongue in her mouth. She grabbed Robin by the shoulders and pushed her against the kitchen counter, never interrupting the contact between them for even a second. Her breasts pressed against Robin's, and a zing of electric awareness shot through every cell of her body. *Oh, yes!*

Robin trailed her hands down Alana's back, cupped her ass with both hands, and squeezed while her mouth and tongue caused shivers up and down Alana's spine.

Her whole body came alive, screaming for her to rip Robin's clothes off. She tore her mouth away to gasp for breath. Without Robin's tongue and lips doing incredible things to her, she could think more clearly. *Too fast!* Robin had been sober for less than two months. *It's too soon for her.*

Robin let go of Alana's ass and let her hands rest on Alana's hips. "Are you all right?" she asked, panting.

Physically, Alana felt more than all right. Every cell in her body that could feel pleasure was firing full blast. Emotionally, though, she was more confused than ever. Lying wasn't an option. She needed to be honest. "No, not really."

A pang of hurt shone in Robin's eyes. She stepped back, breaking the physical contact. "I'm sorry, I thought…"

Alana touched Robin's arm and enjoyed the spark of pleasure between them. "Don't apologize. That was…" How could she describe such an overwhelming experience? "It was incredible."

"But?"

Alana smiled wistfully. "I'm your sponsor. I'm supposed to help you stay sober, not risk your sobriety by getting involved with you." When Robin closed her eyes as if in defeat, Alana touched her chin until Robin's beautiful blue eyes appeared again. "AA advises you to get a plant to start with. If the plant is still alive after a year, get a hamster or something. If both are doing all right after two years, then you can start thinking about a relationship."

Robin regarded her with a stubborn gaze, her jaw set and her chin held high. "I don't like hamsters."

Alana couldn't help smiling. "Well, then get a cat."

A fleeting smirk dashed over Robin's face. "I don't like cats either. Where does that leave us?"

"With a dog, probably."

Robin nudged her gently. "You know what I mean. Do you really want us to ignore this," she pointed back and forth between them, "just because of that two-year rule?"

Alana sighed. She should say yes. Considering that she was a few centuries older than Robin and had been in AA for much longer, she should be the sensible one. But for once in her life, she didn't want to fulfill other people's dreams and wishes—she wanted to act on her own desires. "No," she said. "I don't want that. But we should at least take it slow."

Robin frowned. "Define slow."

Alana found herself staring at Robin's kiss-swollen lips as if she were a lip reader. Then her gaze swept over the rest of Robin's body. Her mouth went dry. *Probably the opposite of where my thoughts are heading right now.* "We take it step by step. First of all, we'll need to find you a new sponsor."

"I don't want another sponsor," she said, heat in her eyes. "I want you."

Static crackled between them, making Alana shiver. "You're not helping."

Robin took a step back and placed both palms on the kitchen counter. "Okay, okay, I'll behave. So, what are we going to do now?"

Alana bridged the space between them, leaned up on her tiptoes, and placed a short kiss on Robin's lips. Before either of them could deepen the contact, she withdrew, took Robin's hand, and pulled her toward the living room. "Now we'll sit down on the couch, and you'll tell me what got you so upset before you came here."

CHAPTER 12

Alana rubbed her forehead for the umpteenth time. How on earth could she get her client Mrs. Schultz to agree to... *Oh no, not now. Not here.*

The familiar high-pitched sound that proceeded Dahir's appearance rang through the office. Dahir materialized, perched on Alana's desk. She raised her hand and wriggled her fingers in greeting. "Hi, girlfriend."

Through clenched teeth, Alana asked, "What are you doing here? I told you you can't come..."

A knock sounded seconds before the door swung open.

Dahir quickly transformed herself into a stack of files on Alana's desk.

Grace stuck her head inside the office. "Did you say something, boss?"

"Uh, no. Just talking to myself. This new case is driving me crazy." She pointed at the top file.

"Ah. I'll just ignore the muttering, then." Grace nodded but paused when her gaze fell on the stack.

Alana looked in the same direction and froze. On top of the Dahir stack was a catalog of sex toys for women. *If she weren't immortal, I'd kill her!*

Blushing, Grace cleared her throat. "I'll be at my desk. Let me know if you need," she coughed, "if you need anything." She closed the door behind her.

Alana buried her face in her hands and groaned.

With a quiet pop, the stack of files with the sex-toy catalog on top transformed back into Dahir's human form.

Alana lowered her hands and shook her head at her. "Hard to believe that you're nearly five hundred years old. You behave like a teenager."

"By djinn standards, I am a teenager. Speaking of the djinn... Have you thought about my offer to help you return to the Great Energy?"

"Of course I have, but..." How could she explain the turmoil she was in? If Dahir had asked this very question six months ago, the answer would have been yes in a heartbeat. But everything had changed since she'd met Robin. Now, it wasn't as easy anymore. *Is it really just Robin?* She mentally shook her head. *Admit it, you like being human.*

"But?"

"Huh? Oh, yeah. It's an important decision. I need more time to think it over, Dahir."

"What's there to think about?" Dahir asked. "You miss your old life; admit it. I saw how you looked at your bottle on my last visit."

"My bottle's destroyed." Even though it had happened a few days ago, her eyes still burned when she remembered that her old home was gone forever.

"Destroyed? Don't tell me you..."

"Robin dumbed it into the trash can."

Dahir sucked in a breath. "You've got to be kidding."

Alana shook her head. "I wish I were. She saw the bottle and your little cocktail umbrella and thought I was drinking again."

"I'm so sorry," Dahir said and covered one of Alana's hands with her own, causing a swirl of colors and a ripple in the ethereal currents that flowed through them. After a few seconds, Dahir's frown disappeared, and she sat up straight. "It doesn't matter. At least I don't think it does. We'll just get you a new reservoir. I've been telling you for decades that you need something more modern." She pulled a gleaming smartphone from her pocket.

"This is my newest home. That way, my masters can talk to me while I'm resting without anyone becoming suspicious."

Alana stared at her. "You live in a cell phone?"

She shrugged. "Stranger things have happened." Dahir pierced her with a disapproving stare. "A djinn who wants to become human, to name one thing."

Alana lowered her gaze. "I need time, okay? It's not as easy as you think."

Dahir opened her mouth as if to object but closed it without speaking. Finally, she nodded. "All right. If you want to talk about it or I don't know…" She trailed off and stood. For a long moment, she regarded Alana, then said, "Come here, I want to give you a hug."

Alana rolled back her office chair and stood. Djinn didn't embrace; they could just come together in the Great Energy. Did Dahir miss that kind of contact with her?

Dahir opened her arms, and Alana stepped into the embrace.

Energy flowed between them in a pleasant buzz. It reminded Alana of the feeling when she and Robin held each other, but it was also different. Robin's touch caused her heart to skip and her hormones to dance a samba. Holding Dahir was as she imagined holding a sister would be: no exciting push and pull of two different kinds of life energy meeting and sparking off each other. It was more like a gentle flow…a sensation of dipping into a tub of warm water.

When Dahir let go and stepped back, she smiled. "Being close like this is…different. But also kind of nice."

Alana smiled in return. "Yes, it is."

Dahir took a deep breath. "Okay, I have to go. Take care." She waved and disappeared.

For a moment, Alana stood beside her desk, shaking her head. Even after centuries, Dahir managed to surprise her from time to time.

The chirping of her cell phone brought her out of her musings. She took the call at the second ring. "Wadd."

"Hi, it's me—Robin. Do you have a minute?"

She sounded so serious. And usually she didn't call Alana at work. "Are you okay?"

"Uh, yeah, I'm fine. And you?"

For a split second, she wanted to tell her about Dahir showing up but then realized she couldn't. "Great. Busy with work, but it's still nice to hear from you."

"I don't want to keep you for long, but I was wondering..."

When seconds ticked by without Robin continuing, Alana asked in a gentle tone, "Tell me what's going on."

Robin chuckled. She sounded nervous. "Sorry, I...I wanted to ask you if you, well, if you've got some time tonight. I have something I'd like to give you."

"Oh, Robin, that's so nice of you. I wish I could, but this week is just crazy. Two of my important cases go in front of a judge on Friday. Until then, I'll barely have enough time for a quick sandwich, much less anything else."

"I see. No problem. Really."

Even though Robin sounded as if she understood, Alana thought she could hear disappointment in her voice. *Or maybe it's just that I wish I could see her.* "I don't have much time, but would it be okay if I send you a text message from time to time?" They usually exchanged text messages only in the evenings, when Alana was home from work and Robin had made her word-count goal for the day.

"Of course," came the immediate answer.

Alana smiled. "Great. I'll keep you updated if you keep me updated how you're doing."

"You've got a deal, Ms. Wadd."

Now grinning from ear to ear, Alana said, "Then type to you later."

Robin's melodic laughter rang through the cell phone. "Yeah, type to you later. And Alana?"

"Yeah?"

After a moment of silence, Robin said in a serious voice, "It was nice to hear your voice."

"Yeah, yours too." She ended the call and grinned like an idiot into the empty office before going back to work.

———— ••• ————

Alana smiled when she spotted Robin's car in the parking lot of the church not far away from where she had just parked.

It seemed that Robin had waited for her, because when she got out, Robin's door opened as well and she flashed Alana a radiant smile. "Hey, stranger," she purred.

Great Energy, that voice. That in combination with her heated gaze was Alana's undoing. She licked her lips and hurried her steps. She didn't want to shove their one-week-old relationship into the group members' faces, but an embrace should be fine even if someone saw them.

As if knowing what Alana wanted, Robin opened her arms and enfolded her in a tender hug.

Alana took a deep breath and inhaled Robin's intoxicating scent, a mix of her fruity shampoo, the leather of her black jacket, and something that was just Robin. "Mmm, why do you smell so damn good?" She rubbed her face against the soft skin of Robin's neck and pulled her closer. After not seeing her all week, she couldn't get close enough.

Robin's pulse pounded beneath her lips, and Alana couldn't resist pressing a kiss to the tender spot. Maybe she'd read too many vampire romances in the last couple of weeks. After reading the first of Robin's novels, Alana had been unable to resist and had bought them all and read most of them by now.

A groan escaped Robin, and she pulled back a little. The hunger in her eyes, which had gone almost black, made Alana swallow.

"S—someone could see us," Alana stammered.

A smile flitted across Robin's beautiful face. "Nobody's here."

Alana tore her gaze away from Robin's tempting lips and took a look around the parking lot. It was deserted. They were early, so they probably had a few minutes before the first members of their group arrived. *Just a short kiss. It'll help me survive the next two hours without touching her.* Alana slid her hand up, into Robin's short hair, and pulled her down. She'd intended to give her a short peck on the lips, just to establish some kind of contact and to enjoy the buzz between them, but when their mouths met, all rational thoughts escaped her. Their tongues danced with each other, sending surges through her whole body with every stroke, especially between her legs. A loud groan, muffled by Robin's mouth, rang in her ears, but she didn't care. She was overly aware of Robin's breasts pressing against her own. Was it possible to come from just a kiss?

"Alana?" said a deep voice next to them.

Damn. Alana wrenched herself away from Robin and swayed, dizzy from the kiss.

Robin wrapped both of her hands around Alana's arm and held on to her as if she needed to regain her balance as well.

Brian stood next to Alana's car, regarding them with a frown.

"It's not what it looks li..." Alana sighed. She didn't want to lie to her oldest human friend. Lying was useless anyway. Their kiss left no room for misinterpretation, and Brian would find out eventually. "Okay, it's exactly what it looks like."

Brian stepped up to them. He looked at Alana, disappointment carved into his tensed facial features. His silence was worse than anything he could have said.

Alana half turned to Robin and caressed one of her arms with her free hand. "Could you give us a minute?"

Robin glanced from her to Brian and back. "It's not just your fault. I—"

"Yeah, but he's my sponsor. Please, Robin."

Hesitantly, Robin nodded and let go of her. "I'll be inside."

When they were alone, Alana said the only thing possible, "We're in love." She paused and marveled at what she'd just said.

Wow. When did that happen? Just a few weeks ago, she'd been determined never to fall for a human again. Somehow, Robin had made her forget all of her resolutions, and Alana wasn't sure yet whether it was a good or a bad thing. For now, she was content to see where it was going. "Well, at least I'm in love with her, and I hope she feels the same."

Brian rubbed his beard. "How could you let that happen?"

"I didn't want to. I swear. I wanted to stay away from her. That's why I didn't want to be her sponsor when you suggested it."

He stared at her. "This has been going on for that long?"

"No!" She didn't want Brian to think that. "No, just since last week, but there was something between us from the very first moment."

"AA is not a dating agency. You're endangering your recovery and hers as well. God, she hasn't even been sober for three months."

Actually, it was even less than he thought, given her relapse two months ago, but Alana chose to keep that to herself. "I know. That's why we're taking it slow."

He arched a brow. "That was slow?"

A blush crept up her neck.

"Alana, you know this is not a good idea."

As much as she wanted to deny it, he was right. "I know. We talked about it, and we're both willing to risk it." She took one of his hands and looked deeply into his warm brown eyes. "It's not just a fling for me. And I'm pretty sure it's more than that for her too. I promise we'll be careful."

He took a deep breath. "I don't want to spoil this for you. I just worry. You know that I care for you. After what happened with Kelly, I'm glad you found someone. Despite the circumstances."

That brought a smile to her face. "Thank you. I care for you too." She nodded toward the church entrance. "Let's go, big brother." She pulled him toward the oak doors.

He fell in step, and they crossed the parking lot in silence.

At the door, Alana paused. "I need a favor."

"What is it?"

"Robin needs a new sponsor."

"You're right." Brian held the door open for her. "I think I might have the perfect candidate for the job. What do you think of Caren?"

Alana forced a smile. Caren was a good-natured elderly lady, who was always there for everybody and often spoiled the other group members with her cakes and pastries. But how could she convince Robin to accept her as her sponsor? It was clear she didn't want a new sponsor, but if they wanted to build a serious relationship, there was no alternative.

Brian seemed to sense her worries and patted her back. "Don't worry. I'll be there for you, no matter what."

Alana looked up at him. She hoped that, against all odds, her relationship with Robin would work out. *It has to.*

"Not hungry?" Robin asked and looked down at Alana's untouched french fries.

Hungry yes, but not for food. "I could ask you the same thing." Alana pointed at the discarded steak in front of Robin.

She shrugged. "I'm not very hungry." She fiddled with the straw of her milkshake, every now and then peeking up at Alana.

The silence between them was charged with sexual tension. Alana fought against the urge to get up, climb into Robin's side of the booth, and kiss her senseless, onlookers be damned.

"Did Brian give you a hard time because of us?" Robin asked after a while.

Alana shook her head. "He's worried; that's all." Considering the circumstances, Brian had been really understanding. Had it been the other way around, Alana wasn't sure she'd have stayed so calm. Thirteen-stepping—beginning a relationship with a newbie who hadn't been sober long—was just wrong. *Am I making a huge mistake?* What if it didn't work out and Robin relapsed because of it? Or what if it worked out, but Robin relapsed anyway? She couldn't be with someone who drank, not without endangering her own sobriety. Even if neither of them relapsed, how could a relationship between them work if she couldn't even tell Robin who she really was—or rather, who she had been? Sometimes, she wondered if Kelly had cheated on her because she had sensed that Alana had held a part of herself back.

Well, Robin will notice sooner or later, if you look more or less the same in twenty years while her hair is getting gray. Gosh, I bet she'll look so sexy. She shook her head at that last thought. *You're hopeless.*

"Hey," Robin said quietly and covered Alana's hand with her own, sending tingles up and down Alana's body. "Are you all right?"

Alana met her gaze. "Do you think we're doing the right thing?"

For some endless seconds, Robin didn't answer.

What if she said no? *What if she says yes?* Alana was so full of doubts. Being with Robin meant deciding for a life as a human and against returning to the Great Energy, if that was even really possible. Was that really what she wanted?

"I don't know," Robin said, making Alana's heart sink. "I didn't want to get involved with you. With anyone."

Alana sighed. "Me neither."

"But," they both said at the same time and then grinned at each other.

"I don't know if it's right," Robin said, "but it certainly feels right."

It feels amazing. Alana tried to focus on the conversation, not on the excitement running through her as Robin brushed her fingertips over the sensitive skin on the inside of her wrist. She cleared her throat. "Thanks for accepting Caren as your new sponsor."

Earlier, when Brian had dragged Caren over to talk to Robin, Alana had been more than a little surprised when Robin hadn't put up a fight and had agreed to the new sponsor. Despite her earlier refusal, she seemed to understand that it was a necessity.

"She's really great," Alana said. "I've known her since I first came to the meetings." It was hard for her to concentrate on this topic when the three open buttons of Robin's blouse revealed a tantalizing bit of cleavage.

"So you said."

Alana pulled her gaze away from Robin's full breasts and watched their joined hands instead. Funny how the energy between them had changed. First, there had been this almost painful spark, which had transformed into an intense but pleasant tingle. Now every single touch seemed to energize and excite her, as if Robin's life energy were pulsing through her, igniting her taqa and bringing her whole body alive.

"You know, I'm not really hungry," Robin said.

Alana looked up.

Robin's eyes reflected the desire Alana felt.

She had to swallow. *Slow, remember? You wanted to take it slow.* Maybe getting out of here, clearing her head in the cool air outside, was a good idea. "Okay, then let's go."

Outside, the fresh air engulfed her. It smelled of spring, making her think of a stroll in Central Park, hand in hand with Robin. She grinned at herself. *Listen to you.* Her hormones were turning her into a romantic sap.

They had taken Alana's car and had left Robin's in the church parking lot, since parking was at a premium around the diner and they hadn't wanted to be apart, even for the ten-minute drive.

When they reached the car, Robin didn't let go. Instead, she used their joined hands to pull Alana into her arms. Her body heat was like a warm blanket on a cold winter day.

That feels so damn good. Being in Robin's arms quieted the insistent voice in her ear, telling her this couldn't work, no matter how much she wanted it to. She had never considered telling Kelly about her life as a djinn. Something, maybe her fear of Kelly thinking she'd gone nuts, had held her back. But with Robin, it felt important to be honest. She wanted to open up to her by sharing this important part of herself. *You don't even know if she feels the same.* If nothing else, Kelly had taught her not to count on her partner returning her feelings.

Hesitantly, Alana let go so they could get into the car.

As she started the car, Robin reached over and tenderly squeezed Alana's thigh. "What's going on in that beautiful head of yours?"

"Just thinking about some stuff." Alana looked away from traffic for a moment to gaze into Robin's sparkling eyes. "Most of it R-rated."

"Oh, yeah? Care to elaborate?"

Robin's voice and the lingering touch to her leg made her shiver. Alana laughed shakily. "I'd better not."

"Uh, you realize that you should have gone right at the intersection?" Robin pointed over her shoulder.

"Shit. You're just too distracting." Alana looked around for a spot where she could do a U-turn, but there was none in sight.

"It's okay. Just keep going. You can drive me home, and we can come back tomorrow to get my car."

At least it would give them another excuse to spend more time together. Not that Alana needed much of an excuse at this point. She nodded and kept driving.

They'd been sitting in the car in front of Robin's condo building for the past fifteen minutes. They had said good night at least four times, but every time, one of them had turned to the other for one last kiss, and that had started another make-out session.

Robin had thought it might get easier to rein in her attraction once she'd admitted it, but now she found that the opposite was true. She was so drawn to Alana—to her touch, the heat of her body, the pounding of the arteries in her neck as they kissed...

Robin tried not to think about it, tried not to imagine licking that warm skin, gently biting down, and tasting Alana's delicious blood, but it was like telling yourself not to think of a pink elephant. When she couldn't take it anymore, she wrenched her mouth away and leaned back in the passenger seat. "Do you want to come up?" *What?* That wasn't what she'd meant to say. Or maybe it was. At least if Alana went inside with her, the clan elders' spies wouldn't see them making out like a couple of teenagers if they drove by. Plus she still needed to give Alana the gift she had purchased with the royalties from her last short story. She would give Alana her surprise and then walk her back to her car.

Alana hesitated and looked at Robin, her gaze full of doubts. "It's not that I don't want to." She stroked Robin's cheek, sending electric flares though Robin's body. "But we said we'd take it slow, remember?"

"Get your mind out of the gutter, woman. I'm not inviting you up for *that*." Robin laughed, even though she wanted nothing more than to drag Alana to her bedroom and not let her out for the rest of the night. But she'd wait until Alana was ready. It would give her a much-needed chance to work on her self-control so she wouldn't bite Alana when she finally got to kiss her from head to toe. If she hurt Alana in the heat of the moment, she'd never be able to forgive herself. "There's something I want to give you."

Curiosity sparked in Alana's eyes. "What is it?"

Robin shook her head. "I'm not telling you. Come on up and find out."

Alana bit her lip while gazing out the side window. Eventually, she turned toward Robin. "Okay, then let's go." She got out of the car.

On the way up, Robin kept her hands wrapped around the elevator's handrail so she wouldn't run them all over Alana. In public, it had been easy to behave, but now that she'd have Alana in her home and would be all alone with her... *Maybe this wasn't such a bright idea. I should tell her she'll get her gift another time and send her away.* But she couldn't bring herself to say the words. Her fingers shook as she unlocked the door to her condo.

Her heart pounded even faster when Alana took off her coat and swept her hair back over her shoulder, revealing her alabaster neck.

Robin forced her gaze away. *The gift, remember?* She sat on the other end of the couch, away from temptation, and fiddled with the gift-wrapped package that had been lying on her coffee table. Nervousness replaced the amorous thoughts from moments ago. *What if she thinks it's stupid or starts crying again?*

"Is that for me?" Alana asked, pointing at the gift.

Robin nodded but didn't hand it over. She ran her hands over the oddly shaped present, remembering how long it had taken her to wrap it properly. She had wrapped several layers of paper around it so the shape wouldn't give away the surprise.

"But it's not Christmas, and I never told you my birthday."

"It doesn't matter," Robin said. "Here." Quickly, before she could change her mind, she placed the gift on Alana's lap.

"Thank you." Still looking puzzled, Alana began to remove the gift wrap from the present. Finally, the red-and-green paper fell away, revealing a blue, womanly shaped bottle with a golden stopper. Alana gasped and ran her hands all over it. "That's..." She glanced at Robin, then back down at the bottle. "How did you...?"

"It's not yours, but it's the closest I could come. I know that doesn't undo what I did, but... I wanted to give you this to show you how sorry I am and..." Robin swallowed. "...to show you how much I care."

Alana stared at her. Tears gleamed in her eyes.

Oh no. Robin helplessly lifted her hands. *I knew it. I shouldn't have...*

Alana put the blue bottle down on the coffee table, safely out of range. Without saying a word, she turned toward Robin, took her face in both hands, and pressed their lips together. The kiss she gave Robin made all others they'd exchanged so far feel tame in comparison.

Heat shot through Robin. She kissed her in return, all the while trying to hold back just a little so she wouldn't lose control and do something stupid.

Alana pulled away just long enough to whisper, "I...care about you too." Then her mouth was back on Robin's.

Gasping under the passionate assault, Robin managed to get out, "We don't need to—"

"Yes," Alana said. "We do. To hell with slow. I want you."

Her words set off little fires all over Robin's body. She pulled Alana up from the couch and toward her bedroom. They stumbled through the hall, kissing and caressing.

Alana struggled to open the buttons on Robin's blouse. "Off, dammit." One of the buttons went flying and ricocheted off the wall; the rest of the buttons cooperated.

Robin was just as eager to feel Alana's bare skin. Ignoring Alana's protests, she interrupted their kiss and pulled the sweater over Alana's head. Then their mouths again collided in a passionate kiss. More stumbling than walking, they made it into the bedroom and fell onto the bed, with Robin on top. Her leg slipped between Alana's thighs.

Moaning, Alana surged up. She clutched Robin's hips and pulled herself against Robin's thigh more firmly.

Robin rained kisses over Alana's upper chest, enjoying her scent and the heat of her skin. When she reached the lacy edges of her bra, she followed its contours with her fingertips. "Nice."

"Can we stop talking about my bra and take it off?" Alana asked, her voice husky.

"I wasn't talking about the bra."

When Alana leaned up on one elbow, Robin reached around her and unhooked the bra. She sat up, straddling Alana, and slid the bra straps down her arms, following them with kisses and little nips. She kept a tight rein on her instincts that urged her to unsheathe her fangs and rake them down Alana's chest.

Alana pulled her back down.

Robin gasped when their bare skin met. Somehow, Alana had managed to get rid of Robin's bra too, without her even noticing. Desire surged through her, but she forced herself to go slow and focus on Alana. She kissed her chin, then along her jaw until she licked that sensitive spot below her ear, making Alana gasp. She skipped the tempting neck and pressed her lips to Alana's collarbone while letting her hands trail up and down her sides, each time venturing a little closer to her breasts.

Clutching Robin's bare back, Alana said, "Stop teasing."

"I'm not teasing. I just want to take my time. I love caressing you." She trailed the tip of her index finger down Alana's breastbone, fascinated by the goose bumps her touch caused, and then cradled one of her breasts in her palm.

Alana gasped and arched into her touch.

So good. So responsive. Robin massaged the breast, enjoying the soft flesh. "And I love licking you." She bent and swept her tongue along the outer curve of Alana's breast, then made the circles smaller and smaller.

Alana moaned and threaded her fingers into Robin's hair, trying to pull her closer.

Robin resisted and continued with her unhurried pace. "Kissing you." She pressed a kiss to one of Alana's nipples, feeling it instantly harden under her lips. "And I love sucking." She drew the nipple into her mouth.

"Oh!" Alana clutched Robin's head, pulling her closer.

"And biting," Robin mumbled around the hardened nipple and gently bit down on it. *Oh, yeah. I especially love biting.*

Tightening her fingers in Robin's hair, Alana writhed beneath her. Her moans and little gasps made Robin's head spin with desire.

She wanted to take Alana, here and now, but at the same time, she wanted this to never end. It had never been like this, not even with a Girah woman. She released Alana's nipple and moved up to kiss her.

Alana used the moment to roll them over with unexpected strength. "My turn to drive you crazy," she said, her voice hoarse.

"You already do," Robin whispered. Then she couldn't talk anymore, because Alana's mouth was on her, kissing her breathless before moving down, licking, kissing, sucking, and biting in an imitation of what Robin had done to her. *Oh my. She's incred*— She gasped when Alana flicked her tongue across her nipple and then rasped her teeth over it.

Alana trailed kisses down Robin's chest and belly. Each kiss sent little electrical thrills through Robin's body, ending in her pounding clit.

Robin clutched the sheets beneath her. "If you keep that up, it'll be over in five seconds."

Her hair tickling Robin's belly, Alana looked up. Her green eyes had gone dark, appearing nearly black. "Ever heard of multiple orgasms?"

Her heated gaze robbed Robin of breath. *She's gonna be the death of me. But what a way to go.*

Alana opened Robin's belt and pulled it from her pants. The metal clanked as it hit the floor next to the bed.

Unable to lie still and wait, Robin helped her, unbuttoning and unzipping her pants before reaching for Alana's. She lifted her hips, allowing Alana to tug her jeans and underwear down over her hips.

Standing for a moment, Alana kicked off her own pants and underwear. Then she was back, their bare skin sliding against each other, setting off sparks that seemed to gather low in Robin's belly. Her whole body tingled with excitement, and she felt the answering tremors run through Alana.

Wet heat pressed against Robin's leg. A growl rose up her chest. She rolled them around. If she took over, it would be easier not to lose control.

But Alana didn't give her a chance. She slid her hand between them, palm up, and trailed her fingers down Robin's belly and between her legs.

The first touch nearly sent her over the edge. Gasping, she clutched Alana's arm.

"Let me," Alana whispered. "Please."

Too weak to resist, Robin let go and allowed Alana to roll over and crawl on top of her.

"It's been a while," Alana said quietly. "So please tell me if—"

Robin shut her up by kissing her. If this was how Alana made love when she was a bit rusty, she surely would be the death of her. "You're doing fine. More than fine. You're incredible." She kissed her again and then moaned into her mouth as Alana started to slide her fingers through her wetness.

With dexterous fingertips, Alana circled her clit and then stroked directly over it. She dipped one finger inside before pulling back. With her lips hovering just an inch above Robin's, she looked down at her, a silent question in her eyes.

"Yes!" Robin moaned as Alana entered her with one finger, then with two. Robin grabbed two well-rounded ass cheeks, pressing closer. Every square inch of her skin came alive as they moved against each other. *So good. Oh.* Her eyes fell shut, and she rolled her head from side to side. Her gums started pounding along with her clit. *Faster.*

She wasn't sure whether she'd said it aloud or just thought it, but Alana promptly changed her pace, setting just the rhythm Robin needed.

A buzzing started in Robin's ears. Her whole system was going into overload, and all she could feel was Alana—inside her, on top of her, her warmth, her skin, the thrumming of her heart.

Alana curved her fingers and moved them even faster.

Groaning, Robin opened her eyes and fell into Alana's darkened green irises. Pressure gathered in her belly. Her clit twitched sharply. She arched up and pressed her face against Alana's damp neck.

When Alana smoothed her thumb over Robin's clit, the pleasure in her belly exploded outward. Her muscles contracted around Alana's fingers. Alana's pounding pulse beat against her lips, and Robin bit down.

A spark of energy that had nothing to do with her orgasm slammed into her, nearly making her black out, and flung them to opposite ends of the bed. Robin crashed against the headboard. Dazed, her clit and her head pounding for two very different reasons, she stared at Alana, who stared back from the foot end of the bed, looking just as surprised as Robin felt.

Alana clutched her neck.

"What the fuck?" they said at the same time.

CHAPTER 13

"Who...what are you?" Robin asked. Alana sure as hell wasn't human. She was too beautiful to be one of the cave-dwelling Nocnos and too nice to be a demonic Alshi, and if she were a shape-shifter, Robin's bite would have put her into fight-or-flight mode, making her shift shape.

"I guess I don't have to ask what you are." Alana rubbed her neck. When she lowered her hand, her skin was unblemished; not even two twin prick marks were visible on her neck.

Robin stared. Had that weird energy that had hit her also stopped her fangs from penetrating?

Alana pulled her knees to her chest as if she needed to protect herself. "You're a Girah."

Robin's mouth fell open. Alana had said Girah, not vampire. That meant... "You...you know? About us, I mean?"

"I know Girah exist, but I had no idea that you're one of them." Alana reached for her pants and started getting dressed. "Why all the deception? Infiltrating AA, pretending to be an alcoholic, becoming friends...lovers with me... All that just for a bit of blood?"

"No!" Robin jumped up and followed her into the hall, where Alana picked up her sweater and put it on. "Please, Alana, don't believe that. I couldn't tell you the truth, but I never lied to you either. I am addicted, just not to alcohol. I joined AA because I want to stop biting humans for blood."

"Then what was that?" Alana pointed at her neck.

Robin's cheeks heated. "I couldn't help it. You're just too delicious, but I never meant to hurt you. I really lo... I really care for you."

Now dressed but still barefoot, Alana glanced back and forth between Robin and the front door and chewed on her lip. "I hate being lied to by someone I trust," she whispered.

Remembering Alana's former lover, who had cheated on her, Robin lowered her head. "I know. But you weren't exactly honest with me either. You let me believe you're human."

"I am human," Alana said.

Robin snorted. "You're about as human as I am. You fake it really well, but these sparks of energy... I should have known that they weren't just static from a sweater, but I guess I wasn't thinking straight—no pun intended. But when I bit you, it felt like being hit by a lightning bolt." She shook her head. "You aren't human."

"I am," Alana repeated. "At least I am now."

Robin frowned. "What's that supposed to mean?"

"It's a long story."

"Then let's sit down and talk. I want to know what's going on." Robin wanted to take Alana's hand, stop her from running away, and pull her to the couch, but after getting zapped so hard, she didn't dare.

Alana eyed her warily. "If you promise you're done with the biting."

Robin rubbed her overly warm cheeks. "I didn't mean to do that. It was instinct. I just came so hard that I must have bitten down."

Now it was Alana's turn to blush. "All right. Let's talk." She threatened Robin with her index finger. "But no funny business with those fangs."

While Alana waited in the living room, Robin hurriedly got dressed and then joined her on the couch, where they sat without touching. She hated the sudden distance between them.

Even though Alana wasn't who she appeared to be, she still felt drawn toward her. "So?"

"Do you remember what I shared with the group the day of your first AA meeting?" Alana asked.

Robin nodded. She remembered each and every moment with Alana in vivid detail.

"When I said that I gave up everything for Kelly, that wasn't an exaggeration. I gave up my former existence, all of my skills, and became human, just so I could be with her."

"Your skills?" Robin's mind flashed back to the skills Alana possessed in the bedroom, but she chased those thoughts away. "What do you mean?"

"The spark you felt whenever we touched is a remainder of the life energy I once possessed. We're beings made entirely of energy and light. We can travel large distances in the blink of an eye, take any shape we want, and materialize any object." Alana looked her in the eyes, completely serious. "I'm a djinn."

Of all the things Robin had expected her to say, that would have been the last on her list. "A djinn? You mean you're…a genie?"

Alana's brows bunched together. "We don't like that word."

Robin could relate. She didn't like being called a vampire either. *A djinn…* She didn't know what to say, having always assumed these powerful creatures that could fulfill every wish existed just in the imagination of humans. "You don't look anything like Barbara Eden or a belly dancer." Not that Alana wouldn't look good in a beaded bra and a sheer chiffon skirt.

"You don't look anything like Count Dracula either," Alana countered with a small smile.

"Touché." A thought hit her. "Oh, Zeus on a bike! That blue bottle I smashed…was that…?"

Alana sighed. "It was mine. We use objects like that as a reservoir to focus our energy."

"I'm sorry. If I'd known..." Robin reached out to squeeze Alana's hand but pulled back at the last moment. "I really thought you had a drinking problem and had relapsed."

"I do have a drinking problem. I guess we djinn like bottles just a little too much for our own good," Alana said with a self-deprecating smile before her face grew serious. "At least I do."

Robin leaned back against the couch and stared at the wall. Her head was still spinning, and it had nothing to do with the intense orgasm or with being thrown against the headboard. "Wow. A djinn." Something occurred to her. "A djinn who couldn't get enough of gin."

"And a Girah who wants to stop drinking human blood," Alana murmured, looking just as dazed.

Robin turned her head and made eye contact.

They looked at each other, and after a moment, they both smiled before sobering.

"Where does that leave us?" Robin asked.

"I don't know," Alana said. "I can imagine that it must have been a pretty big shock for you." She grimaced. "No pun intended either."

Robin chuckled. "It hit me pretty hard. All this time, I assumed you were human."

"I'm sorry. I couldn't tell you, probably for the same reasons you couldn't tell me."

Robin nodded and thought about it for a while. "Actually, it's not a bad surprise."

"It's not?" Alana asked, a hopeful tone in her voice.

"No. I struggled with my attraction to you because I couldn't tell if it's just bloodlust or more. O negative is for me what gin is for you."

Alana frowned. "How do you know my blood type?"

Robin just pointed at her nose. "And now it turns out you come with a built-in bite deflector."

"I take it that's a good thing?"

"Oh, yeah. I really care for you, and it's not because of your blood type."

They looked at each other. The currents of emotions made the air between them crackle with static. Alana reached across the couch cushion between them and laced their fingers together.

Robin stared at their entwined hands, halfway expecting to be zapped and thrown across the room, but all she felt was a pleasant tingling that ran through her entire body.

They sat on the couch, holding hands, for several minutes until Robin cleared her throat. "Do you want to...?" Her earlier boldness gone, she pointed in the direction of the bedroom. "I didn't mean to leave you high and dry."

"You didn't exactly leave me dry, believe me," Alana mumbled. More loudly, she said, "I think we should just call it a day for now. We both have a lot to think about."

Robin nodded, knowing Alana was right. Still, she couldn't help feeling disappointed and a little abandoned when Alana got up.

At the door, Alana turned back around and touched her fingertips to Robin's chin, making her look her in the eyes. "I just need a little time. And so do you."

"Okay."

Before Robin could say anything else, the door closed behind Alana, leaving behind the tingling in Robin's chin and the whirlwind of thoughts and emotions in her mind.

Groaning, Alana plopped down on her couch. "What a disaster," she mumbled and rubbed her face.

The familiar high-pitched sound announced Dahir's arrival before she had fully materialized. "I hope you're not talking about me."

Alana wasn't in the mood for her friend's quirky sense of humor. "Cut it out, will you?"

"Wow, someone is sexually frustrated, and it's not me."

"Yeah, well, djinn don't have sex or sex drives, unless they take human form," Alana muttered. Sometimes, she didn't know whether to envy or pity them.

Dahir dropped onto the couch beside her. "The last time I looked in on you, you and Robin seemed in a hurry to get between the sheets and—"

"You spied on me?"

Dahir straightened. "I did no such thing. After all these weird things that happened with her and her family, I thought I'd keep an eye on you." She brushed an imaginary piece of dirt from her sleeve. "When I realized where things were heading, I retreated into my smartphone of course."

As much as she hated to be observed, Alana knew that Dahir really had just wanted to protect her. She touched her arm. "Thank you. That was nice of you." As an afterthought, she asked, "When will you ever take a more classic home?"

Dahir waved dismissingly. "Bottles and lamps aren't classy; they're boring. But back to the topic at hand. Your little encounter didn't last very long, did it? Was it at least good?"

Alana pulled one knee up and rested her chin on it. Even after almost an hour, her body was still humming and screaming for release. She sighed. "It was fantastic, but it had a bit more bite to it than I normally like."

"Huh? What's that supposed to mean?"

"She bit me."

Dahir whistled. "Is that what humans do when they're getting hot and heavy with—?"

"Robin isn't human," Alana said. "She's a Girah."

Dahir's mouth fell open. "You've got to be kidding! Did she tell you that?"

Alana shook her head. "She didn't exactly tell me. When she came, she tried to bite me."

"You mean *came* as in…?"

"Yes, when she had her orgasm."

"Oh."

"Yes, oh."

Dahir was silent for a moment before saying, "You said she *tried* to bite you...so she didn't hurt you?"

"It seems my residual taqa protected me. She was slammed against the headboard in the blink of an eye."

"That's what I call a climax."

"Dahir, please. It's not funny."

Sobering, Dahir nodded. "I'm sorry. It must have been a rude awakening."

"You could say that." Tears threatened to escape Alana's burning eyes, but she didn't allow them to fall. "I really like her. I think I even..." Her voice broke. Could she love and trust someone who had lied to her since the first moment? *You're one to talk. You didn't tell her who you are...what you were either.*

"You even what? Don't tell me you fell in love with her."

"I don't know," Alana whispered. "I don't know anything anymore."

Raising an index finger, Dahir said, "Now I understand why I felt this strange energy signature with Robin's family. And I think the woman we thought was drugged was just thralled."

This got Alana's attention. "She was what?"

"Thralled. I hear Girah can control the minds of people. Well, of humans to be exact."

"Yeah, I heard that too, but I thought it was just a rumor."

"I don't think so." Dahir's gaze pierced Alana as if she wanted to see right through her. "Wait. If Robin is a Girah, how can you be sure she didn't thrall you into...you know, sleeping with her?"

Alana's eyes widened, but then she shook her head. No, that couldn't be. "Robin wouldn't do something like that."

"Maybe she just wants you to believe that."

"No. I wanted it just as much as she did. I didn't need any thrall to sleep with her, believe me." A thought occurred to her. She remembered how baffled Robin had seemed when she had tried to send Alana away and Alana had refused to go. Had Robin used her mind control skills on her?

Alana suppressed a sigh. It didn't matter. That had been months ago, when they'd barely known each other. She wanted to believe that Robin wouldn't do something like that to her now. "Besides, if she controlled my mind, why didn't she make me forget about her trying to bite me?"

"Mmh, you've got a point there. But maybe she—"

"No, I just know that my feelings are true." She looked into Dahir's eyes. "She makes me feel more alive than I've ever been, even in the Great Energy. I really think I'm in love with her."

One of Dahir's eyebrows shot up. "A djinn and a Girah? Well, stranger things have happened, I suppose."

"I'm no longer a djinn."

"But you could be one again. I'm still waiting for your answer, you know?"

Why did all of this have to happen at once? It was too much. She scratched at her knee. "What about Robin?"

"Of course you couldn't be a couple in the traditional sense, but if you take on human form every now and then, a little hanky-panky should still be possible, I guess."

"No!" The word burst from her lips before it was even formed in her mind. "We didn't have the best of starts, but I really care for her, and if she feels the same, I want more than just 'a little hanky-panky.' I want us to be a couple."

Dahir groaned in exasperation. "Oh, no. Not again. Didn't you learn your lesson with Kelly?"

"That's just it. Kelly was a human; Robin isn't. I swore to stay away from humans, and that's what I'll do." She wasn't sure if all Girah were like that, but Robin's focus while they'd made love had been entirely on her, as if she'd never been with any other woman and would never even think about another woman again after Alana had touched her. "Robin and I might have the same lifespan, so we could grow old together."

"Or you could return to the Great Energy and never grow old."

Slowly, Alana shook her head. "I'm not saying it's not tempting. But if I have to choose between a life with Robin or eternity without her, eternity loses." If she already felt like this after just a few months, she hoped she would never regret this decision.

Dahir took both of Alana's hands and looked deeply into her eyes. "Are you sure that's what you want?"

A shaky breath escaped Alana. "Yes, I'm sure. It'll take a while for Robin and me to work everything out and be able to fully trust each other again. She needs to tell me everything, really everything about her family, her life, and her…"

"Bloody past?" Dahir supplied.

"Yeah."

"For what it's worth, I'll always be your friend, and if she's what makes you happy, enjoy your Girah girlfriend." Dahir engulfed her in a tight hug and whispered in her ear, "Rumors have it Girah are fantastic lovers, but I guess you already know that."

The pulsing between Alana's legs returned full force, making her jerk back from Dahir. "I wouldn't know," Alana murmured and got up. "But thanks for letting me know."

"What do you mean? I thought you two… Hey, where are you going?"

"What do you think? After you so kindly informed me about what I missed, I'll take a shower. A cold one." She strode toward the door but stopped before she reached it and turned around. "Thank you, Dahir."

"For what?"

"For being my friend no matter what."

Dahir winked. "Always. If you'd excuse me now. A mistress in Saudi Arabia who still has one wish left is calling for me. Enjoy your shower." As fast as she had appeared, she vanished.

CHAPTER 14

ROBIN WAITED UNTIL EVERYONE ELSE had left the meeting room in the church basement, glad to see that Alana didn't seem in a hurry to leave. They had exchanged texts a few times this week and had talked on the phone once but hadn't been together since each had found out who the other really was.

Now that she was facing Alana, all alone, Robin didn't know what to say. *Come on. You slept with her already, and now you can't even talk to her? Get your ass over there!* Shuffling her feet, she walked closer. "Hi."

"Hi." Alana shoved her hands into the pockets of her jeans as if she didn't know what to do with them.

Good to know I'm not the only one feeling like this. "Want to go for a burger and some fries?" Robin asked. The past few weeks, they had gone to the diner after every meeting. It had become a sure thing, neither of them having to ask. But now things had changed.

"Sure," Alana said, and Robin was relieved that she didn't seem to hesitate. "But, uh, do you even need to eat? I mean other than…" She looked around and whispered, "Blood."

Robin smiled. At least Alana didn't appear to be grossed out. "I don't have to, but I can."

"Okay, then let's go."

Side by side, they crossed the parking lot.

Robin glanced down, wondering whether it would be okay to take Alana's hand.

Before she could decide, Alana entwined their fingers.

Little thrills of energy pulsed through Robin's palm and flowed up her arm until they warmed her chest from the inside out. Grinning, she followed Alana to her car.

They left Robin's Prius in the church parking lot and drove to the diner together. The familiar routine felt wonderful because it indicated that not everything between them had changed.

By the time Alana had eaten her last french fry and Robin had finished her milkshake, things felt normal. Well, almost. Speaking so openly about her life, her family, and her need for blood would take some getting used to.

"And you're really the only Girah who thinks like that?" Alana asked.

"There must be others, but I don't know any of them personally." Robin hadn't allowed herself to linger on it, but now she realized how lonely that made her feel. She used her straw to draw patterns in the bottom of her empty glass.

Alana reached across the table and squeezed her hand, starting the familiar tingling again. "I had a feeling from the start that you're pretty special." She grinned. "I just didn't know how special."

Robin laughed. "Well, seems I'm not the only special one." Over dinner, she had listened with fascination to Alana's descriptions of the ethereal plane and the community of djinn, which she called the Great Energy. It sounded like a wonderful place where no one ever felt lonely. "You must have loved her an awful lot to give up that existence for her." Jealousy gripped her, but she tried not to let it show.

"Back then, I thought so. But it turned out I had no idea what love really was."

Robin peeked up from the milk foam at the bottom of her glass. "And now?" She cursed herself as soon as she'd asked it. *It's too soon, idiot.*

Alana licked salt and oil off her fingers, taking her time answering.

Robin's heartbeat accelerated, not just because of Alana's sexy gesture, but also because she was afraid of the answer.

"Now," Alana said and looked up, "I'm hoping to have enough time to find out."

A sigh of relief escaped Robin. She could live with that answer. "Well, we Girah are a pretty long-lived species."

"We former-djinn-turned-human are too," Alana said. "At least the Great Energy thinks so."

They grinned at each other.

A shadow fell across the table.

"I'm having a weird sense of déjà vu," someone said next to them.

Robin looked up.

Meghan stood before them. She stared at their entwined hands on the table. "I thought she's just your editor. Is that how you got your little romances published? By sleeping with your publisher's staff?"

Plates rattled as Alana jumped up from the table. She stepped so close to Meghan that their noses almost touched. "How dare you! Have you bothered to read even one of her books? Scratch that. You probably don't even know how to read."

An unhealthy scarlet color crept up Meghan's neck. She looked ready to explode.

Robin scrambled out of the booth and pushed between them, protecting Alana with her body.

"You little..." Meghan lunged, trying to reach around Robin and grab Alana.

"No!" Robin shoved her back. Her fangs unsheathed in an instant, ready for battle.

When the guests around them started to look up, Meghan sent them a glare, no doubt thralling them into going back to focusing on their food.

Alana put one hand on Robin's hip. "Don't worry. She can't hurt me."

Relief trickled through Robin when she remembered the energy that surrounded Alana like a protective shield. It might not prevent her from accidentally cutting herself with a knife, but somehow the energy reacted to anyone touching Alana, especially in a threatening way. Still, she wouldn't allow Meghan to threaten Alana. "I think it's time for you to go, Meghan."

"Go? I'm hungry, and this is a diner, so…" Meghan looked at the other guests dining all around them and made a show of licking her lips.

Robin would have liked nothing better than to drag her out of there and stop her from hunting for her dinner, but she knew it was a losing battle. She couldn't get the rest of her species to stop drinking human blood. "Then we'll leave." Without looking, she reached back and found Alana's free hand. "I'm through hanging out with you."

After Robin had paid for their dinner, they left the diner hand in hand.

"Why do you have friends like that?" Alana asked when they reached the car.

"She's not my friend," Robin said. "Not really. She was just the only clan member my age that would have anything to do with me."

Alana took Robin's hand in both of hers and pulled her closer. "God, you must have been so lonely."

Robin shrugged. "A little. I admit it felt good to have you defend me just now."

Gently, Alana cupped her cheek with one hand. "Everybody needs someone to defend her every now and then, even someone with big fangs."

A smile chased away the memories of how lonely Robin felt sometimes. "Well, they're not that big," she murmured.

"Really? Let's see." Alana pulled her closer, leaned up on her tiptoes, and kissed her.

The tingling sensation flowed through every cell of her body until Robin thought she'd melt on the spot. Alana's lips moved slowly against her own, caressing, exploring, reconnecting.

After a while, Alana teased the corner of Robin's mouth with her tongue.

Both of them moaned when Robin opened her mouth and their tongues met.

Robin let go of Alana's hands, grabbed her hips, and pulled her closer.

Alana darted her tongue along Robin's teeth.

Breathing heavily, Robin pulled back. "What are you doing?"

"Searching for your fangs," Alana said with an impish grin.

Robin rolled her eyes. "Let's get out of here."

Alana unlocked the car without having to be told twice.

———•••———

When Robin's phone rang, she groaned into Alana's mouth but didn't pull back from their kiss.

With her hands in Robin's hair, Alana crawled closer on the couch until she nearly sat on Robin's lap.

The ringing of the phone stopped and then started again seconds later.

Alana tore her lips away. "Someone really wants to talk to you," she said breathlessly.

"And I really don't want to talk to them, whoever it is." Robin nipped at Alana's bottom lip. "It's probably just my parents anyway. They keep calling, trying to get me to see the err of my ways."

"Hmm, I love your ways." Alana hummed into the kiss but then pulled back. "Tell them you'll call back later." She moved away so Robin could reach the phone on the coffee table.

Grumbling, Robin snatched up the phone and glanced at the caller ID. It wasn't her mother or her father. Her editor's name flashed across the display. She quickly accepted the call. "Hi, Nicole. Did you get my manuscript?"

"I just finished reading it."

Robin reached for Alana's hand as her tension rose. Waiting to hear what her editor thought was always nerve-racking. "What did you think?"

"It was well written, as usual," Nicole said.

Uh-oh. By now, Robin knew her editor well enough to read between the lines. "But?"

Nicole sighed. "You'll have to do a lot of revisions, especially in the second half of the manuscript. Some of the romance and the characterization of your main character won't work for our target audience."

Robin frowned. "What do you mean?"

"We talked about this before, Robin. People who buy books about vampires have certain expectations. They either want to read something scary or something sexy. Making your main character not very good in bed is funny, but it's not sexy. It won't sell."

"How do you know if we don't try? Maybe readers have just been waiting for something different."

"Take a look at my comments in the document," Nicole said. "I explained it in more detail there."

Robin didn't want to take a look at the comments. She wanted to yell at her editor and throw the phone across the room. But she was a professional, so she gritted her teeth, reined in her temper, and said, "I'll take a look."

"Good. Take your time, okay?"

Grumbling, Robin said she would, said good-bye, and hung up. She picked up her laptop from the coffee table, opened it, and logged into her e-mail account to download the edited manuscript. "My editor sent me her feedback. She says I have a lot of revisions to do."

"May I?" Alana nodded toward the laptop screen.

Robin wrapped one arm around her and pulled her closer. "Sure."

Together, they watched as the document opened.

"Six hundred comments?" Robin groaned. "You've got to be kidding me!" She read a few of them. "Why does she think that drinking blood makes them sex gods?"

Alana leaned over and softly kissed Robin's cheek. "Maybe because some of them are," she whispered, her breath hot on Robin's ear.

Robin shivered, for a moment distracted from Nicole's critique. Then she forced her attention back to the laptop and continued clicking through the comments. She could understand where Nicole was coming from, but she wasn't sure she agreed with all of her comments. "What do you think?"

Alana shrugged. "I think you and your editor will never be on the same page about how to portray vampires. She's human, so she has certain expectations."

"What expectations are those?"

"What humans like about vampires is that edge of danger," Alana said.

"Edge of danger," Robin repeated and tilted her head to regard Alana with a questioning gaze. "Is that what you like about me?"

"No. Believe me; I've had enough excitement in the last few centuries."

Robin looked at her curiously. She had a hard time getting it into her head that this beautiful face belonged to someone who had been born centuries ago...if djinn were even born the conventional way. "How old are you anyway?"

Alana playfully tapped her on the nose. "Didn't your mother teach you not to ask a lady her age?"

Robin grinned. "No. She just told me not to ask a lady her blood type as soon as I met her, but she didn't say anything about the age thing."

"We don't keep track of time the way you do, but I think I'm about four hundred and fifty years old."

Robin fell back against the couch. Even her Girah mind couldn't process living for that long—or giving up an existence like that to become human. "Wow."

"Yeah. I'm kind of robbing the cradle with you." Alana grinned at her.

Robin directed her gaze back to the document on her laptop. "So with your vast experience, you think Nicole, my editor, is right?"

"Maybe she is. A vampire who doesn't drink blood directly from humans lacks that edge of danger. It just isn't sexy."

"Oh, really?" Robin put a purr into her voice.

"To your readers," Alana added hastily. "Maybe your next book should be about something else."

"Hmm, so if I'm not writing about vampires anymore, what other devastatingly sexy supernatural creature could I write about?" Robin stroked her chin, pretending to think hard.

"I'm sure you'll think of something. Maybe some research will help."

"Research?"

"Yes. Very hands-on research." Alana softly closed the laptop, put it on the coffee table, and pulled Robin up from the couch.

Robin grinned and followed her to the bedroom. "Some days, I just love my job."

───────── ··· ─────────

Alana pressed her hips urgently against Robin's, pushing her toward the bed. The tingle of electricity between them ratcheted up her desire another notch. Her lips devoured Robin's hungrily while she let her hands roam all over Robin's strong back.

Robin stopped abruptly when the back of her knees hit the bed. She broke the kiss. Her blue eyes sparkled in the dim light of the bedroom. Between two gulping breaths, she panted, "What if I can't control myself and bite you again?"

It took a few seconds before Alana's passion-clouded mind had processed the words. She looked into Robin's eyes and stroked her cheek as if she could wipe away her fear. "My residual taqa will protect me. Like it did the last time when you, um, slipped." Alana nibbled on Robin's enticing lower lip before adding, "But don't you dare bite before I come."

"Yes, ma'am. I mean, no, ma'am."

Alana drew back a little. "Enough talking."

One of Robin's eyebrows hiked up, accompanied by a smirk. "You think so?"

How could anybody look so smug and so sexy at the same time? Alana licked her lips. Instead of answering, she grabbed Robin by the collar and pulled her down for a passionate kiss.

Robin moaned into Alana's mouth.

Alana let go of Robin's collar and moved her hands to the front, opening the buttons of Robin's blouse. It seemed to take forever until the garment fell to the floor. When Alana came up for air, she looked at Robin's black silk bra. Her mouth went dry, and she pressed her lips to one breast.

"Wait!"

Alana immediately drew back. "What is it?"

Robin reached behind her, opened the bra, and let its straps slide off her arms. Her beaming smile was mirrored by Alana.

Without hesitation, she captured one nipple with her mouth and started sucking.

"Ah!" Robin held Alana's head into position. "You drive me totally crazy."

Alana's answer consisted of swirling her tongue around Robin's hardened nipple. She just couldn't get enough of her intoxicating taste and smell.

Robin's legs buckled, and she sank onto the bed with Alana on top of her.

When Alana wanted to switch to the other breast, Robin grabbed her shoulders and whirled her around until she was lying on top.

"Hey," Alana protested half-heartedly.

Panting, Robin shook her head. "It's my turn now."

Before Alana knew what was happening, Robin had gotten rid of her sweater and bra and was feasting on her breast.

Alana leaned into the contact and couldn't stop a moan from escaping her lips. She wanted more. "Let's take off the rest of our clothes."

"Oh yeah." Robin backed off and tore her pants open. Within seconds, she was standing in front of the bed gloriously naked.

Urgency gripped Alana, and she lifted her hips to peel off her remaining clothes. "Come here," she said hoarsely.

Robin obviously didn't need to be asked twice; she covered Alana's body with her own in the blink of an eye.

Both groaned at the oh-so-sweet contact.

Alana spread her legs and shuddered at the intense spark where Robin's lower belly pressed against her center.

A moment later, Robin swirled her tongue down Alana's neck and nibbled carefully below one ear.

Alana's eyes fell shut, and she trailed her hands up and down Robin's spine.

Hot breath bathed Alana's skin as Robin moved her mouth away from her neck, over her collarbone, back to Alana's waiting breasts. But instead of lingering there for long, she moved up Alana's body again.

Alana's eyes fluttered open.

Robin's gaze was so full of emotions that it made Alana even more breathless than their kisses had.

Slowly, Robin caressed one of Alana's cheeks with the back of her hand. She gave Alana a short, almost shy kiss and said, "I love you."

Tears sprung to Alana's eyes. Robin's expression and her words left no doubt about her sincerity. She took Robin's face between her hands and touched Robin's lips with her own in a tender kiss. Her tongue stroked Robin's without the hurried urgency from before. This was not just about passion and lust, but also about love. For maybe the first time in all the years of her existence, Alana understood the meaning of the term *lovemaking*. She wanted to make love with Robin, and she wanted her to make love to her.

Robin seemed to have the same goal because she took her time caressing and kissing every available inch of her body.

When Robin's lips moved lower and lower on her body, Alana gulped for air. Her heart was beating so hard, it seemed as if it were about to burst out of her chest. Eagerly, she spread her legs wider.

But Robin didn't seem in a hurry and trailed one hand down the insides of her thighs, driving Alana totally nuts in the process.

"Robin, please."

"Huh?" Robin looked up, an expression as if she'd just awakened from a thrall on her face. "Oh, I'm sorry. You're just so…"

"I'm what?"

Robin's eyes radiated awe. "You're so incredibly beautiful. You're perfect."

Kelly had said the same thing, and Alana hadn't been sure if she would ever be able to believe those words again, but the admiration in Robin's eyes didn't leave any room for doubt. The sudden sting behind her eyes made Alana look away. Forcing herself to make eye contact, she croaked out, "And so are you. You really are."

For a few moments, they lost themselves in each other's eyes, and then Robin trailed her gaze down Alana's body. She dipped her tongue through the slippery folds. "Mmhh."

Robin's moan vibrated through Alana, making her tingle to the tip of her toes.

She let her head fall back but clasped both of Robin's shoulders in a strong grip.

Again and again, Robin's tongue reached out as if she was trying to lick every single drop from Alana's center without even once grazing her clit.

Alana squirmed under the attention, sure she would come without direct stimulation if Robin kept that up. It was all she could do to control her ragged breathing and not moan too loudly.

Slowly, Robin's mouth engulfed Alana's clit and began a careful sucking. Her tongue flicked rhythmically over the swollen nub.

"Yeah, yeah, just like that." She clutched Robin's shoulders so strongly that she was probably leaving marks, but she couldn't help it. Her body was on fire. Robin's touches set off little sparks that turned into a full-out explosion in her belly. Behind her closed lids, she saw stars, and the world started spinning. "Oh, Robin!"

Robin slowed and then stopped moving her tongue and tenderly caressed Alana's thighs and hips. After one last kiss to Alana's oversensitive clit, Robin climbed up her body.

Their lips met, and this time it was both passionate and tender. Alana tasted herself and moaned into Robin's mouth.

When the kiss ended, Robin's flushed face appeared in her line of sight. *So beautiful.*

Alana had never told anyone that she loved them, not even Kelly, even though she had thought she loved her. But right now, even the tiniest bit of doubt about her feelings toward Robin vanished like a fulfilled wish. As if Robin were the most precious thing in the world, Alana touched Robin's lips with her fingertips. When their gazes met, it was as if they were one, as if Robin could read her mind.

Robin smiled.

"I love you with all my heart," Alana whispered.

Robin's smile broadened before she engulfed her in a tender embrace. "I love you too."

Alana's eyes fell shut. She'd always thought that the Great Energy was the most peaceful place to be, but being held by Robin brought her a contentment she hadn't thought possible. *I'm home.*

CHAPTER 15

SMILING, ALANA STROLLED BACK TO the couch. She took a sip of her hot chocolate before placing it on the coffee table. With a low groan, she lay down and reached for the last of Robin's books she hadn't yet read. Since their relationship had developed into romance, the stories Robin had written about women falling in love with each other and having a happily ever after didn't seem like an illusion any longer.

Quite the opposite.

Alana took another sip of the hot cocoa and sighed. Life was good. Okay, maybe it would have been even better if Robin hadn't left to meet with her agent, but the novel in her hand was the second-best company she could wish for. After all, Robin had written these words.

She giggled. *God, I'm so smitten.* And it felt fantastic.

The doorbell rang.

A peek at the wall clock revealed that Robin's appointment had begun just twenty minutes ago. Who could it be? Maybe Kenison had come over to say hello. Since the incident more than three months ago, they had become friends. Alana still remembered the shock she'd felt when Robin had told her what her relapse with Kenison had really been about. But now, after the three of them had spent a few evenings together over dinner, even Robin seemed to relax around her. Seeing that Kenison was doing fine seemed like a balm to her soul.

The doorbell rang again, pulling Alana out of her musings. With long strides, she hurried to the door and looked through the peephole.

The smile she seemed to have plastered on her face permanently since she'd started to date Robin vanished as if she'd been slapped. "Meghan," she growled.

Keeping the safety chain in place, she opened the door a few inches. "What do you want?"

"What kind of greeting is that? Hello." Meghan's smile was as fake as Pamela Anderson's breasts. "You didn't think I would just walk away, did you?"

"I was hoping you would," Alana mumbled. More loudly, she repeated, "What do you want?"

Meghan jumped forward, slamming against the door.

The chain rattled and then snapped. Wood splintered.

The door flew open, throwing Alana back.

Her head bounced off the wall. Pain exploded in her skull, and dizziness threatened to take her out for a moment. Blinking, she saw Meghan sauntering into the apartment with a predatory grin on her face before she closed the door. Fear gripped her. *Shit, she's strong. This could get ugly.* Suddenly, she wasn't so sure that her taqa could protect her from a Girah determined to do some serious harm. On wobbly legs, Alana moved away from Meghan, who snarled at her like a rabid dog.

"See, that's what happens when you have no manners. You should have asked me in."

When the low side table in the hall stopped Alana's retreat, she paused and looked Meghan in the eyes, not wanting to give her the satisfaction of seeing her tremble. "What do you want, Meghan?"

"What do I want? Just a little chat about my friend Robin." Meghan took a menacing step closer. "And you will listen."

As much as she tried, Alana couldn't control her ragged breathing. Without taking her eyes off Meghan, she reached behind herself, hoping to grab something she could use in defense. But all she could get her hand on was a scarf. She threw it back down. *Dammit!*

Meghan stepped closer until they were just inches apart.

Meghan's breath on her face chilled Alana to the bone, but she forced herself not to back away. "Leave," she said. "But first, pay for the damage done to my door."

Meghan burst out laughing, throwing her head back. "God, you're hilarious. Highly entertaining. I can see why Robin keeps you around." Sobering, she added, "This has got to stop. Stay away from Robin. If I catch you hanging out with her again, I will hunt you down and suck you dry—to the very last drop of your blood. Do you understand?"

"N-no."

Meghan blinked. "What did you say?"

She's trying to thrall me. Alana pressed her hands against the wall behind her. "No, I won't stop seeing Robin."

Meghan stared into her eyes. "You will never see Robin again."

With a braveness she didn't feel, Alana pushed her chin forward. "No. You heard me the first time. I won't stop seeing Robin, and nothing you do will change that."

"Oh, yeah? Let's see." A dangerous fire sparked alive in Meghan's eyes.

Alana reacted instinctively. When Meghan made a grab for her, she ducked and dashed into the kitchen. A weapon. She needed a weapon to defend herself. Her hip collided with the kitchen island, but she ignored the pain and rushed toward the drawer that held the knives.

Just when she closed her fingers around the drawer handle, Meghan gripped Alana's sweater from behind and jerked her back.

Alana crashed into the kitchen island, clutching it to keep herself upright.

"Gotcha," Meghan said and stepped closer, crowding her. Her fangs shone in the bright kitchen light when she smiled.

"Unlike Robin, I'm not a big fan of O negative, but I'll make an exception for you." She placed her hands to either side of Alana on the kitchen island, trapping her, and slowly leaned forward.

With nowhere to go, Alana bent back until she was almost lying on the kitchen island. "If you harm one hair on—"

"Oh, don't worry. It's not your hair I'm after." Meghan's fangs came closer and closer.

Alana screamed and tried to kick.

Lowering her head even more toward Alana's neck, Meghan grabbed her.

A spark of energy zapped Meghan, shoving her back against the counter.

"What the fuck?" Dazed, she stared at Alana. A flush of anger crept up her neck, and an artery in her temple started to pound. "I'm gonna drain you!" She lowered her head like an attacking bull and then charged Alana, moving too fast for Alana to flee.

This time, it was an all-out attack that made her previous attempt look like a cat playing with the mouse.

Her fangs connected with Alana's neck.

A force field hit Meghan with more power than before, throwing her across the small kitchen and slamming her against a counter. She hit her head on a kitchen cabinet with a loud bang and went down.

It took a few seconds before she started to move. With a stunned look on her face, she reached up and touched the back of her head. Her hand came away bloody.

Alana's chest heaved. On trembling legs, she stepped closer and looked down at Meghan. "Leave. Now."

Meghan stumbled to her feet, but instead of moving toward the door, she just stared at Alana.

"Get out!"

Meghan shook her head as if that would help clear her mind. "What the fuck are you?"

"I'm Robin's girlfriend, and I'm part of her life whether you like it or not."

Meghan opened her mouth to answer, but Alana didn't want to hear what she had to say. "Leave it to Robin to decide what she wants or doesn't want." She had enough of this woman. Alana took a threatening step toward her. "Now go, or I'll zap you again."

Meghan's eyes widened. Slowly, she backed out of the kitchen. She snatched the door open and half turned. "This isn't over. You have no idea what you're getting into," she said between clenched teeth before she left the apartment.

Alana leaned against the kitchen counter and exhaled loudly. She raked a trembling hand through her tousled hair. *Calm down.* Meghan could threaten her all she wanted. As scary as the incident had been, it had proven that her taqa could protect her even from a serious attack—and if need be, it would protect Robin too. Alana would step between her and any attacker.

Pushing away from the counter, she rubbed her hip, where she'd collided with the kitchen island. Good thing her taqa made her a fast healer. Robin would go ballistic if she found her covered in bruises. Alana went in search of her phone. If she was lucky, she could get the security chain replaced and the door frame repaired from where the screws had been ripped out before Robin returned.

───── ••• ─────

When Robin stepped out of the elevator, a guy in blue overalls was leaving Alana's apartment, carrying a toolbox.

Frowning, Robin sprinted the rest of the way and put her hand on the door before it could close. "Alana?"

Alana pulled the door open and let her enter. "Oh, hi. How was the meeting with your agent?"

"Good," Robin said, but her thoughts weren't on the meeting. "What's going on?"

Alana fiddled with the security chain on the door. "I, uh, had to call in a repairman to repair the doorjamb and replace the security chain."

As far as Robin remembered, the door had been fine when she had left Alana's apartment not even two hours ago. "What happened?"

"Nothing," Alana mumbled but stared at the floor.

Robin stepped closer and tipped up Alana's chin so she could see her eyes. "What happened?" she asked again.

Alana's shoulders slumped. "I had a visitor while you were gone."

"A visitor? What does that have to do with the security chain having to be repl—?" Realization hit her midword. Anger boiled up in her, making her temples pound. "Hell and tarnation! They paid you a visit, didn't they?"

"Just Meghan."

Robin took Alana's face in both hands and searched her eyes. "Are you okay? Did she hurt you?"

"I'm fine, but not from lack of trying. She tried to turn me into a pincushion, and let me tell you, it was a lot less pleasant than when you are using your fangs on me."

A low growl rose in Robin's chest. "I'll kill her!"

Alana gripped Robin's hips, keeping her in place. "Don't do anything stupid."

"Stupid? Stupid?" Robin was nearly shouting. "She was trying to hurt you, probably even kill you."

"Yeah, but she lost her appetite when my taqa hit her." Alana clutched Robin's back, pulling her closer. "I can defend myself, Robin. I don't need you to run out of here like an avenging angel, getting yourself hurt."

Alana was putting up a brave front, but Robin felt the tiny tremors running through her body. She smoothed her hands over Alana's shoulders and down her arms, hoping the energy flowing between them would help calm Alana. She wasn't sure if it helped Alana, but it had a calming effect on her. She took a deep breath and pulled Alana into her arms, holding her tightly. "If she had harmed even one hair on your head…"

"She didn't," Alana whispered, her warm breath brushing Robin's ear, making her shudder. "I don't think she can."

Robin slumped against her. She hadn't realized how worried she'd been, but now she felt as if a giant boulder had been lifted off her shoulders. Knowing Alana's taqa would protect her, even against a serious attack from a Girah, was a big relief. Still, she couldn't allow Meghan or any other Girah to scare Alana so badly. She would march over to Meghan's apartment and—

Alana pulled back a little so she could look into Robin's eyes. "Promise me you'll let it go and won't try any of that avenging-angel stuff."

Robin shook her head. "I can't promise you that."

Alana gripped Robin's arms. "Promise me. I don't want you to ever see Meghan again." She shook Robin lightly. "Promise me."

"All right," Robin finally said. "I promise I won't pay Meghan a visit." Her parents, though, were a different matter. After her mother had voiced her concern about Robin's seeing a human, Robin wouldn't be surprised if her parents had sent Meghan to remove the bad influence from their daughter's life.

"And your parents," Alana said, not letting go of Robin's arms. "Promise me you won't get into a standoff with them either."

Damn. Was she that easy to read, or did Alana really know her that well already? "Alana, I have to face them some time. The ultimatum they gave me is nearly up. And didn't you say I have to face them to complete my step work?"

"Yes, but…"

Robin leaned forward and kissed her gently, stopping her protests, before pulling back again. "This is something I have to do."

"Okay," Alana said after a while. "Then let's do it this weekend, when I can go with you."

"Oh, no. You're not coming with me." No way was she bringing Alana into this mess. "This is between my parents and me. They won't react too well to the presence of a human."

"I'll wait in the car."

Robin snorted. "And sit out there like Girah bait? No."

"I can defend myself." Alana's tense face relaxed into a teasing smile. "After all, I watched all one hundred and forty-four episodes of *Buffy*."

"Oh, yeah, that makes me feel so much better," Robin grumbled.

Alana's grin disappeared as fast as it had come. "Robin, if you want to be my partner, you have to let me be your partner too. I won't sit around at home while you head into danger."

"They're my parents," Robin said. "They won't hurt me."

"Maybe not physically." Alana laid a hand on Robin's chest, right over her heart.

The warmth of her skin seeped through Robin's blouse, and a tingling sensation flowed through her, binding them together. *Partners.* Robin sighed. "All right. But at the first sign of trouble, I want you out of there."

"At the first sign of trouble, I'm coming in after you."

Robin opened her mouth to protest, but this time it was Alana who leaned forward and stopped her with a kiss.

"If it makes you feel better, I can tell Dahir to keep an eye on me," Alana said when the kiss ended.

Robin raised a brow. "Your friend who leaves little pink cocktail umbrellas all over your place?"

"My *very powerful* friend who leaves little pink cocktail umbrellas all over my place," Alana said. "If any bloodsucker tries to hurt me, she could turn them into…let's say a mosquito."

Robin grinned as she imagined squishing Meghan with a well-aimed slap of a newspaper.

Alana lightly pinched her ass. "Don't get any ideas."

"I thought you liked my ideas," Robin said, making her voice a seductive purr.

Alana shivered against her and cleared her throat. "Not this one."

"Well, I have a few others that you might like better," Robin whispered into her ear.

"Oh yeah?"

"Oh yeah."

Alana pulled her into the bedroom, making them both forget about Meghan, Robin's parents, and mosquitos for a while.

CHAPTER 16

ROBIN TURNED OFF THE ENGINE but didn't get out of the car. Still clutching the steering wheel, she stared at the sprawling colonial home across the street. *What is it with me and staring at buildings?* "I really have to stop doing this."

"Doing what?" Alana asked from the passenger seat.

"Oh." Robin hadn't realized she'd said it out loud. "Nothing."

Alana reached over and rubbed Robin's thigh, setting off tingles that made Robin forget her nervousness for a few seconds. "Are you sure you want to do this?"

No. Truth be told, Robin didn't want to do this at all, but at least this way, it would be her decision. "Yeah. I have to go in. I told them I would be over around five, and now it's already five thirty because someone who shall not be named wouldn't let me out of bed."

"Me? You're the one who kept saying 'one more time.'"

Robin's cheeks heated. It was true. She'd been insatiable in a whole new way, so she and Alana had spent most of the weekend in bed. Now she wished she were back there. Sighing, she turned her head and stared at the house again.

"You're mumbling," Alana said.

"Oh, sorry." Robin realized she'd been counting windows to calm herself. It wasn't working. "I was just…" She'd never admitted it to anyone, but now she took a deep breath and said, "I was counting. It's a stupid habit when I get nervous."

Alana leaned over the middle console and kissed her cheek. "It's cute." She rubbed Robin's leg again. "Listen, I know this is hard. You don't have to do this right now if you're not ready."

Robin sighed. "I don't think I'll ever be ready. But the ultimatum they gave me is running out, and if I don't come to them, they'll show up on my doorstep, probably with Meghan in tow—and I think you'll agree that there are nicer things than having her visit." She undid the seat belt. "I'd better get it over with. Are you sure you wouldn't rather wait at home? I can take a cab back."

"I'm sure," Alana said. The expression on her face left no doubt that she wouldn't move an inch before Robin was back.

"Okay. But please stay in the car and lock the doors after I'm gone. Are you sure Dahir will hear you should you call for help?"

Alana glanced at a pink smartphone on the dash of the car. "She's just a call away."

For a moment, Robin wondered where the ugly piece of technology had come from and why Alana would call a djinn on her cell phone, but then she shrugged and reached for the door lever.

"Wait!"

One brow raised, Robin turned back around.

"I'll be right here, waiting, okay? You're not alone in this."

Robin forced a smile. "Thanks. I appreciate it." After one more fortifying kiss, she got out of the car and closed the door. Their gazes met through the side window, and they nodded at each other. Squaring her shoulders, Robin marched toward her parents' Scarsdale home, past a well-manicured lawn and a series of plastic deer and bunnies that her parents thought would help them fit in with their suburban neighbors.

Her mother opened the door before Robin could ring the doorbell. "Finally! Come on in. Everyone's waiting."

Everyone? Robin's brows knitted as she stepped into the house.

"Well, well, well, look who's home." Meghan came out of the kitchen, carrying a tray.

Robin moved so fast that even her mother's quick reflexes couldn't stop her. A porcelain teapot rattled as she shoved Meghan against the wall. The tray crashed to the floor.

"Robin!" Her mother pulled on Robin's arm. "What are you doing? Meghan is a guest in our home, and she's your friend!"

"Nice friend! She attacked my…" Robin bit her lip, not sure what to call Alana in front of her mother.

"Your little human toy?" Meghan supplied, smirking. So low that only Robin could hear, she added, "If she really is human."

So she didn't want the other Girah to know what had happened in Alana's apartment. Robin pressed her forearm against Meghan's throat. "If you ever lay so much as a finger on her again, I swear I'll—"

"Let her go," Robin's father said as he stepped into the hall.

Robin hesitated, still staring into Meghan's eyes. She leaned forward and whispered into her ear, "Stay away from us, or I'll let everyone in the clan know how a lowly human kicked your ass."

"Now!" her father shouted.

Slowly, Robin let go and stepped back from Meghan.

"Clean up that mess, please," her father said to Meghan, pointing at the tray and the broken teapot on the floor.

"Yes, sir." With one last glare at Robin, Meghan disappeared into the kitchen.

Her willingness to follow his orders made Robin think. She narrowed her eyes at him. "It was you, wasn't it?"

Her father regarded her with a calm gaze. "I have no idea what you're talking about."

"You ordered her to attack Alana." The thought made her queasy.

He snorted. "If I wanted that human dead, she wouldn't be sitting outside in the car, still alive."

Fear gripped Robin. *I shouldn't have left her alone in the car.* Her first impulse was to whirl around and run to the door, but she held herself back. Alana had already proven that she could defend herself with the help of her taqa, and she had a powerful friend who was keeping an eye on her. She didn't need Robin to come to her rescue.

"Whatever Meghan did, I assure you we had nothing to do with it," her mother said. "I promise we won't harm your...that human. But you have to listen to what we have to say." Her mother looked at her with a pleading expression.

Even her father met her gaze as if he didn't have anything to hide. Were they really not responsible for Meghan's attack? Well, even if they hadn't sent Meghan, they didn't seem too broken up about it either.

"Okay, I will listen—if you promise to stay away from Alana." Even with the taqa that protected her, Robin didn't want Alana to have to look over her shoulder for the rest of her life, always on the lookout for Girah trying to attack her or find other ways to make her life a living hell.

"Your mother already promised," her father grumbled.

"But you didn't."

He rolled his eyes. "Fine. I won't harm her."

That still didn't rule out sending others to harm Alana. Robin opened her mouth to demand another promise, but her father cut her off with an impatient wave of his hand.

"Enough. Come." He pulled her into the formal dining room.

Three elders sat around the large table, sipping blood from dainty porcelain cups.

Robin stopped in the doorway and sent her mother a reproachful gaze. "You called the elders?" She sighed. Of course they had. She should have expected it; after all, it had been the elders who had made the ultimatum.

"They are the clan elders," her father boomed. "Show some respect."

"Sorry," Robin said, knowing it was expected of her. She gave them respectful nods. "Greetings, Elders. I hope you are well."

They tilted their heads in a minimal acknowledgment and kept sipping their drinks. Finally, one of them set his cup down and regarded her with eyes so dark they appeared black. Something in his gaze revealed how much he had seen in his long life. "Robin Caldwell," he said, making her name sound like a reproach. "This childish rebellion must stop. Here and now."

"Elder, I—"

"If you continue with this unnatural behavior, you'll make us the laughingstock of every other species. Is that what you're trying to do?"

Robin swallowed. "No, Elder, of course not, but—"

"Then maybe you're intent on embarrassing your parents?" The elder's gaze and his words cut like a sword. "People are talking about them at clan meetings. Is that what you want?"

Robin forced herself to stand still and not fidget under his intense stare. "I'm not trying to embarrass anyone, Elder. I made a choice for myself, the choice not to hunt humans and drink their blood ever again, but that has nothing to do with you or my parents."

Robin's great-great-great-grandaunt looked up from her cup of blood and shook her head. "Young people nowadays. I don't know where they get these exotic ideas."

"It's that human she hangs out with," her mother said with a sorrowful expression.

"It has nothing to do with—" Robin stopped herself before she could say Alana's name, just in case the elders didn't know it already. "I decided not to drink fresh blood long before I met her."

"That is unacceptable!" her father said, his voice becoming louder with every word until he was shouting the last one. "No daughter of mine will live that way. I won't have it!"

"It's not your decision to make, Dad," Robin said as calmly as possible. "After nearly killing a woman—a mother of two—on New Year's Eve, I made up my mind to never again take any blood that isn't given willingly, and I'm sticking to that decision."

"They are humans, child," her father shouted. "Humans!"

Robin sighed. She could argue until she was blue in the face; it wouldn't change a thing. Girah were taught that they stood at the top of the food chain, so it was their right to take whatever they needed. "I know you don't understand. I just hoped you could at least accept it…accept me."

Her mother took a step toward her. "It's not that we don't accept you, Robin, but…"

"No, Mom." Robin pulled away before her mother could touch her. "You either do or you don't. There's no but."

The oldest of the elders, the only one who hadn't said anything yet, rose and slowly rounded the table. Robin thought she could hear his bones creaking as he walked toward her and stopped just inches away. No one knew how old he was, but rumor had it that he'd been one of the men who had promoted the career of young George Washington.

Everyone else grew silent, even Robin's father.

"You're right," the elder said, his voice so calm it was as if he were merely reading a story from the newspapers aloud instead of discussing Robin's life. "There is no but. Clearly, you're too young to see the err of your ways and too stupid to listen to what older, wiser people have to say. I'm giving you one last choice. You either follow our age-old traditions and start hunting again, or…"

A lump formed in Robin's throat and refused to go away, no matter how many times she swallowed.

The elder's gaze drilled into her. "Or we'll cut your clan ties forever."

Forever. The word echoed through Robin's mind until she thought her skull would burst. Her vision blurred, but she forced herself to look the elder straight in the eyes. "I don't want to spend my life without my clan," she peered at her parents, who stood in the middle of the dining room, frozen, "but I want to spend it without the woman I love even less. I don't want to drink her blood—or that of other humans. If you can't accept that..." She faltered for a moment but then forced herself to continue. "If you think that's reason enough to cut my clan ties, then so be it."

She strode to the door, hoping that someone would call her back.

No one did.

The door closed behind her with a loud click that echoed through her all the way to the car.

Alana frowned when the door of the house opened after less than ten minutes. That couldn't be a good sign.

With drooping shoulders, Robin trudged toward the car. She averted her gaze as if she was ashamed. Or deeply sad. Still not looking at Alana, she opened the driver's side door and got in. The slam of the door reverberated in the silence between them. Instead of saying something, Robin stared at her hands.

Even without an explanation, it was obvious that the conversation with her parents hadn't gone well.

Oh, Robin. Alana's heart hurt for her. She bent toward her, ignoring the middle console pressing into her side, and enfolded her in a tender embrace. "Everything's gonna be all right. I'll be your clan now."

Robin held on to her and leaned her head against Alana's. "I love you."

Drawing back a little, Alana looked deeply into Robin's eyes. "I love you too. Let's get out of here."

Nodding, Robin started the car.

Out of the corner of her eye, Alana saw a woman standing at the window, hugging herself, half hidden behind the curtains.

Was it Robin's mother, watching them, maybe even wishing Robin would turn around and come back? *Maybe*, Alana thought, *maybe there's still hope.* Time would tell.

EPILOGUE

Robin clutched the lectern with both hands to stop the trembling of her fingers. She had read from her books in front of hundreds of people without batting an eye, but somehow, this was different. In here, she couldn't hide behind her characters. This was about her. Hoping to calm herself, she let her gaze sweep through the basement, counting the members who had gathered to hear her speak. *Twenty-one. Just like my first meeting.* She took it as a good sign, even though the only person whose presence really mattered to her hadn't shown up yet.

The door opened, and someone else slipped into the room.

Instead of being annoyed that her lucky number had been destroyed, Robin beamed. "You made it," she mouthed.

Alana gave her a thumbs-up and took a seat next to Brian in the first row, closest to Robin. Since she'd come straight from court, she was still wearing a pencil skirt and an emerald silk blouse that contrasted nicely with her copper hair.

As much as Robin enjoyed seeing her dressed like this, she planned to undress her as soon as they made it home, maybe using her fangs to bite off the buttons if they refused to cooperate. But first, she had to make it through this speech.

Drawing a deep breath, her gaze firmly on Alana as if she were the only one in the room, she stood up straight and said, "Hi, my name is Robin, and I'm an addict."

"Hi, Robin," the group said in unison.

An unexpected surge of power swept over Robin, and she let go of the lectern, no longer needing its support. "I come from a long line of drinkers. You could say it's a family legacy."

From her place in the second row, Caren gave her a nod.

Robin knew that her sponsor also came from a long line of drinkers. *Not quite as long as mine, of course.* "For years, I drank too, sometimes several times a day. I didn't think anything of it. It seemed to be the normal thing to do. Until I went out with a friend—or someone I thought was a friend—on New Year's Eve, eager for a drink. Just one little drink. But then I couldn't stop. I..." She bit her lip and stopped herself before she said too much. "Someone nearly died that night. I nearly killed someone. That was my final wake-up call."

Several members nodded. They'd all had a wake-up call of some kind.

"So I found myself here because I didn't know where else to go." Robin spread her arms, indicating the church basement. "The first few meetings, I really wasn't sure I'd be back. In fact, I was positive that I wouldn't return. I thought my problem was so different, so unique that no one could possibly understand and help me. I couldn't see why everyone else seemed to find these meetings so helpful. All they did was remind me of what I'd given up. But then I started working on the twelve steps with Alana."

"Is that what they call it nowadays?" Brian called. "Working on the steps?"

Everyone laughed. By now, their relationship was pretty much common knowledge.

Alana gave him a gentle shove. "Shut up, Brian," she said affectionately.

Robin rolled her eyes, long since used to his ribbing. "Yes, working on the steps, Brian. I realize that you have to work on it for it to work. Getting—and staying—sober is not like making a wish to a genie, who will snap her fingers and solve the problem for you." She looked at Alana, who smiled at her. "You have to work on it every single day. Some days, it's easy. Other days, it's still as hard as it was in the beginning."

It had taken her a long time to accept that it would always be a struggle, just as Alana would always remain an alcoholic, no matter how many years she stayed sober.

"But, unlike in the beginning, I now know that I don't have to do it alone. There are people who'll give me a hug or a kick in the ass if I need it." She looked at Alana. "So thank you."

When she moved to leave the podium, Brian jumped up. "Wait a minute." He bent and opened the case at the bottom of the lectern. Grinning, he held out a sobriety chip with the gleaming number six on it.

Robin took it and clutched the chip so hard that her fingers hurt. When she stepped down from the podium, people around her patted her shoulders; Brian and Caren even hugged her.

She let it happen, no longer trying to stop them with her thrall, even though there was really only one person she wanted to hug. Their embraces brought their necks too close to Robin's mouth for her liking. Her mouth watered reflexively, but it wasn't too hard to resist temptation—not with Alana in the same room.

Finally, the crowd around her dispersed, and Alana stood in front of her. "Good speech. I knew you could do it." She pulled Robin into her arms, pressing their bodies together from hips to shoulders.

The tingle running through Robin, familiar yet still exciting, made getting up on the podium worth it.

"I'm so proud of you," Alana whispered into her ear. "But as soon as we get home, I'm gonna get you for that genie comment."

Robin laughed and swung her around. "I'm counting on it."

If you enjoyed this book, check out Jae's award-winning paranormal romance *Second Nature,* the first book in her popular shape-shifter series.

OTHER BOOKS FROM
YLVA PUBLISHING

www.ylva-publishing.com

SECOND NATURE
Jae

ISBN: 978-3-96324-359-2
Length: 379 pages (146,000 words)

For solitary novelist Jorie Price, true love is as fictional as the shape-shifting creatures she writes about. But when her work gets too close to the truth, shape-shifter Griffin Westmore is sent in to investigate. Problem is, Griffin's supposed to kill the human, not fall in love with her.

A compelling, standalone, lesbian paranormal romance, part one in the award-winning Shape-Shifter series.

TRUE NATURE
Jae

ISBN: 978-3-96324-360-8
Length: 394 pages (141,000 words)

CEO Rue has no idea that her adopted son Danny is a wolf-shifter or that his beautiful tutor Kelsey isn't there to teach him algebra.

When Danny runs away, the race is on to find him before his first transformation. In the frantic search, Kelsey and Rue unexpectedly find something else: each other.

A gripping lesbian paranormal romance about family bonds and being true to yourself.

MANHATTAN MOON
Jae

ISBN: 978-3-95533-013-2 (mobi), 978-3-95533-012-5 (epub)
Length: 29,000 words

Nothing in Shelby Carson's life is ordinary. Not only is she an attending psychiatrist in a hectic ER, but she's also a Wrasa, a shape-shifter who leads a secret existence.

To make things even more complicated, she has feelings for Nyla Rozakis, a human nurse.

Even though the Wrasa forbid relationships with humans, Shelby is determined to pursue Nyla. Things seem pretty hopeless for them, but on Halloween, during a full moon, anything can happen...

BANSHEE'S HONOR
Shaylynn Rose

ISBN: 978-3-95533-475-8
Length: 389 pages (155,000 words)

Honor. It was torn from Azhani's grasp by the sorcerer whose hatred of her family is decades old.

Love. Ylera, Azhani's beloved, was murdered, her death no more than one callous act in a chain meant to put a noose around Azhani's neck.

Once, not long ago, Azhani had been hopeless, lost, and without any desire for a future, but now, the rimerbeasts have come, and she is needed. Can she put aside her yearning for justice and face this ancient menace as honor demands, or will the bonds of love lost hurl her into a mire of death and revenge?

ABOUT JAE

Jae grew up amidst the vineyards of southern Germany. She spent her childhood with her nose buried in a book, earning her the nickname "professor." The writing bug bit her at the age of eleven. Since 2006, she has been writing mostly in English.

She used to work as a psychologist but gave up her day job in December 2013 to become a full-time writer and a part-time editor. As far as she's concerned, it's the best job in the world.

When she's not writing, she likes to spend her time reading, indulging her ice cream and office supply addictions, and watching way too many crime shows.

CONNECT WITH JAE

Website: www.jae-fiction.com
E-Mail: jae@jae-fiction.com

ABOUT ALISON GREY

Alison has been writing since the age of ten. Her first works were poems and short stories; then she wrote her first novel-length book when she was eleven. It was a *Star Trek: The Next Generation* fanfiction

In addition to writing, Alison likes spending her spare time with her friends. The vegetarian also loves cooking and baking. If she's got enough time, she reads books about history and about social and political sciences.

CONNECT WITH ALISON
E-Mail: Alison-Grey@web.de

Good Enough to Eat
© by Jae & Alison Grey

ISBN: 978-3-95533-242-6

Also available as e-book.

Published by Ylva Publishing, legal entity of Ylva Verlag, e.Kfr.

Ylva Verlag, e.Kfr.
Owner: Astrid Ohletz
Am Kirschgarten 2
65830 Kriftel
Germany

www.ylva-publishing.com

First edition: February 2015

Credits
Edited by Nikki Busch
Cover Design by Streetlight Graphics

Made in the USA
Middletown, DE
04 July 2020